Sylvie and the
Songman

Sylvie *and the* Songman

Tim Binding

With illustrations by Angela Barrett

David Fickling Books

OXFORD · NEW YORK

A DAVID FICKLING BOOK

Text copyright © 2008 by Tim Binding
Illustrations copyright © 2008 by Angela Barrett

All rights reserved. Published in the United States by David Fickling Books, an imprint of Random House Children's Books, a division of Random House, Inc., New York. Originally published in Great Britain by David Fickling Books, an imprint of Random House Children's Books, a division of the Random House Group Ltd., in 2008.

David Fickling Books and the colophon are trademarks of David Fickling.

Visit us on the Web!
www.randomhouse.com/kids

Educators and librarians, for a variety of teaching tools, visit us at
www.randomhouse.com/teachers

Library of Congress Cataloging-in-Publication Data is available upon request.
ISBN 978-0-385-75157-5 (trade) — ISBN 978-0-385-75159-9 (lib. bdg.) —
ISBN 978-0-375-85363-0 (e-book)

Printed in the United States of America

August 2009

10 9 8 7 6 5 4 3 2

First American Edition

This is for all of Chloe's friends who came through our house over the years, especially Jessica, Lydia, John, Vanessa and, of course, Miss D

Every creature has a song
The song of the dogs
And the song of the doves
The song of the fly
The song of the fox
What do they say?

Adin Steinsaltz
From Steve Reich's *Three Tales*

Chapter One

Tyger, Tyger, burning bright,
In the forest of the night:
What immortal hand or eye,
Could frame thy fearful symmetry?

Sylvie recited the poem along with the rest of the class. It was the last lesson of the day. George was sitting next to her trying to kick her legs. Their form teacher, Miss Coates, stood in front of them, her eyes scanning the room for anybody who hadn't yet learned it properly. The first lines of the poem seemed straightforward enough, the tiger with his bright shining eyes prowling through the jungle, but she couldn't get her head round the second half too well. Immortal hand – what did that mean? And symmetry? She'd never even heard of the word. But despite it all, it did make a sort of sense, this fabulous beast with its great rippling body and huge padded paws.

She and Dad had been to the zoo the Sunday before last. The zoo was down by the coast, with large pens for the animals that ran down to the marshes. Beyond lay the sea and the abandoned lighthouse that always seemed shrouded in mist. It had been a strange day. All the animals had seemed on edge, running back and forth in their compounds, calling to one another in shrill, agitated voices – all except one: the solitary tiger. He lay stretched out on the ground, his great head on the packed earth, as if he was listening to something far away. His cage was set back, a fenced-off no man's land in between him and the path. He was lying near the bars. Sylvie had stood as close as possible, drawn to his immense size, his frightening weight, the strange, unsettling quietness of him.

'I wonder what he's thinking,' she had said.

'A man once wrote, If a tiger could talk, we wouldn't understand a word he said,' Dad told her.

Sylvie frowned. 'I don't get it,' she said.

'What he meant was that tigers don't see the world as we see it. No animal does. If the tiger could paint you a picture of how the world looked to him, you wouldn't recognize it. How we talk – well, that's a way of describing our world: a tall tree, a brown cow, a red sky. So if a tiger could speak, he would not describe what we saw, but what he saw, and it would sound as strange to us as if he was an alien from outer space. Do you understand?'

Sylvie had nodded her head, but she didn't really. Yet looking at the tiger that day, she had an inkling of what her father had meant. What lay behind those eyes? What went on in that great head? When he looked at her, what did he see? A thirteen-year-old girl with long fair hair, thin and strong and small for her age? A friend? A foe? A snack in-between meals? As if in answer to her silent questions, the tiger had raised his immense head and stared back, first at her hands, and then straight into her eyes. She could feel his presence boring into her. It was almost as if he was trying to tell her something. Then, without warning, he bared his teeth and, throwing back his head, gave a huge roar, a wild animal sound, fit for a untamed forest, standing proud on the point of a craggy rock, not hemmed in on a patch of arid ground in a corner of Kent. She had stood back, ashamed.

George kicked her legs again. A sharp voice broke in from the front of the class.

'Sylvie! Did you hear what I said?'

'What?' Sylvie jumped back to the present, still thinking about that day. She was completely lost. The class murmured. Trouble ahead.

Miss Coates tapped her fingernails on her desk, making a hollow drumming sound, like rain on a tin roof. She was a nice enough form teacher but, like most teachers, hated it when you didn't pay attention.

'So enlighten us all please, Sylvie: symmetry. What do you think it means?'

Sylvie glanced around. George was looking down at his desk, trying not to be noticed. He was staying over in two days' time. Then it was the last day of school and the beginning of the summer holidays.

'Well, Sylvie,' Miss Coates intoned. 'All agog, we are, waiting.'

There was a ripple of laughter. Miss Coates glanced triumphantly around the room.

Sylvie didn't know what the word meant, but in her mind she saw the tiger in front of her, pacing up and down in his cage, sunlight falling on the length of his massive body, his muscles rippling under his skin with each step he took; his domed head, his slow sweeping tail, his heavy trembling mouth all waiting, watching, every part of him ready to jump into action, to tear the world apart.

'Perfect, Miss Coates. Does it mean something like perfect? Like everything about a tiger is just so.'

And Miss Coates had to admit that, yes, it did mean something like that: there was something about a tiger that was just so.

The bell rang. School was over for another day.

On Mondays and Tuesdays Sylvie stayed behind. Mondays she worked in the library, doing her homework, Tuesdays she learned the flute. But today was Monday, and after an hour and a half's homework she caught the bus down to the station and the train home. Sylvie and her dad lived on the edge of their small Kentish vil-

lage, at the end of a row of semi-detached houses, red brick and ivy on the outside, wooden floors and high ceilings inside. It was an ordinary sort of house, a bit messy, in need of a coat of paint – though, being at the end, they had a bigger garden than most of their neighbours. However, the one out-of-the-ordinary part of the house was Sylvie's bedroom.

Once it had been the attic, dark and uninviting, full of broken furniture and cardboard boxes, but on Sylvie's twelfth birthday Dad had converted it into her very own room, as long as the whole house, with a huge window knocked into the roof from where she could look down onto the back garden and the disused railway track that ran along the back of it. The stairs leading up to it were not fixed onto the walls but were attached to the inside of the trapdoor, and were pulled down onto the landing by means of a long rope. Sylvie had hung Mum's last photograph, the one with her waving in her green swimsuit, on the wall facing the stairs, so every time she went to bed, it was as if Mum was wishing her goodnight. Most of the time the steps were left down, but when she felt like it, Sylvie could climb up to her bedroom and pull them up like a drawbridge, sealing the bedroom off from the rest of the house. She liked shutting herself away sometimes, having the world and her room all to herself. It made her feel strong, as if nothing could stop her from being who she was, and who she wanted to be.

Mum had disappeared three years ago, before Sylvie and Dad's very eyes. The three of them had been out at Durdle Door, where the cliffs form a great arch into the sea and the beach shelves deeply into the water. Sylvie wasn't allowed to swim there because the tow was so strong, but Mum loved it, riding the waves, playing with the current as it washed her to and fro, in and out of the arch. The greater the swell, the longer she stayed, laughing at its strength. She'd come back, her eyes shining with excitement, her skin glowing as if the water had brought it alive. She always seemed restless and a little sad after a good swim; she seemed sorry to be back on dry land. But that day she went in and vanished. Coastguards were called out, lifeboats and fishing boats searched the coastline for days on end, but they never found her.

Sylvie missed her. Every day she missed her. There was a part of her that was hollow now. She could feel it somewhere between her heart and her stomach, an aching gap she knew would never be filled. Sometimes it ached more than she could bear, but good or bad it was always there – always would be too. Sometimes she felt as though she would see her mum again one day, not in heaven or as a ghost – things she didn't quite believe in – but here on earth, standing by her bed or coming out of the waves at Durdle Door, but she knew it would never happen. Her mum was gone for ever.

Opening the back door, she called out, 'Wakey-wakey, Mr Jackson. I'm home.'

The old dog blinked and wagged his way out of his basket. Mr Jackson was nearly as old as she was – older if you counted him in dog years. Part collie, part Labrador, he was a black, comfortable, obstinate dog, with inquisitive eyebrows and devoted brown eyes. When he was young, he used to bark at almost everything – bicycles, prams, skateboards – but even in his old age the two things that still set him off were hot-air balloons and the moon.

A few days earlier, he'd disappeared on one of his walkabouts, as Dad called them, and come back looking tired and hungry and with his voice completely gone. At first it was something of a relief, but it still hadn't returned, and he was beginning to look rather miserable. 'Where the bloody hell have you been?' Dad had shouted in mock anger, and Mr Jackson had wagged his tail sheepishly, happy to be home. During that terrible holiday he'd lost his name tag and Mum had sewn a leather pouch onto his collar, and folded a letter inside which read, *My name is Mr Jackson and I'm a bit lost. Here is my address and telephone number. Please get in touch. My family need me.* She'd written it only a few days before she'd disappeared herself. Every once in a while Sylvie took the note out, unfolded it and stared at the bold handwriting with the swirled flourishes, the last thing her mum had ever written. *My family need me.*

Perhaps the letter he carried was the reason why Mr Jackson liked the letter song so much. It was one of Dad's favourites, and when Sylvie was young, he used to hold her in his arms and sing it to her while she fell asleep. Every time Mr Jackson heard it, the same thing happened.

'I'm gonna sit right down and write myself a letter
And make believe it came from you . . .'

Mr Jackson would come up beside them and try and sing along in a soft, whispering howl. Dad would keep on singing:

'I'm gonna write words, oh so sweet
They're gonna knock me off my feet
A lotta kisses on the bottom
I'll be glad I got 'em . . .'

Mr Jackson would roll around on the floor and stick his legs in the air. Sylvie would chuckle sleepily as the last verse came.

'I'm gonna smile and say "I hope you're feeling better"
And close "with love" the way you do,
I'm gonna sit right down and write myself a letter
And make believe it came from you.'

And along with Sylvie, Mr Jackson would curl up and fall asleep. He just loved that song.

Sylvie took a slice of bread from the bread bin. 'Come on, Mr Jackson,' she said. 'Time for your constitutional.'

Outside, the old blackbird with the one white feather in his tail flew down and perched on the roof of the little bird table, chirping away while she broke the bread into pieces. He was almost tame, the way he followed her about. Then it was time for flute practice. She'd rather have watched television, but Dad would be upset if she hadn't done her regulation half-hour by the time he got home.

Although Sylvie looked forward to him coming home, the evenings weren't always the success they both wanted them to be. Sometimes she had too much work to do and would get in a temper if he refused to help out. Sometimes he came home smelling of beer, his eyes a little too bright, his manner a little too friendly, as if he wanted everything to be, yes, just so, and the day would end unfinished, with a nasty taste in their mouths. But sometimes the evenings were perfect: Mr Jackson lay in front of the fire, nice and cosy, while she and Dad talked and watched a murder mystery; if the weather was good enough, he stretched out on the little patio watching them play a game of badminton on the back lawn. Then it was just the three of them, Sylvie and her dad and Mr Jackson, against the world.

Dad's name was Daniel. He played bassoon in a London orchestra, the Orchestra of Light. He didn't earn a lot of money. Sylvie didn't even have a mobile phone yet, though he'd promised her one this coming birthday. As well as working in an orchestra Dad was also a composer. When he wasn't working in London, he was busy in his wooden hut at the bottom of their garden. The trouble was, no one wanted to listen to his music except Mr Flowerdew, Sylvie's music teacher at school. Mr Flowerdew was Dad's oldest friend, a sort of unofficial uncle to her. Although at home she called him Uncle Alex, at school she had to call him Mr Flowerdew. Sometimes she got it all mixed up and called him Uncle Alex in class and Mr Flowerdew at home, but he just laughed it off with an understanding wink.

Back in the kitchen, she opened up the sack of feed. 'Dinner time!' she called out. 'Where's your bowl, Mr

Jackson? Where's your bowl?'

Mr Jackson came trotting over, his enamel bowl gripped between his jaws, his tail wagging furiously. She measured out three handfuls, topped it up with cold water and laid it on the floor.

'Wolf it down,' she said. He set to it with abandon, pushing the bowl across the floor as he buried his nose deep into the mixture.

She could still hear him crunching it down as she climbed the stairs and set up her music stand. On the wall above her bed was the poster of this year's summer concert in Hyde Park. All the top stars were going to be there, their names ranged in importance. At the very bottom, in much smaller letters, she could read, *Also Appearing: The Orchestra of Light, Conductor Walter Klopstock.* Dad playing in a pop concert! They were booked to play in the early evening, in between the afternoon and evening events. Walter Klopstock had even promised that Dad might be able to perform one of his own compositions. Dad had become both dreadfully excited and desperately nervous. Every spare waking hour was spent in the hut, trying to get everything exactly right.

Sylvie had just started her practice when the back door opened and Dad called out. He was home early, and by the smell coming up the stairs, he'd brought back an Indian takeaway. She clattered down the stairs. They hadn't had curry in weeks.

Dad was holding the bulging paper carrier high in the air and his round face was smiling.

'Chicken tikka masala, king prawn biriani, two onion bhajees, one pilau rice, one peshwari nan and four poppadoms. How's Mr Jackson? Still not a hundred per cent? Voice not back yet?'

Sylvie shook her head. Dad stood over him.

'Well, he doesn't look ill, does he?' He felt Mr Jackson's nose. It was perfectly cold and wet. 'Nothing wrong there,' he said.

'Well, something's not right,' Sylvie insisted. 'I mean, he doesn't look happy, does he?' Mr Jackson raised his baleful eyes. She was right. He didn't look happy at all.

'You know, it may not just be him,' Dad declared, setting out the containers. 'Apparently half the animals at the zoo have lost their voices too. There's some sort of virus going round. Perhaps we brought it back with us on that last visit.' He reached down and ruffled Mr Jackson's head. 'In a bad way, are you? Not ticketyboo? Well, if it doesn't clear up in the next day or two, we'd better take him to the V-E-T – eh, old boy? Now come on, let's have this food before it all gets cold.'

Sylvie prised the lids off the silver-foil boxes while Dad fished a can of beer out of the back of the fridge. Mr Jackson sat by the table, licking his lips in anticipation, his spirits momentarily raised. Takeaways usually meant extra grub.

Sylvie sat down and helped herself to the steaming food. 'How's it going?' she said, breaking a poppadom in two.

'Great.' Dad poked his rice about the plate. That meant it wasn't going well at all.

Sylvie bit into the dark red chicken. It was hot and spicy, just as she liked it. 'Did Klopstock agree?' she asked. Walter Klopstock was famous for his fiery temper. It seemed to go with the territory.

Dad nodded. 'I get fifteen minutes, all the instruments. Me and Uncle Alex.'

'No, Dad, I meant the backstage pass.'

'Oh, that. I haven't asked him yet.' Sylvie looked disappointed. 'Don't worry. I will. It just slipped my mind. There's so much to do. Alex is coming round this Thursday and I want to have everything ready by then.'

She looked at his worn suit and his shock of uncombed hair and the big baby face that tried to hide his thoughts and feelings but revealed so much.

'Don't worry, Dad.' She patted his arm. 'It'll come right in the end.'

'Perhaps, but it's not right yet. There are some adjustments I've got to make. I don't suppose you'd care to lend me a hand this evening? It's not easy, all by myself.'

'I've got my own work to do. Miss Coates expects, and all that.'

'Can't it wait a bit? I'll help you afterwards if you want. What is it?'

'French, but I can do that in the morning. There's that poem too, about the tiger. I've got a test on Wednesday.'

'William Blake? That won't take you long. Come on, just for a while.'

There were no windows in Dad's shed. It was longer and wider than most, with a wooden floor, and walls lined with egg boxes. They helped keep the sound in. Down one side ran a long table covered with sheets of music.

The stuff Dad wrote was weird. It was so weird he'd invented strange instruments to play it all. They had strange cumbersome names too: there was the Shinglechord, the Featherblow and the Furroughla. The Shinglechord was built of old beer barrels and huge shells, with valves made out of dried sea urchins and conkers, and when he turned the handles, it sounded like the sea was singing, restless and deep. The Featherblow was shaped like a church organ on wheels, only fashioned out of bullrushes and bamboo canes and feathers. When he worked the bellows, it hummed and shimmered like still air on a summer's day. The Furroughla looked a bit like a piano, but one that had been crossed with some old farm machinery. It had pedals and keys made out of thick blocks of wood, but also wheels of leather flaps that delved into its unknown heart. Lodged inside were hollowed-out pumpkins and rams' horns. It was deep and throaty; it could rumble like thunder and squelch like wet mud, and when it hit the low notes, it felt as if the very earth was trembling.

Dad had once tried to explain to her what his music was all about, but it was rather like that stuff about the tiger, a bit above her head, just out of reach. He'd sat her down at the piano in the living room and run his fingers up the scales.

'You know how the music you play is made out of octaves, rising from the lowest notes to the highest?' Sylvie had nodded. 'And you know that in each octave there are twelve notes; on this piano, for instance, the seven white keys and the five black ones – twelve notes in all.' Sylvie nodded again, a little impatiently. Who didn't know what a piano looked like? 'Well,' Dad continued, 'I believe there are other notes in between, notes that we're not used to hearing, or don't think of as notes. How many times have you heard the wind blowing through the trees or a branch rubbing against a windowpane and thought, That's a note I've never heard?'

Sylvie had never thought any such thing, but had kept quiet. Dad had been in full flight.

'Everything is made out of notes, vibrations. Many people think the universe started with a great big bang. What's that if it isn't a note, albeit a rather loud one? Somewhere there's probably a note that brings the whole universe together.'

'Is that what you're looking for, this note?'

'Me? No. Goodness knows what will happen if anyone finds it.' Dad had laughed. 'We'll probably all be blown up; either that or we'd find ourselves in another universe.'

'Sounds like something from a sci-fi film.'

'Don't worry. It won't happen. But what I am trying to do is make music out of those other lost notes – the sounds and music that we've forgotten. There are so many songs that most of us never get to hear.'

'What sort of songs?' she had asked.

'The songs of the sea, the songs of the earth and, the most precious of all, the songs of the animals.' He had leaned forward, his eyes sparkling. 'Every animal has a song, Sylvie. It's how they talk to each other and the world around them. If only we could get close to it, close to all the other music in this world, think how wonderful it would be.'

Daniel dragged the Furroughla, the Shinglechord and the Featherblow into a rough semicircle so that he could quickly move from one to another. There was another instrument there too, one that Sylvie had never seen before, made out of long hollows of highly polished wood. It was shaped like one of those three-sided washing lines people have in their gardens, the wooden slats hanging down like Venetian blinds; in the centre hung a huge, upended glass bowl.

'That's the Clattercloud,' Dad said proudly. 'The vibrations just drop into the glass and produce the most wonderful resonance.'

At one end of the building were stacked the instruments' spare parts: pumpkins, bundles of bamboo, boxes of feathers and wing bones, a variety of rams' horns all arranged in order of size. Placed behind Daniel's stool was the only other device in the shed, the Harmonograph. It was the most complicated instrument of all, with pendulums and tuning forks and a large sheet of paper over which four pencils were poised. When Dad played his music, the vibrations set the pendulums in motion, which in turn moved the pencils across the paper. Strange fantastic forms would appear, which looked familiar but somehow defied definition. It was like seeing shapes in ink blots, feeling that something was nearly there, but not quite.

Dad plonked Sylvie down on the old piano stool in front of the Furroughla. He had in his hand what looked like a bag of conkers, only with a series of holes drilled into them.

'I'm increasing the number of variables,' he explained. 'What I want you to do is work the pedals on the Furroughla with these stops out, while I adjust the setting on the Shinglechord with these. I want to see how they combine against the higher vibrato of the Featherblow. I should be able to work both. Hang on a moment while I set the Harmonograph.'

Standing over the machine, Sylvie started to pedal while Dad bent down beside her, opening up a flap at the side of the Shinglechord with one hand, while the other worked the bellows of the Featherblow. The pitch began to rise slowly. The pedals of the Furroughla grew harder to work.

'Come on, Sylvie, keep it up,' Dad urged.

Really, she thought, this was just what she shouldn't be doing when she had a poem to learn. She pumped and pumped, her legs beginning to get tired. Dad was working the Shinglechord with one hand while trying to adjust the Featherblow with the other. Suddenly Sylvie foot's slipped off the pedal, and instinctively she grabbed at one of the stops to prevent herself falling. It broke off in her hand, sending her crashing into Dad, who was kneeling beside her. A low humming sound started to fill the hut, rather like one of those spinning tops she'd had as a child, but lower in tone, like a slow undulating wave. Then she heard another noise, higher up but coming down, as if it were trying to meet the other one coming up. Sylvie couldn't work out where it was coming from but she could feel the two notes converging on one another. They sounded far away, like a plane's engine in the distance, growing more insistent as they drew closer. She looked across.

Dad was lying awkwardly on the floor, his foot jammed underneath the Featherblow.

'Are you all right?' she said, but he didn't answer.

Although no one was pedalling or working the keys, the notes were still there, as if the instruments had taken on a life of their own. The Furroughla was shaking slightly; the Shinglechord's reeds were rattling against each other. Behind her, the arms of the Harmonograph had sprung into life, the pendulums swinging back and forth, the paper twisting and turning as if trying to escape. The notes grew louder. Sylvie's head started to pound. It was as if someone had stuck a bicycle pump in her ear and was filling her head with pressurized air. She clamped her hands against her temples, wincing in pain. Just when she could stand it no longer, in a split second of time which seemed to last for ever, there was nothing, nothing at all; her ears and her eyes and everything outside floated in silent black space. Then her brain seemed to explode, booming like a paper bag bursting inside her skull, and she was flung backwards across the room. There was a sucking noise, and the door burst open, throwing Sylvie headlong out into the garden. A howling wind pulled at her hair, her skirt billowed out, Dad's music sheets swirling around her in a chaotic spiral. Then, as quickly as it came, it was gone. Paper floated down like oversized confetti. Dad stood in the doorway, clutching his head.

'Dad! Are you all right?'

'Yes. Yes.' His breath was short. He looked about him, dazed. 'Quick, Sylvie! My music! Before it's all ruined.'

She ran round snatching up the sheaves of paper. Dad limped out into the garden. He had a bump on his forehead the size of a bird's egg. He looked suddenly older, shaken. Soon Sylvie had all the sheets bundled up in her arm.

'Here, Dad, sit down.'

She led him to the little wooden seat on the porch, and began handing them back one by one, counting out the page numbers as he tried to shuffle them back in order. There was one smaller than the rest, covered in a mass of irregular squiggles, as if a child had been let loose with a biro.

'That's the Harmonograph,' Dad told her. 'Surprised it didn't blow up altogether. That was some bang.'

Sylvie looked at the sheet again. There was something there, in amongst the tangle. 'What's that, Dad, in the middle?'

Her father peered down. In the very centre was a small black dot, only it wasn't really a dot, more like a bulbous head on a thin neck peeking up from the ground.

'Looks like a mushroom,' she said. Dad stared at it for a moment, then folded the paper in two and stuffed it into his top pocket.

Sylvie was still shaken. 'What happened?' she asked.

Her dad ran his fingers through his hair, still out of breath. 'I'm not sure, to tell the truth. But whatever it was, better not tell anyone, eh? Better not tell anyone at all.' He looked at her seriously. He meant it. She nodded. He reached up and squeezed her hand. 'I'll be OK from here on in. I want to write all this down. You'd better go and do that homework.'

Hours later, Sylvie heard her father come in from the garden. She could hear him wandering around the house, muttering to himself, and then talking to someone on the phone, a long conversation, held in a low voice as if he didn't want her to hear what he was saying. Perhaps he had found a girlfriend. It was going to happen one day, whether she liked it or not. Trouble was, she didn't like it. For all his faults she wanted Dad all to herself.

Sylvie got into bed thinking of who it might be. Someone at work? The leader of the violins, the woman with the long hair? No, she'd tried last winter and failed. Julie, the PE teacher? Too young, surely. What about her form teacher, Miss Coates? No, that was too ridiculous for words. No one could fancy Miss Coates. Not even her dad could be that desperate. Sylvie fell asleep with a smile on her face.

Chapter 2

Next morning Dad was sitting at the kitchen table in his best shirt, skewering holes in another heap of conkers, as if nothing had happened.

'Morning, Dad.'

He looked up. 'Sleep well?' He pushed the conkers aside apologetically. 'Sorry about the mess. Just having a bit of a tinker.' He held one up. 'I don't suppose you have any more of these?'

'Dad, I stopped playing conkers years ago. Did you work out what happened?'

He seemed hardly able to remember it. 'That? Something funny going on with the acoustics, that's all. Hasn't done my hearing any good.'

'But you seemed so worried.'

'Worried in case it broke any of our neighbours'

windows. I don't want to have to fork out money we can ill afford.'

He looked at his watch. 'Heavens, time for the off.' He swept the conkers into his pocket and stood up. 'Big day today, Sylvie. And I will definitely ask about that backstage pass, OK? Now, I have to make a good impression. Klopstock's introducing me to the concert promoter. What do you think? The pink shirt or the pale blue?'

Sylvie smiled to herself. Though Dad tried to dress smartly, he never got it quite right: the colours clashed or his shirt tail hung out at the back, or his jacket had an ink stain at the front where his fountain pen had leaked. When he had a concert to perform, he had to dress up in a bow tie and tails. He still couldn't tie the bow, even after years of trying. Mum used to have to do it for him. These days Sylvie did it, standing on a chair as her dad stretched his neck in the air, fingering his collar, begging her not to tie it too tight. It summed up their relationship perfectly, Sylvie thought. Although from the outside it looked as if it was he who was looking after her, very often Sylvie felt it was the reverse, that it was she who looked after him, made sure he was presentable and didn't get too stressed, helped him to see beyond his worries.

'The pale blue,' she said. 'It suits you better.'

'Yes, but the pink is more fun, wouldn't you say? What about a tie? The purple striped?'

'Only if you want to look like a stick of rock. Your grey one would be best.'

'It's a bit boring though, isn't it? I don't want to look boring, Sylvie. I want to look . . .' Dad waved his arms about, trying to snatch the word out of the air.

'Like a deck chair?'

'Lively. Eager, full of vim and vigour and . . .' He couldn't work out what the third ingredient should be.

While he went to get dressed, Sylvie made herself two banana sandwiches to eat before Mr Flowerdew's flute lesson and then went to put out the bird food. The blackbird with the one white feather in his tail was standing there, his head to one side.

'Morning, your blackness,' she said, but he flew off without a sound. 'Please yourself.' She watched him wheel round the garden before disappearing out of sight.

Back upstairs, she crossed the landing and went into the bathroom. She brushed her teeth, washed her face and tied back her hair in the mirror on the door of the little medicine cabinet. When she came down again, Dad was struggling with his blue music folder, his bassoon and an oblong contraption wrapped up in sacking.

'The Clattercloud,' he explained. 'I want to show Klopstock.'

'Here, let me,' offered Sylvie, taking his music

folder. 'I'll carry it to the station for you.'

She stuck her father's folder into the front pocket of her rucksack, grabbed her flute and said goodbye to Mr Jackson.

'See you later, Mr Jackson,' she said, ruffling his raised head. 'See you later.'

In normal weather, walking to the station took exactly seven and a half minutes. If they had to run, which happened on average once a month, it took four. There was no need to run this morning. Halfway down the road though, Sylvie stopped and stood still.

'What's the matter?' her father asked.

'I'm not sure. Something's not quite right. Not there.' She looked about her, as if searching for something.

'What do you mean, not there?' He looked at her anxiously. 'You haven't forgotten my music, have you?'

'No, not that. Can't you feel it? Something's missing.'

'Sylvie, the only thing that's missing is going to be our train. Now come on.'

Four minutes later they had crossed over the station footbridge and were standing on the platform, watching the train approach. Sylvie travelled only a few stops, to the market town up the line, while Dad carried on all the way to London. The seating on the train never varied. They got into the third carriage, second door down, and sat next to the window on the left-hand side. Across the corridor perched the man with big ears and protruding rabbit teeth, his silver-topped walking stick held between his legs. Opposite him sat the woman with kid gloves, a ball of green wool stuck with thick wooden knitting needles lying on her lap, her bulging canvas bag on the rack above. More wool, Sylvie supposed, not that the woman ever did any knitting. She just sat there, with a straight back and her long straight neck, staring straight ahead. The two were related, Sylvie supposed, but couldn't quite work out how. Husband and wife? Brother and sister? It was hard to say. All she knew was they looked out of place on this morning commuter run.

Further along, the business-suited solicitor, portly and slightly balding, was squashed against his thin, dour-looking companion. He was one of those men who was always complaining: public transport, teenagers, where all the good tunes had gone – those were his favourite topics, though he was an expert in complaining about almost anything. Today he was back on his favourite subject: the state of the railways and, more particularly, this train.

'We must be the only line in Kent with the old slam-door carriages.' He wriggled in his seat, squashing his friend a little closer to the window.

'We are,' his friend sympathized. 'They've been promising us the new ones for months.'

'It's a disgrace. Do you know what I am going to do?'

But Sylvie never heard what the plump solicitor was going to do, for just then the man with rabbit teeth raised his hand in greeting.

'Morning, young miss. School today?' He inclined his head, waiting for an answer. Every day he asked the same question and every day she replied in the same way.

'Yes,' she said.

'Top of the class, I bet,' the woman with kid gloves added and, turning, grinned inanely at her. She meant well, but the sight of her always slightly unnerved Sylvie.

'Not me,' she said softly.

'Practice makes perfect,' Rabbit-teeth observed, and the two of them nodded to each other, as if the phrase was meant for them rather than for her.

Routine kicked in. Dad took out his newspaper, the solicitor booted up his laptop, his thin companion wrestled with the day's crossword. At the next stop the scruffy lad with muddy boots hopped in, earphones clamped to his head. He took his place opposite the solicitor and stretched out his feet. Sylvie always wished he'd sit a bit nearer so she could discover what sort of music he liked.

'Wretched thing!' the solicitor exclaimed. His mobile started to ring. 'Yes,' he barked. 'Braithewaite here.'

The train horn hooted. The passengers settled into their seats. It was all so curious, Sylvie thought, these people I see every day. They read their papers, talk on their mobiles, yet I haven't a clue who they are, or what they're really thinking. Perhaps they're like tigers too. Perhaps they see the world in a different way to me. Perhaps everyone does.

The train pulled away. Sylvie gave Dad's leg a surreptitious kick. It wouldn't be long now. She leaned forward, trying to hide her excitement, looking for the rise in the embankment and the little platform of earth under a canopy of trees where the old dog fox would be. Every day they passed by and every day he'd be there, lying on the flattened ground, his head raised, taking it all in. You could tell he was old by the white on his front and the grey on his muzzle and the way he lay, as if he'd seen it all before. The first time she'd caught sight of him she'd pulled her father's arm and cried, 'Look, Dad! A fox!'

Dad had put his finger to his mouth. 'Shh,' he had murmured in her ear. 'Foxhunters. Anyone in this carriage could be one. You wouldn't want any of them to know about him, would you?' Leaning forward, he had licked his finger and on the dirt of the window-pane drawn the outline of a large unblinking eye. 'Eyes and Ears,' he had whispered. 'Always remember. Eyes and Ears are everywhere. Look out for the fox, follow his movements, but don't tell a soul. You never

know who's listening,' and he turned in his seat, as if anxious that someone might have overheard.

From that day on, Sylvie had looked for the fox on every journey she made, through that summer term and, after the holidays, through the wet autumn and the dark of the winter, into the light of the spring. She had seen him with the sun on his face and she had seen him with the rain pouring down his back. She had seen him sitting with the cold wind blowing through his fur and she seen him surrounded by great banks of fluffy snow, his grizzled head peering patiently over the powdery white. Every day she looked out for him and every day he'd be there, sitting and watching; but watching for what? Surely not the trains? Surely not Sylvie, though sometimes he put his head to one side, following them as they clattered past. If only she could ask him!

The train rounded the bend and she held her breath, excited at the thought of seeing him again. She never got tired of it. Over the last few months his coat had grown quite glossy. He must be eating well. All the more reason to keep quiet. The train sped along-side. Sylvie squinted and shielded her eyes. The ledge came into view. It was empty! She couldn't believe it. She tugged on her father's arm.

'Dad! He's not there!'

Her dad looked up from his paper. He seemed worried. 'What? Are you sure?' He strained to see for himself but the train had already whisked them past.

'Course I'm sure. You don't think . . .' She looked around, as if one of her fellow travellers might have been responsible.

She didn't mean to speak so loudly, but no one seemed to be taking any notice.

Dad shook his head. 'No, I don't think so. Quite bare, was it? No sign of him at all?'

Sylvie shook her head.

'Maybe he's looking for food,' he suggested brightly, trying to hide his feelings. 'We'll look out for him tomorrow. I dare say he'll be back by then,' and Dad rattled his paper and started reading again.

The train pulled in to the station. Sylvie could see the school bus waiting. Kissing Dad goodbye, she opened the door and jumped down. As she walked towards the bus, she noticed an extraordinary thing. On the telegraph wire that stretched over the car park sat a line of plump green woodpeckers, fifteen in all, their bright red heads all turned in the direction of the train. Sylvie had never seen one green woodpecker sitting on a telegraph wire before, let alone fifteen. They were such shy, solitary birds.

The guard blew his whistle, and in response they

rose en masse, flying away in their exaggerated undulating flight, their harsh cry suddenly filling the air with birdsong. Sylvie stopped in her tracks.

'That's what was missing!' she said out loud.

She ran back onto the platform, waving to get Dad's attention, but he was staring out of the window, across the fields to the wood where they thought the old fox must live. The train started to move off.

'Dad! There were no birds singing this morning. That's what was missing!' she shouted, but he couldn't hear. No matter. She'd tell him tonight.

Chapter 3

On the bus, George, her best friend, had kept a seat for her. They had plans to make about Wednesday's sleepover – what dvd they should rent. George had joined the school last September. He was a dumpling sort of boy, with thick square glasses, the sort scientists seemed to wear, and short little legs and short stubby fingers which often held one of those inhalers to ward off asthma. He was a bit of a loner, was George, slow to make friends, slow to join in. Although he was quite bookish, and sounded as if he should be top of the class, George wasn't especially good at anything – not at sport, not in class – and was the worst singer Sylvie had ever heard. Being a bit overweight and a bit shy, he was mostly ignored by the rest of the class. And by Sylvie.

And then one day Miss Coates had asked everyone

in the class to tell them about their hobbies. The next morning he'd brought in a huge paper kite shaped like a hooded bird with long sickle-shaped wings and a snaking red tail. Miss Coates had marched the class out onto the playing fields and asked George to give them a demonstration. Most kites need two people to launch them – one to hold the kite in the air, the other to hold the controls – but George had simply laid the bird out on the ground, walked back, given the stick a little twist, and up she had flown, swooping in long elegant curves in the autumn breeze. The class had stood with their necks craned as the kite climbed and cut through the sky. They were amazed that such an awkward-looking boy as George could have made something so graceful, so swift and so agile. Miss Coates was as surprised as the rest of them.

'Surely you didn't make this all by yourself, George,' she said, in a tone that implied an adult must have helped him.

'Of course I did,' he replied indignantly.

Miss Coates looked at it critically, as if expecting it to fall out of the sky. 'Can't it go higher?' she questioned. 'You've lots more string.'

'Twine,' George corrected. He pointed to the end of the field. 'If I let it out too much and the wind drops, it could get caught in the trees. I didn't bring it here to get caught in trees.'

Miss Coates sniffed the air. 'I'm an experienced

sailor, you know. That wind's not going to drop. Perhaps your kite can't go any higher.'

George tipped his glasses to the end of his nose and peered over the top of them. 'This kite,' he said carefully, 'will go as high as the twine is long. It's that sort of bird.'

'I don't think that could be true,' Miss Coates countered. 'What if the string was a mile in length? You're not telling me that kite could climb that high!'

George thought for a moment. 'The twine would need to be stronger, for the pull would be greater up there, but otherwise, yes, it could, though you'd need binoculars to see it.'

Miss Coates wasn't satisfied. She looked on impatiently. 'Why don't you let someone else hold it?' she suggested.

George was doubtful. 'I don't know, Miss Coates. They can be quite tricky if you don't know what you're doing.'

'Nonsense.' Miss Coates was adamant. 'It flies in the air, it falls to the ground. What could be simpler than that? Who'd like to have a go?'

The class held back. It was George's kite, not theirs.

'Here. Let me.' Miss Coates snatched the controls out of George's hand. The kite quivered.

'Careful,' said George. 'Don't let it run away with you.'

'Don't worry. I'm completely in control. See? First this way, then that.'

The kite swung to and fro, like a pendulum in the sky. For a minute Miss Coates was lost in the simple beauty of it, unaware of her class standing behind her, watching. Though no one could see her, she was smiling – the child she'd never been, alone and happy. Then the kite gave a sudden pull. Miss Coates stumbled forward.

'Hold your ground!' George warned. 'Keep it level!'

Miss Coates braced herself and wound the twine around her right wrist.

'No, don't do that,' George warned. 'It's dangerous.'

The words were hardly out of his mouth when another gust of wind sent the kite soaring into the air. The twine tightened round Miss Coates's wrist, cutting into her flesh. Her arm was yanked into the air, her feet scrabbling on the ground, trying to find a hold. She was half running, half dancing in the air, twisting and turning like a puppet with half its strings cut loose.

'Help, George!' she cried. 'Help me!'

Another violent blast and the kite lifted her clean off her feet. George started to chase after her.

'Hurry!' he shouted. 'We'll lose her!' The rest of the class quickly overtook him, jumping up at Miss

Coates's legs as she flew screaming towards the edge of the field. One of the taller girls managed to grab hold of her left ankle; another, her right. Then, with four more hanging on, they began to haul her down.

'My hand!' Miss Coates was yelling. 'It's cutting off my hand!'

Sylvie tried to pull the twine towards her, to give it some slack, but it was no use. The kite was too strong, the wind too fierce. The twine cut deeper; Miss Coates's face screwed up in agony.

'Do something,' she begged.

George took one last look at his kite, then opened up his penknife and cut the twine free. The kite shot into the air, its long tail drifting up towards the trees. For a moment it seemed as if it might escape and sail away, never to be seen again, but then the tree's bare fingers seemed to reach out, snatching at it like over-eager fans chasing a celebrity. The kite spun round, trying to break free, jerking like an angry dog on a chain, then sank back in a slow, doomed spiral.

Miss Coates rubbed her wrist tenderly. There was a livid purple ring just above the hand, and on either side the flesh had puffed up, swollen. She was pale and shaken.

'That,' she pronounced, her voice trembling slightly, 'is a very dangerous toy.'

'That's just it,' said George. 'It's not a toy.' He stood there, looking up at his lost kite. 'I'll never get that down,' he said despondently. 'She's there for good.' He looked desperately unhappy, as if he'd just lost a favourite pet.

Sylvie had stepped forward. 'No she's not,' she announced, and before Miss Coates could stop her, she ran across, gripped the lowest branch and swung up.

Sylvie had always loved climbing trees, but in the last year it had almost become a compulsion. It was something she had to do. Sitting in their nooks and crannies, watching the world below, she felt as if she belonged there, safe amongst their leaves and boughs. Somewhere, she knew, was a tree waiting just for her. She knew what it looked like too. It stood on top of a smooth green hill, flat country all around; a single oak, perfectly shaped, looking out across the land. Awake, she was always on the lookout for it; asleep, she dreamed of it. Whenever she practised her scales, she imagined herself climbing up and down through its branches, and whenever she had a pencil in her hand, it was its limbs, its sturdy trunk that she drew. That's why she liked her attic bedroom so much. With its wooden floor and its angular beams and the way it was perched at the very top of the house, it was a bit like a tree itself.

Sylvie brushed her hands together. Above, the branches forked out in irregular intervals, some close, some barely within her reach. She could see the kite quite plainly, caught in a tangle of treetop limbs. It didn't look too difficult. She began to climb.

At first it was easy, the bark a little damp to the touch, her foot- and hand-holds a little slippery, but she didn't mind. She was strong, and her grip was sure. Three metres, five . . . she rose steadily. At seven metres she realized that although she was quite high up, she still had a long way to go. Now the branches seemed to crowd in on her, making it difficult for her to twist round for the next hold, or squeeze her body through the narrow gaps. The wind began to blow harder than ever.

'Sylvie Bartram' – Miss Coates's worried voice pierced the air – 'come down this instant.'

Sylvie pressed on, pretending not to hear. The branches were thinner now, weaker. She swayed back and forth, buffeted by the gusty wind, her hands gripping tightly, her feet riding the sways like a fairground attendant. She felt a little frightened, a little excited, determined not to give in. She climbed higher, clinging to the central trunk; above her the red tail of the kite flapped furiously in the air, egging her on. She was almost level with it now. It lay a couple of metres away, fluttering against the spindly branches like a wild bird desperate to escape from its captor. To get it she'd have to edge out along a branch no thicker than her arm.

'Sylvie, I absolutely forbid you to . . .'

Miss Coates's voice died away as Sylvie stepped out. Down below everything went quiet: the rest of the class held their breath. Grasping onto the branch above, she edged out, inch by inch. The ground seemed very far away. Though she dared not look down, she could tell that her feet were now balanced on a length of wood no thicker than a climbing rope. What if she missed a step? She hesitated. What was she doing here, all alone, fifteen metres up, out on a limb, with no one to help her? Her legs started to shake. She wanted to go back, to close her eyes and wish herself down, but she could not. She had to get the kite. She took a deep breath. As long as she kept her head straight and didn't panic, it would be all right. She moved her foot along.

Suddenly the branch sagged under her weight. Her right foot slipped. The gasp from below hit her in the face as her foot first dangled dangerously in the air, then, miraculously, found the branch again. She held on tight, gathering her thoughts, then looked up. The kite was within reach. Balancing carefully on the balls of her feet, she untangled the tail before pulling the kite towards her, folding its torn wings in her arms, then slowly descended. Jumping down the last two metres, she handed it back to George, who inspected it carefully, examining the extent of the damage.

Miss Coates called her over, her pale face now red with anger. 'Sylvie Bartram, didn't you hear me up there?'

'No, Miss Coates.'

'I don't believe a word. You deliberately ignored

me. What if you'd fallen off? Who do you think would have got the blame then? George and his stupid kite or me? I'm putting you on report.'

She stomped off. The class began to straggle back. George fell in beside Sylvie.

'I can't believe you did that. I couldn't have done that to save my life.' And he ran his fingers over the kite's frame, just like Dad would touch one of his instruments. He spoke in a slow, measured voice, quite unlike most boys of his age. Sylvie was intrigued.

'And I couldn't have made something like that. I had a kite once, you know, for the beach, but it wasn't a bit like yours,' she replied.

'Those things aren't proper kites,' he said, dismissing them with a wave of his hand. 'They're kids' stuff. Mine are serious malarkey.'

Serious malarkey. It was a phrase she had never heard before. He spoke as if he had a whole room of kites.

'Do you have many?'

George considered for a moment. 'Thirty-three.' Sylvie blinked in disbelief. 'Would have been thirty-two if it hadn't been for you. And of course there's always the spare collapsible I have in my rucksack, just in case.'

'Just in case of what?'

George looked at her as if she were particularly stupid. 'Just in case there's a good wind blowing, of

course. A collapsible kite, a compass to find the direction of the wind and a spare ball of twine – I never leave home without them. It's a serious business, making kites. One day I'm going to build one like a glider. I'll strap myself under it and fly away from all this rubbish. There's a competition, you know. The first person to fly a mile under his own power wins a million pounds. One special kite and I wouldn't have to go to school any longer. I could buy a hill somewhere with a castle on it, and fly kites all day, and throw boiling oil over anyone who tried to stop me. Or water.'

Sylvie had thought of her bedroom. 'Forget the boiling oil. A drawbridge would be all you need, then no one could get in. Save the oil for lamps and the water for drinking and cooking and . . . washing.' She looked at his hands. They were scratched and rough, the nails chipped with a ridge of black dirt underneath them; just like her father's.

'My dad makes things,' she told him. 'Musical instruments that only he and Uncle Alex' – she corrected herself – 'Mr Flowerdew can play. He'd like you.'

George shrugged his shoulders. 'I doubt it. I don't have a musical note in my body. It's not that I'm just tone deaf. I have no sense of tune, pitch or rhythm. I just don't get it.'

'Not even pop music or anything?'

'Nothing,' George said proudly. '*Rien*. It all sounds the same to me, like a rusty lawnmower. Flowerdew has banned me from singing altogether. Apparently I undermine the vibrant image of the school. Even the rents can't stand it. When I have a bath, they leave the house.'

Sylvie was puzzled. 'The rents?' she questioned, not understanding. There it was again, the look.

'Parents. You know, the desperate double-act: the good cop, bad cop. I'm a disappointment to them. I expect I'll be a disappointment to your dad too.'

But George had been wrong. Dad had taken to George immediately. He liked his obstinacy and his love of his kites. When George was older, they planned to join forces and make an instrument that flew in the wind and never came down, but crisscrossed the globe, playing music from the clouds.

Now Sylvie climbed onto the bus and walked down the aisle to where George was sitting, gazing out of the window. There was an air of excitement about. The holidays were just on the horizon.

'Did you see all those woodpeckers on the telegraph wire?' she asked as she plonked herself down beside him.

He turned. He face was grave, his manner glum. 'I've more important things to think about than a few moth-eaten birds, Sylvie,' he intoned, shaking his head. 'It's the holidays soon, if you haven't noticed.'

'Of course I've noticed. It's great.'

George snorted. 'Great for you, maybe. Great for everyone on this bus, except me. First day I'll come down to breakfast hoping to try out my new kite, and it'll be, "George, why don't we go to the Science Museum today, see how a lift works?" Or, "George, wouldn't it be fun if we all talked French at meal times?" *Fantastique, Maman. Écoutez-moi* one more time. *Je n'aime pas le muesli ou le* grated carrot. Then there's the extra maths tuition and the swimming lessons. And you know what they've promised me at the end of it all? A ride on the London Eye. I mean, what is the point of going round and round on a wheel? Do I look like a hamster?'

Sylvie bit her lip and said nothing. As a matter of fact, without his glasses, he did look rather like a hamster, and a well-fed one at that. The bus swung out of the station car park, taking its chattering passengers through the busy streets to the school, set almost in the very heart of the town. George, however, was uncommunicative and Sylvie was happy not to talk. She kept thinking about those fifteen woodpeckers watching the train, and the strange silence on the way to the station. She thought of Mr Jackson, unable to bark, even at the moon. It seemed like everything was losing its voice.

Once through the wide gates, and hurrying down the tiled corridor to the old, draughty classroom, she had no time for such thoughts. Tuesdays were always bad: double science, double maths, with French and geography and history thrown in for good measure. The day went excruciatingly slowly. No one really wanted to be here, not even the teachers, but, as if to prove that holidays meant nothing to them, they all acted as if some dreadful exam were just around the corner – eyes down and no messing about.

At half past three she went back into her classroom to collect her flute. Although she was running late, she couldn't help but stare at her picture, hanging up on the classroom wall. There it was again – her tree. She'd drawn it so many times. And every time it seemed to take a little more out of her, grow a little stronger. This one seemed almost luminous. George's kite hung beneath it, pinned up like a giant butterfly.

'Sylvie Bartram! Shouldn't you be at a music

lesson?' Miss Coates's bad-tempered voice rang out.

Sylvie whipped round. Mr Flowerdew was standing right behind her.

'Uncle Alex! But I thought . . .' She looked around. Miss Coates was nowhere to be seen.

Mr Flowerdew touched his throat. 'A little trick of mine,' he said sheepishly. 'I couldn't resist it.'

'But it was exactly like her!'

'Wasn't it.' Mr Flowerdew beamed. 'I've often thought of playing a trick on her. Ring her up, give her a good ticking off about something, using her own voice. That would keep her quiet for a bit, don't you think?'

He laughed. Sylvie laughed with him. That was Uncle Alex all over. There was a mischievous side to him that usually she only saw when he came over to see Dad. He was quite a bit older than Dad, tall and craggy, with an unruly shock of white hair that sat on his head like waves crashing against the shore. He had long bony arms and long bony wrists, and when she was younger, he used to throw her up high in the air and catch her in his long bony hands and, when she couldn't sleep, sing her soft, sleepy lullabies. Though he was only part time, teaching the flute, he also ran the school choir. He had the most marvellous voice. He'd been helping Dad with his instruments ever since Daniel got started. She couldn't quite remember a time without Uncle Alex.

'It's very good, you know,' he said, pointing to her picture. 'When did you do it?'

'The beginning of this term,' she said. 'It's coming down tomorrow.'

'Well, I think it's marvellous – wonderfully alive.' He took a pace back, gazing at it intently. Sylvie couldn't help noticing that he had odd shoelaces on his scuffed suede shoes, one brown, one black. Typical. Just like Dad.

'Where's it of?' he asked casually.

'Nowhere really. It's just a tree I keep dreaming about.'

'Ah.' Uncle Alex turned to her, smiling. 'We all have dreams we'd like to come true.' He scratched his head, a little embarrassed. 'Look – would you mind very much if we cancelled our lesson today? The car's making a terrible racket and it's the only time the garage can see me. You can go to the music school if you want. Bang on the drums for an hour. I won't say anything.'

Sylvie tried not to show her delight. 'No, that's OK. I'll get off home. You're seeing Dad tomorrow, aren't you? Perhaps we could have a quick lesson then.'

'You mean Thursday? Yes, I don't see why not. How is he?'

'A bit frazzled. He's got a new instrument, the Clattercloud. He was working yesterday and it nearly burst our eardrums.'

'Really? He never said.'

'You talked to him?'

'Last night. Only briefly.' Uncle Alex tut-tutted, a schoolmaster-ish face coming to the fore. 'Those instruments of his! They'll get him into trouble one day. Look, I must run. Catch you soon.'

He ruffled her hair and walked out. Sylvie hit the air with her fist. She'd catch an earlier train, do what little homework there was, and delight Dad with a surprise dinner. She'd cook a Spanish omelette. It was the easiest thing to make.

She walked down through the town feeling light and happy, wondering how Dad's interview had gone, hoping too that in his excitement he'd remembered to get her that backstage pass. If she'd had a mobile she'd have been able to call him and remind him. Down by the station she was surprised to see Uncle Alex flying past in his green Morris Traveller. He didn't notice her, but he almost jumped the lights in his hurry to get out of town. There seemed nothing wrong with the car's engine at all. Perhaps he just wanted the afternoon off.

The train was pleasantly empty – no bad-tempered solicitors, no knitters, just a railway workman snoozing in the far corner and a couple of happy women back from a good morning's shopping in London. For the first few miles the train rumbled alongside the road, then branched off through the orchards and fields and hop gardens, the great old wood of the Weald stretching beyond. The fox's ledge was still empty, but that wasn't surprising. He was usually gone by the afternoon. As Sylvie walked back from the station, the road seemed quieter than ever. Of course, birds didn't sing as much in the afternoon as in the morning.

Mr Jackson was surprised to see her back so early. He sat up in his basket, thumping his tail. She took his lead off the hook and rattled the chain.

'Time for your constitutional, Mr Jackson. There's a good boy.'

He jumped up excitedly, his mouth open. He wanted desperately to tell her how pleased he was, but his voice was still hushed. There it was again, that sad, puzzled, almost reproachful look.

'There, there, Mr Jackson,' she said, tickling his throat. 'There, there. It'll get better soon.'

She led him down the back garden and out onto the old disused railway track. The air was warm, the grass soft under their feet. Sylvie loved the old railway track − its seclusion, the thick wall of brambles and hawthorn that sealed it off from the rest of the world. It was hard to believe that only a few metres away were ordinary gardens and roads. Though the railway line had long gone, the way it ran, half hidden from all the fields and houses nearby, still gave it that sense of mystery, that feeling of a journey. Long ago people had travelled along this route, sitting in railway

carriages, staring out of the windows, looking at the fields and passing farmhouses, thinking of things to come, of their future, of their past. All that remained now was this overgrown, intensely silent track, which stretched away into the distance, as if it could go on for ever. Sylvie had often felt that if you walked far enough along it, it would lead you somewhere unexpected, somewhere magical.

Coming back, she went into the kitchen, fed Mr Jackson and started on supper. It was an old-fashioned kitchen, with an old table in the middle and dark cupboards along the walls. Before Mum had died they were going to put in a new kitchen, but afterwards Dad didn't want to change anything. Memories, he said, were more important.

She started on the omelette. Mum had shown her how to make it the year before she died. First she chopped the onion into thin slices, then did the same with two large potatoes. She put them into a large frying pan with two tablespoons of oil, turned the heat down very low and put a lid on the top. It always looked like too much to begin with, but Sylvie knew that after twenty minutes it would have reduced to a soft melted mass. Sure enough, by seven they were ready. Dad would be home by ten past. She broke five eggs into a bowl, beat them with a fork, then stirred in the potatoes and onions before pouring the mixture back into the frying pan. It would take twenty minutes or so to cook. Dad would get home with time to change his clothes and have a wash before sitting down to supper. He might even like a glass of wine. Seeing what she'd done, he might even let her have a taste. She deserved it. She went to the cupboard, laid the table and put out two of their best glasses.

Ten past seven came, fifteen minutes past, but no sign of Dad. Sylvie wasn't worried. The train might have been delayed, although he usually left a message on the answerphone for her if it was. At twenty past the omelette was almost ready and no key turning in the door, no voice calling out, 'Sylvie?' Perhaps he had stopped off in the pub. Sylvie called but Jim the landlord said he hadn't been in all week. She slid the omelette onto a plate and put it out of Mr Jackson's reach. It didn't matter if it got cold. A cold Spanish omelette was as good as a hot one – better, Mum used to say. Mum had been funny that way. She'd preferred most things cold: tea, toast, Yorkshire puddings, roast potatoes. Even fish. When they bought fish and chips at the seaside, she used to open up the paper and wait until the fish was stone cold before eating hers. Then she used to gulp it down like a hungry penguin.

'Mum!' Sylvie would say. 'That is so gross.'

'Nonsense,' her mother used to reply. 'Nothing nicer than a bit of cold fish,' and she'd lick her fingers and sigh, as if missing something.

By eight o'clock there was still no sign of Dad. Sylvie

called his mobile, heard his quick, friendly voice:

'Hello. Daniel Bartram here. I can't take your call right now, but if you leave a message, I'll get back to you as soon as I can.'

'Dad! Dad! It's me. Please call me. I'm worried and I don't know what to do.'

Half past eight came and went. The house felt cold, the rooms strangely empty, as if the walls were waiting for someone who wasn't there. Even Mr Jackson looked unsettled. At nine o'clock the phone rang. Sylvie leaped upon it.

'Dad? Is that you?'

'The pest from the west here.'

'George. Get off the phone. I'm waiting for my dad to call. He hasn't come home yet and I don't know where he is.'

George detected trouble in her voice. 'Are you OK?' he asked.

'A bit worried. It's not like him not to call.'

'Perhaps he's in a meeting. My dad's always in meetings – least that's what Mum says. That's what you do when you go to work apparently. Have meetings. I mean, what's the point of all these lessons if at the end of it all we have to do is sit around jawing?'

'George.'

'Sorry. I'll get off. Call me if you want. I'll leave the mobile on silent so that the rents can't hear.'

George rang off. Sylvie looked around, not knowing what to do. Usually, if Dad was going to be very late, she stayed over at George's. When the orchestra were on tour, Dad's sister, Aunt Penny, came round, but that was never a success because she didn't approve of dogs. Once when the train had broken down and Dad couldn't get back, and the neighbours were away, Sylvie had locked the door and taken Mr Jackson upstairs, pulled up the steps to her bedroom and spent the night all alone. It hadn't been too bad. She could do things on her own now, things that she couldn't do before. It wasn't simply that she was older. Since Mum's death she was more used to thinking things out for herself, making decisions without the benefit of a grown-up's advice.

She ate half the omelette and poured herself a glass of wine. She sat at the kitchen table, waiting for the door to fly open and Dad to fall in, bursting with apologies. But nothing happened. Sylvie chewed mouthful after mouthful. The house was silent, except for the hum of the fridge and the occasional swish of Mr Jackson's tail on the floor. After the omelette she went into the living room and started to watch a quiz show. She couldn't concentrate on homework but she couldn't concentrate on the television either. Why wasn't Dad home? If anything had happened to him, surely the police would have called?

She was drifting off into troubled thoughts when the doorbell rang. Sylvie raced down the hall and, without thinking, opened the door. A small, clipped man stood on the doorstep.

'Sylvie Bartram?' He was carrying a large black case and, although it was summer, wore thick black leather gloves.

'Yes.' Her voice was flat, noncommittal. Mr Jackson padded up beside her. The man looked down, unperturbed.

'I've an appointment to see your father,' he said brightly.

'Oh.' Sylvie pressed her foot against the door.

'Yes, I represent the Song Company. Your father was most anxious to examine our product – songs for use in a domestic environment.' Out of his pocket he brought a squat glass bottle. It looked like the bottles they had in chemistry, only instead of having a stopper, the glass seemed to be twisted at the top like a stick of liquorice.

'This,' he said, 'is the very latest thing in home entertainment. We call it the SongGlass – one word, capital S, capital G. For an appropriate fee we can deliver any song you like to your doorstep.'

'What sort of songs?' Sylvie demanded, momentarily intrigued.

'What sort, young lady? What sort? Any sort you like. Songbirds are very popular. Better than that budgie you have in the house.'

'We don't have a budgie. I don't like caged birds.'

'My sentiments entirely.' The man smiled, revealing a row of little tobacco-stained teeth. 'With the SongGlass you don't need a cage or a budgie. All you need is one of these.' He waved the bottle in the air. 'Now, if I could just come in for a moment, I could give you a demonstration. Wouldn't you like that?'

He took a step forward and peered in. His breath smelled of stale tobacco. Suddenly Sylvie felt terribly small and vulnerable. She knew she had done the stupidest thing in her life, answering the door like that. There was no way she could prevent him from forcing his way in if he chose to. Did he really want to see Dad? Or was he after something else? Whatever he wanted, she knew she mustn't let him in. If he realized she was alone, there'd be no stopping him. She had to bluff it out. She stood back and flung the door wide open.

'You'd better come in and join the queue,' she said, keeping her voice as light as possible.

'Queue?' The little man stopped short, hovering at the door.

'Yes. My teachers, Mr Jackson and Miss Coates, are in the back room. They've been waiting for Dad for over an hour. Why don't you come in and show them too? I'm sure they'd love to see it.'

She pointed down the hall, towards the low murmur of voices coming from the half-opened door.

The man stepped back. 'You're very kind, Sylvie,

very kind, but I have other, pressing engagements. And it doesn't do to disappoint one's prospective customers, does it? Will he be in tomorrow?'

'Yes, as far as I know.'

'Working in that cabin of his. Do you know what we call it? The Loudest Little Hut in Hertfordshire.'

'We don't live in Hertfordshire.'

The man raised a finger in the air. 'Precisely.' He shuffled his feet. 'Well, I must be off. But before I go . . .' Holding the SongGlass in the air, he snapped off the top with a flick of his hand. All at once something fluttered past Sylvie's face and the hall was filled with the sound of a lark singing high in the air. It hovered above her head for a moment, then flew up and down the corridor before disappearing out of the open door.

'How did you do that?' she asked, open-mouthed.

'Ah.' The man wagged a finger. 'Trade secret.' He tipped his hat. 'Till the next time, when I can come in and show you properly. Toodle-pip.'

She watched as he ducked down the garden path. Quickly she locked the door and, running into the safety of the living room, pulled the curtains together before bursting into tears. No one could see her now, but she didn't feel safe at all. Mr Jackson trotted over and nuzzled up against her. She buried her head in his thick black coat. He smelled reassuring. He was warm and solid, the one living creature she could depend on. He stretched out on the carpet and sighed.

'He'll be back soon, Mr Jackson, you see if he isn't.' She put her arms around him. She stroked his head and looked into his deep brown eyes. Did he know what she was feeling? Did he know something was wrong? If only he could talk! She closed her eyes, wishing that everything would just jump back to normal. The wine had made her sleepy. If she lay down for a minute, then perhaps it would all come right.

Then she woke, all cold and stiff, unsure of where she was or what had happened. The house lights were on but the rays of the sun were shining through the gaps in the curtain. Mr Jackson lay fast asleep on the sofa, his head on a cushion, his feet twitching on the edge of a dream. She shivered. She looked at the clock. It was six in the morning. Dad still hadn't come home.

She was all alone.

Chapter 4

She went into the kitchen, made herself a cup of
tea and sat down at the kitchen table, trying to
work out what to do. She knew what she should do:
tell someone what had happened. The trouble was,
she was afraid of the consequences. She knew what
would happen as soon as she reported Dad missing. She'd be made to go and stay with Aunt Penny
in Hemel Hempstead. Mr Jackson would be put in
kennels. As if that wasn't bad enough, Dad might get
into trouble for leaving her alone all night. She might
even be taken into care. She'd always been terrified of
something happening to upset the balance of her pre-
carious family. When Mum had died, it was like one
of the legs of a sturdy table had been knocked away.
Everything seemed to wobble a bit. Something like

this could bring the whole world crashing down.

The best thing would be to go to school and act as if nothing had happened. Dad would be bound to get in touch. If she hadn't heard anything by the end of the day, she would go to Uncle Alex. Until then, she would keep her fingers crossed and hope for the best.

She ate a slice of toast and let Mr Jackson out into the back garden. The blackbird with the white feather was in his usual place waiting for his breakfast. Sylvie threw the crusts in, listening carefully. It was still unnaturally quiet. Coming back inside though, she noticed something even more extraordinary. Dad's bassoon case was standing in its usual place under the coat rack, half hidden behind his disreputable mackintosh. How was that possible? He'd had it with him on the train yesterday morning, she was absolutely certain. So how come it was here? It could only mean one thing. He had come home. But when? Before she'd come back, or after? Surely not while she'd been asleep! Her heart began to beat wildly.

'Dad! Dad! Are you here?' She raced through the house calling his name, then dashed out into the garden and down to the shed. She pulled on the door furiously.

'Dad! Dad! Are you in there?' But it was firmly locked, the padlock impervious to her entreaties. Back in the house, she stopped in the kitchen, trying to collect her thoughts. If he'd come back, surely he'd left a message, a note. The thought hadn't occurred to her last night. Frantically she started looking: on the pad near the telephone, through the piles of letters and unpaid bills stacked up on the little table in the hall, on the notice board hanging on the kitchen wall. Nothing. But at every juncture she noticed that things were not quite right. The pad by the telephone was upside down; the bills were on top of the letters, whereas Dad always hid them underneath; the post-cards pinned to the notice board were all askew. He'd been searching for something.

She checked the computer for post-it notes and e-mails. Again, nothing. Nothing in the letter box hanging on the back of the front door, nothing in her room, nothing, nothing, nothing. She stood on the landing, staring at the photo of Mum looking so happy, so alive.

'Oh, Mum,' she cried out. 'I need you back here,' but Mum said nothing either; just stared back as she always did, smiling and glistening with water. Downstairs, the clock in the hall struck eight. She had fifteen minutes to get ready and catch the train. She had to catch the train. She knew that if she was late for school and Miss Coates demanded to know why, she'd break down. She was only just holding on as it was.

She hurried into the bathroom and, grabbing her toothbrush, picked up the toothpaste. The tube was empty, which was odd, considering they'd gone shopping last Saturday and bought a brand-new one. She washed her face and took hold of her scrunchy to tie back her hair. The door to the little medicine cupboard stood open, and as she swung it shut, there on the mirror stared a huge, unblinking eye, just like the one Dad had drawn on the carriage window when they had first seen the fox. She touched it. The surface was hard, but underneath it was soft. She smeared a blob on her finger and held it to her nose. Dad had drawn that eye again, in toothpaste! He had left her a message. But what did it mean?

She stared at the mirror. In the reflection she could see her own worried face and, shining out from the middle of her forehead like a third eye, Dad's drawing. It seemed to be burning its way into her memory. 'Eyes and Ears,' Dad had whispered. 'Always remember. Eyes and Ears are everywhere. Look out for the fox, follow his movements, but don't tell a soul. You never know who's listening.'

She grabbed her things and ran down to the station, the words pounding in her head. As she reached the little footbridge, the train was pulling into the station. Waving her arms, she ran over and raced along the platform. The carriage door swung open. Sylvie jumped in and flopped down. She could hear the fat solicitor whingeing on as usual.

'. . . and I told him, I don't like beetroot. It stains the mashed potato. And do you know what he did?'

But Sylvie never heard what he did, for the man with the rabbit teeth pulled the door shut and said, 'Morning, young miss. That was a close thing. School today?'

Sylvie nodded, out of breath. The man tapped the empty seat opposite her with the tip of his stick.

'Your father not here today?' he enquired.

'No,' she stammered, thinking quickly. 'He's not very well.'

'I'm sorry to hear that.' He turned to the woman with the kid gloves. 'He's not very well,' he repeated.

'Nothing serious, we hope.' The woman with kid gloves looked concerned. Sylvie could have kicked herself. Now they'd start asking questions about doctors and thermometers.

'It's just a bit of a cough,' she explained, 'but he's going away for a few days and doesn't want to take any chances. I had to make him breakfast. That's why I nearly missed the train.'

'That's why she nearly missed the train,' Rabbit-teeth repeated. His nose started to twitch.

The woman with kid gloves leaned across and placed a hand on Sylvie's arm. Her fingers curled round like a claw. She had extraordinarily strong hands. 'What a lucky man your father must be to have such a caring daughter.'

'Very lucky,' Rabbit-teeth agreed. 'I wouldn't mind catching cold with a daughter like you to look after me.'

'Or anything,' the woman with kid gloves added. 'Mumps, measles, spots before the eyes, it's all the same to her,' and she opened her mouth and laughed. Her breath smelled of old seaweed.

The journey carried on as usual. One by one they got in, turned on their machines, answered their phones, concentrated on their puzzles, but Sylvie barely noticed them. All she could see was that eye, staring at her from the bathroom mirror. Something had happened to Dad and he didn't want anyone to know. But what?

The train reached the fox's bend. She tensed herself, hoping against hope that he would be there. It would help to restore things to normality. But the little earthen platform was as empty as the day before. First the fox, then her dad. She could feel tears rising up. If she wasn't careful, they'd start running down her face and her secret would be out. She took out a paper handkerchief and blew her nose.

'I hope it's not catching.' The woman with kid gloves sniffed.

'Whatever it is,' echoed the man with the rabbit teeth. And the two of them stared at her hard. She was glad to get off the train.

George was waiting for her in the school bus.

'Well?' he demanded. 'Did he turn up?'

It all tumbled out: how her dad must have come

home some time during the day, the drawing she'd found on the mirror, and how it meant to keep quiet, not tell anybody. Then she told him about the explosion the night before.

'A big bang, eh? Serious malarkey,' intoned George gravely. He took off his glasses and rubbed the lenses with the end of his tie. 'But you've told me.'

Sylvie looked at his big red face. 'Yes, but Dad didn't mean you. I can trust you.'

George smiled. 'Yes, you can. So is that everything? Did anything unusual happen on the train yesterday?'

'Not when I was on it. Except—' She stopped.

'What?'

She took a deep breath. She might as well tell George about the fox too.

'Dad didn't like it when he realized the fox wasn't there. He tried to hide it, but he was worried, I could tell. Then there were the birds. When we were walking to the station that morning, there were no birds singing. Or this morning. And Mr Jackson's lost his voice too.'

'I don't see what that has got to do with anything,' he said. 'Anything else?'

'There was a man who called yesterday, trying to sell Dad this weird birdsong that came out of a bottle.'

'What was he like?'

'Scary. He said Dad had made an appointment to

see him, but I didn't believe him.'

The bus pulled up outside the school gates. The doors hissed open. Everyone jumped up from their seats, gathering their books. The car park was awash with cars and bicycles. Alex Flowerdew waved at Sylvie as he got out of his Morris Traveller. When he put his feet on the ground, she noticed that he was wearing the most beautiful shoes she had ever seen, light grey, slim and polished. They didn't go with the rest of his outfit at all.

George turned towards her, his face grave. 'I don't think you should be there alone, Sylvie. It doesn't sound safe.'

'But he doesn't want me to tell anyone, George. I've got to find out what's happened. He's in some kind of trouble. He needs my help, I just know it.'

The tears that she had held back all morning started to well up inside her.

George put his arm around her and handed her a crumpled tissue. 'I'm not saying that. What I'm saying is, we must be very careful.'

'We?'

'Well, you helped me get my kite back. It's only right and proper that I should help you find your dad. And I'm meant to be staying over tonight, remember. The rents will be very disappointed if I tell them it's off. Quite spoil their evening. I tremble to think what they get up to when I'm not there.'

Sylvie smiled through her tears.

'So what now?' George asked gently.

She gathered herself together. 'First we should find out when he came back and why. At break, if it's OK, I'll borrow your mobile, ring his work, see if he went in at all yesterday. Tonight we'll go through the house from top to bottom, see if we can find any more clues. Tomorrow we'll retrace his footsteps. The people on the train – the ones Dad and I see every day – maybe they saw something. Then it's the last day of school. After that, I don't know. But I've got all holiday to find him, haven't I?'

George wasn't listening. He was looking up at a hot-air balloon floating high in the morning sky. A little way in front flapped a flock of black-necked swans, their long white wings beating in slow unison.

'That balloon is going the wrong way,' he said, screwing up his eyes.

'How do you mean?'

'The wind – it's blowing in the other direction.'

Sylvie put her hand to her eyes. It was too far away to see clearly. 'Don't you get different currents that high, cross winds and things?'

'Yes.' George sounded doubtful.

Sylvie stared up as the balloon drifted past, the swans keeping steadily ahead. It looked so peaceful up there, so quiet, so ordered. That's what here must look like from up there, she thought, quiet and peaceful, and yet it was anything but. All at once the swans swerved east, towards the coast. There was a surge of fire from the burner and the balloon seemed to change direction too. The school bell rang. She tugged at George's sleeve. He was still transfixed.

'Come on,' she said. 'We've got work to do.'

All through the day Sylvie could barely concentrate. She kept looking out of the window, wondering where her dad might be. At break she rang the orchestra to see if he'd gone to work that day, but he hadn't. All they'd had was a message left on the answerphone, saying that his aunt was ill and he'd had to go away for a few days.

The day dragged on. She tried to eat her lunch but couldn't. Her heart was twisting, wrenched inside. Maths was a nightmare. In English, Miss Coates gave her a ticking off for not reciting the tiger poem properly and made her promise to learn it for tomorrow. And to cap it all even Uncle Alex came down on her. At singing practice he was quite sharp with her.

'Sylvie Bartram, is the outside so much more interesting than what we're doing here?'

'Yes, Uncle Flowerdew.'

'What!' His face went bright red. A ripple went around the room. Mr Flowerdew hated people making fun of him.

'I mean, no, Mr Flowerdew. Sorry.'

'Sorry won't help you get this piece right. Perhaps you should stay behind until you do.'

Sylvie answered back without thinking: 'I can't do that, not today.'

Mr Flowerdew stretched himself to his full height, his mouth set, ready for a fight. 'Can't? What do you mean, can't? You will if I say so.'

Sylvie was adamant. 'No, I can't, Mr Flowerdew. Not today.'

'Actually she really can't,' George put in. 'My mum's arranged everything. Sleepover and that.'

'Oh.' Alex Flowerdew rapped his baton on the music stand. 'Very well. But next time, Miss Bartram, I won't be so lenient.'

The bell rang. Sylvie gathered her things together. As the others trooped out, he beckoned her over.

'Sorry about that, Sylvie. I have to do it, you know, in front of everyone, even if I don't like to.'

'I know, Uncle Alex.' She could feel herself trembling inside. She bit her lip, trying to keep everything back.

'Is everything all right, Sylvie?' His face softened. It would be so easy to tell him. She looked down.

'What happened to the shoes?' she said, glad of the distraction.

'What?'

'Your shoes this morning. They were fabulous. They must have cost you a packet. You're not wearing them now.'

'Oh, those. No, I didn't think they were quite suitable.' He looked flustered, caught out. 'Go on, cut along to your sleepover,' he said, and waved her away with a smile.

It was strange going back to the house, even though George was with her. It had a cold, empty feeling, as if drained of life. Mr Jackson rushed out into the garden and squatted behind the bamboo canes. Sylvie took George upstairs to show him the mirror.

'You sure it's an eye?' George sounded doubtful. 'It looks more like a fish to me.'

'Of course it's an eye.'

'Whatever it is, I don't understand. If your dad wanted to leave you a message, why did he leave it here? And why did he draw it rather than write it? It would have been so much simpler. And why this?' He pressed it gently with his fingers. 'I mean, we all know your dad's a bit weird, but toothpaste!'

Sylvie sprang to his defence. 'He's not weird.'

'No? And what other father comes to parents' evening in a bow tie and Wellington boots? Look, I'm not dissing him. Weird is the best. One day I'm going to be weird too.'

'I don't think you can plan to be weird, George. You either are or you aren't. And as a matter of fact, you are a bit weird too.'

'Too?'

'All right. I accept it. My dad is weird.'

'Good. So he draws this thing in toothpaste and leaves it here for you to find. That's another thing I don't get. How come you didn't spot in right away?'

'The mirror door had been left open,' Sylvie explained. 'I only saw it when I closed it to brush my hair.'

George shook his head. 'That doesn't make any sense either. He wants to leave you this message, but he paints it in toothpaste and leaves it where you won't see it? It's almost as if . . .'

'What?'

'As if he didn't want you to find it, as if he was hiding it.'

Sylvie jumped up and down so hard, the floor shook. 'George, that's it! You're right. What if he was hiding it? Not from me, but from someone else – someone who must have been in the house with him, who brought him back perhaps, to look for something. That would explain everything being out of place. Dad knew I would see the message eventually, because that's where I always do my hair in the morning. But whoever was with him wouldn't know that. So Dad came up here, drew the eye and left the cupboard door open so that the other person wouldn't see it. Then he took Dad away. He's been kidnapped, George!'

George looked unimpressed. 'Who'd want to kidnap your dad? He's not a spy.'

'I don't know. But it's the only explanation that I can think of.'

George ran his fingers over the toothpaste drawing. It had grown quite hard. 'Well, if someone else was here, they might have left something behind. A footprint, a button, a strand of hair. We'd better start looking.'

In Daniel's bedroom they found his purple tie, the one he was wearing that morning, draped over the back of the chair. George held it to his chest, then threw it down in disgust.

'It's worse than the school tie,' he said. 'Tell you what though. It would be helpful if we knew what he was wearing now. Can you do that?'

'Of course. Who do you think does the ironing?'

It didn't take Sylvie long to find out what was missing. A pair of green cord trousers, a brown jacket with a funny green collar that Mum had sewn on when the mice had nibbled through the original one, a yellow checked shirt and, strangely, the joke pair of socks that played Jingle Bells whenever he crossed his legs, which she had bought him last Christmas. His dress suit – the one he wore for performances – was gone too, as was the bow tie.

'Perhaps he's moonlighting as a waiter to earn more money,' George suggested. 'Perhaps he's ashamed, doesn't want you to know.'

'Perhaps you're talking rubbish,' Sylvie replied.

They searched every other room but found nothing else, except Mr Jackson's squeaky toy down the back of the sofa and a toenail clipper nestling in the fruit bowl amongst the apples.

'That is truly revolting,' George said, holding it at arm's length. 'One trembles to think where the toenails are. Now what?'

Sylvie looked out of the kitchen window. 'The music hut. I haven't looked there. I didn't have time this morning.'

It took several goes before the padlock sprang back. As soon as the door swung open Sylvie knew that something was wrong. It sounded hollow, smelled empty. She stepped inside. All the instruments, all Dad's papers were gone. All that was left was the Harmonograph standing forlornly in the centre of the room. She held her hand to her mouth.

'They've taken everything. The Shinglechord, the Furroughla, everything.'

'Look, here,' said George, pointing down. 'You can see where they've dragged them out into the garden.

They followed the trail through the gate, out onto the old railway track. They could see tyre marks and a flurry of footprints – one in particular of a very pointed boot.

'They came this way because no one would see them from the road. There's an entrance down by the station. It's not used much now, but—' She stopped. This was all getting too much for her.

'Well, at least we know why he was taken,' George said gently, poking the long grass with his foot. 'It's got something to do with this music of his. Maybe that explosion you talked about – he didn't want you to talk about that, did he?' He bent down. 'Hello? What's this?'

A metal rod about half a metre in length lay in the flattened grass. One end was blunt, but at the other was a loop with a hole in it, like a metal eye.

'Looks like part of a machine,' George said. 'A piston or something.'

Sylvie took it from him. It was cold and smooth and surprisingly heavy. 'I've never seen it before. What do you think it's made of? Silver? Lead?' She passed it back.

'Maybe. It weighs enough.' He shivered. 'Come on. It's getting dark.'

Back inside, he placed the object on the kitchen table. It lay there, a dull shine to it like a dead fish. It made them feel uneasy, as if it wasn't dead at all, but merely asleep. George walked round it a couple of times.

'You're sure it doesn't belong to your dad?'

'Positive. It's too' – Sylvie searched for the right word – 'too metallic. His instruments are more natural.'

'Metal's natural,' George objected. 'And so is my hunger. How about some nosh?'

She walked over to the fridge and took out the rest of the omelette. She cut it into two.

George looked at it with suspicion. 'What is that exactly?'

'An omelette.'

He lowered his nose to the plate and sniffed. 'Correct me if I'm wrong but most omelettes are served hot. A cold omelette? Why bother to cook the eggs at all? Why don't we just drink them raw?'

'George, it's meant to be this way. It's a Spanish omelette. They're often eaten cold.'

'In Spain maybe, where it's boiling hot. What else you got?'

Sylvie sighed and from the freezer pulled out the largest pizza she could find. Thirty minutes later they were chewing their way through pepperoni and cheese. George was right. It was good to have something warm and comforting. The kitchen almost felt like home again. She was glad George was here, for she knew she couldn't have endured tonight on her own. In a strange way she was enjoying herself.

'How about a glass of wine too?' she suggested. 'I opened a bottle for Dad last night.'

'Fabuloso.'

Sylvie took the bottle and pulled the cork out with her teeth. They listened to the gurgle as she filled their glasses. George took his glass and held it out.

'Cheers,' he said, trying to sound grown up.

They clinked glasses. George lifted his glass to his lips and took the tiniest of sips. Sylvie could see him trying hard not to pull a face.

'Have you drunk wine before?' she asked him.

'Loads.' He wiped his mouth with his sleeve. 'I drink it all the time, you know, my dad being half French.'

'You never told me you were half French.'

'Didn't I? Oh yes, we had chateaux all over the place. Unfortunately my great-great-great-grandfather got his head chopped off in the Revolution. What you might call *dommage*. Wine's all we've got left.'

He took an even bigger gulp. His eyes started watering. 'The fact is, I shall probably make my career in wine – grow the stuff, supply to all those grand dinners people have, with footmen and speeches, and everyone in penguin suits. You know the sort of thing.' He picked up the wand and rapped it against his glass. 'My lords, ladies and gentlemen, pray silence for *le grand—*'

'That's it!' Sylvie jumped up.

'What?'

'What you're holding. It's the striking part of a triangle – wands, they're called. That eye is for hanging the wand on the triangle's base. Only this one's a lot bigger than most.'

'So what's it doing here? Your dad doesn't play the triangle.'

'Perhaps it belongs to the person he was hiding

the message from.' She bit her finger. 'Maybe he and Dad had a fight and it fell out in the struggle. Perhaps Dad's hurt.'

She couldn't say any more. George tried to comfort her.

'That might not be it at all. It could have fallen out by accident. Anything might have happened. The point is, it's our first clue.'

Sylvie's face brightened. 'Yes, and whoever dropped it might come back looking for it.' She started to clear plates from the table. 'Come on, George, we're going up to my room to keep watch. You can see every inch of the garden from there.'

They took the wand, a plate of chocolate biscuits and two glasses of milk up to the attic. Sylvie laid the wand on her bedside table, turned off the light and they sat together in silence. One by one, the neighbouring bedroom lights went off. The room seemed to disappear. All they were aware of was the moonlit garden below. They could see it all laid out in the silvery light: the brick path, the bird table, the apple tree where Mum used to lie in her hammock, singing softly to herself. On the other side was Dad's hut, with its porch and bird feeders and little lantern hanging over the door. It wasn't a big garden, but looking down on it, Sylvie thought what a lot of life it had seen: the time she'd fallen and cut open her knee; the day Mr Jackson had buried Dad's hat in the flowerbed; the afternoon when she had crept up to a sleeping, sun-bathing Mum and poured a watering can of cold water all over her. And Mum had just wriggled a bit and murmured, 'Oooh, lovely, darling – any more?' Every garden had memories, every house; the walls and hedges kept them close.

The night began to stir around them: a hooting owl flitted into the subdued light; a lone white cat emerged from a side hedge and cleaned her paws under the bird table, before setting off for a night's hunting; intermittent shrieks broke the hush, as if some predator had broken in upon a startled bird. Every now and again a blur of hurried shapes would scurry past the gate, but what they were – badgers? foxes? – Sylvie couldn't say. Two hours, three hours they sat, the night growing ever deeper, the world enveloped in a heavy stillness that seemed unwilling to move. It was hard to imagine daylight ever returning, so firm, so fixed was this dark intensity. Sylvie felt herself falling asleep. She looked over. George was picking his nose.

'This is silly,' she said, 'both of us getting tired. Let's take turns to sleep. An hour each. Me first, then you. And be careful what you do with that,' she said, pointing to his finger. 'I do not want to come across it in the morning.'

Sylvie settled down. She thought she wouldn't be able to sleep, but she did, almost right away. And right away she began to dream the dream she always dreamed when she was troubled: she was back at Durdle Door, the afternoon her mum disappeared.

As always, they were walking along the pebble beach, Mr Jackson slinking along after them, not wanting to go out at all. There had been a violent storm the day before, and though the afternoon sky was clear and bright, the sea was high and fierce, snow-white waves pounding in, smashing against the beach, dragging the shingle back and forth like an angry animal in a cage.

'Listen to that sound,' Dad was saying. 'The music it makes. If I could capture just a fraction of that tune, find a way of incorporating that rhythm!' and as usual he started to walk ahead, looking for shells and stones and anything else that might prove useful.

'Dad's got his head in the clouds again,' Mum laughed. Sylvie wanted to call out and stop him, but she could not. She did what she always did: kept hold of her mother's hand, trying to keep her following Dad's path, but every time the sea came crashing in, Mum took a step closer, drawn to it like a magnet. Then they were at the arch itself, and though Sylvie knew how it would end, she could not prevent it. Mum pulled her hand free and, stepping out of her dress, plunged in, striking out into the water rushing through the great rock.

She shouted a warning, but Mum just laughed and dived under the foam, emerging moments later, the water running down her face.

'This is wonderful,' she trilled, her voice echoing under the arch. 'Wonderful!'

Sylvie called out to her dad, but he could not hear her above the wind and the water and the screaming gulls. The water swept Mum back and forth, taking her almost to the very top of the arch before plunging her down into a great swirling hollow. It threw her this way and that, tossing her about like a dog with a ball. She was having such fun.

'Mum!' Sylvie cried. 'Be careful!'

Then the sea began to stir, churning like a whirlpool with her mum in the middle of it. Round and round she spun, her arms stretched out, her body twirling faster and faster, like on a crazy fairground ride. There was a rushing sound, then a gurgling, as if a plug was being pulled.

'Mum?' Sylvie shouted. 'Are you all right?'

'Of course I am, poppet. It's just . . .'

Then it happened as it always happened, as it happened that day and every day after in Sylvie's memory. The sea under the arch grew suddenly still. Sylvie's mum seemed to rise up out of the water, the bubbling green streaming off her sleek body and her long black hair. She was smiling.

'Love you, Sylvie,' she cried. 'Love you both, very much,' and then she went under for the last time, her legs giving a little flip in the water, as if they were joined together. Sylvie began to scream.

'Mum! Mum! Mum!' but she knew it was no use. Dad would come running back and would hurl himself into the sea; the air would be full of their cries, but Mum would not return. The water would grow uneasily still, the seagulls would wheel and call in vain, and Dad would come stumbling back, his face wild and empty. If only she could dream it all differently. If only Mum could come back from the sea, hold her in her arms, speak to her again, even if it was just in a dream. But however hard she wished, the vision never changed.

She woke with a start. Something was wrong. Although the room was quiet, there was a restlessness in the air. She could feel it rolling round the foot of her bed: a sense of prowling, of searching, of eyes locked on the ground. George lay across the foot of the bed, fast asleep.

'George,' she whispered. 'George, wake up. I think there's someone outside.'

They crept over to the window. Up in the sky the moon had lost its colour; dawn was not far away. Below, the ground seemed to sparkle, as if covered in a hoary dust. Her father's hut, the apple tree, the bird table – they all looked like they'd been hewn from blocks of ice. Sylvie felt that if she cried out loud, the garden would shatter into tiny pieces. But there was no one there.

'False alarm,' George said.

From out of nowhere came a flurry of silent birds circling the garden in long low sweeps before settling on the roof of the hut and on the lawn: green woodpeckers, their beaks dark and inquisitive in the pallid light.

'Just like the ones at the station yesterday,' Sylvie whispered, 'only there must be fifty of them here.'

The gate swung open. Sylvie gripped George's arm. Close to the ground, his arms stretched out, his long black fingers patting the ground, came a long, bent, angular man. He was dressed in a livid green coat, and his hair fell in great tangled ribbons onto his shoulders. On his head was perched a top hat of brilliant red. It seemed to glow and quiver in the dark, as if it were breathing.

'Don't you see?' Sylvie mouthed. 'The red hat, the green jacket? He's dressed just like them. A Woodpecker Man.'

The Woodpecker Man began to hop forward, his nose nearly touching the ground. The glow from his hat shed an uneasy light, as if the grass were bathed in blood.

'He must be looking for the wand,' George whispered. They both turned round. The wand lay cold and inert on the bedside table. Straightening up, the Woodpecker Man drew something from inside his jacket. He turned it slowly in his hands and then held it out straight in front of him.

George squinted. 'What's that? A metal detector?'

'It's a triangle, George. A triangle. But bigger than any I've ever seen.'

The Woodpecker Man began to sweep the triangle back and forth over the garden, like a water diviner searching for a hidden spring. They could see his face now, drawn and sharp, with sunken cheeks between a long pointed nose and thin, bloodless lips that seemed to be muttering to an invisible companion. Slowly he hopped forward, his fingers curled tightly round the triangle's base, the woodpeckers fluttering in his wake. As he passed the triangle across the back of the house, it began to twitch. The Woodpecker Man froze and slowly raised his head. Holding it at arm's length, he licked a finger and ran it lightly over the three sides. There was a low humming in the air. On the bedside table the wand began to vibrate, as if someone had switched on a little battery inside it. The Woodpecker Man stared up at their window, took off his hat, brushed it with his arm and bowed. George pulled Sylvie back, frightened.

'Do you think he saw us?' he gulped.

'He can't have done. It's too dark,' but Sylvie wasn't sure. They edged forward again. The Woodpecker Man and his birds were nowhere to be seen.

'Perhaps they've gone,' she said hopefully.

There was a loud thud. The whole house shook. The man was throwing himself against the kitchen door. Then came the sound of broken glass, a key skittering across the tiled floor.

'He's breaking into the kitchen,' George cried.

Sylvie tried to smother her own doubts. 'Mr Jackson wouldn't let him.' They could hear the dog jumping up, paws against the door. A high-pitched whistle stung their ears, then silence. The house was still again.

'What's happened?' Sylvie was as frightened as George.

The kitchen door was scraped open. There was a fluttery *whoomph* in the air, like the sound of a train plunging into a tunnel, fast and feathery. Something fell onto the kitchen floor – a mug or a plate – then a whole sideboard full seem to smash to the ground. The air below was filled with beating wings. The wand began to buzz again, as if sending out a signal. Sylvie ran across the room.

'He knows it's here. Quick, George, the trapdoor, before they find their way up.'

George scrambled over, and together they began to pull on the rope. Below, they could hear the Woodpecker Man hopping through the room, and the scratch of the birds' feet as they followed him down the corridor towards the stairs.

'Hurry, George. If they get in . . .'

They threw all their weight behind the pulley, bracing their feet against the floor as if they were in a tug of war. To Sylvie the attic steps had never seemed heavier. George's presence didn't seem to make any difference at all. The steps began to rise slowly as the hop-hop-hop of the birds scratched up the stairs. A plump green woodpecker flew up over the landing rail, screeching loudly before colliding with the light fitting and crashing to the floor, stunned.

'Come on, George, pull!'

The Woodpecker Man's hat began to fill the well of the stairs, then a hand, thin and black, curled round the banisters. They could hear the rasp of his breath, the low mutter on his lips, and through the air came a cloying smell of mildew. Another bird flew up past him, then another, the two of them blundering into the wall opposite, knocking Mum's picture off its hook. The Woodpecker Man looked up. His eyes were hard and black and flashed with dark malevolence. He saw the trapdoor rising and uttered a thick guttural cry. The birds rushed past him, squawking and flapping, hurling themselves against the closing door.

'Harder, George!' Sylvie urged. The Woodpecker Man leaped up and grabbed the lip of the trapdoor, his fingers wrapped around the edge, his feet lifted clean off the floor. He hung there, raising himself up by his arms, trying to pull the trapdoor down.

'I can't hold on,' George warned.

'Yes you can. Pull with me. One, two, three . . . !'

The trapdoor jerked up. There was a shriek as the

Woodpecker Man's fingers were caught in the gap. They slackened their grip for a second and he fell howling to the floor. Sylvie and George pulled once more and the trapdoor snapped shut. Sylvie dropped to her knees and shot the bolt home. Through the crack she could see the Woodpecker Man picking himself up, blowing on his bruised fingers. Flexing them, he grabbed the loose rope and began to pull as hard as he could. All over the landing, on the banisters, on the floor, on every inch of stair, stood the woodpeckers, tapping their beaks in encouragement.

'They can't get in,' Sylvie whispered. 'Not now.'

They stood in silence, hardly daring to breathe. The trapdoor strained against the lock as the Woodpecker Man tried to pull it free. Then came an uneasy quiet. The tapping stopped, the rope hung loose. Then they heard him shuffling into Daniel's room, riffling through cupboards and wardrobes, mumbling to himself in agitated pain.

'What's he doing now?' George asked.

Sylvie pressed her ear to the gap. 'Sounds like he's looking for something.'

'But he's after the wand, isn't he?'

They listened intently as he hopped from room to room, woodpeckers scattering under his heels. The bedrooms, the bathroom, back down the stairs he went, searching methodically from room to room. They could hear books and papers flung down, desks and drawers opened, furniture moved, accompanied all the while by malevolent, throaty whispers. Then, abruptly, silence.

Over by the window, they watched as the Woodpecker Man emerged on the path, the woodpeckers following.

'He's going,' George whispered, more in hope than belief. 'We've beaten him.'

'Don't speak too soon,' Sylvie replied. 'Look.'

Turning off the concrete path, the Woodpecker Man ploughed his way through the flowerbeds until he stood directly beneath their window. Thrusting his arm deep into the ivy, he began to climb up the wall towards the attic window. Sylvie and George stood rooted to the spot. Slowly the top of his red hat drew closer. They could see it clearly now. It was alive, wriggling with light thrown by a thousand fireflies, their tiny legs trapped on the sticky surface. Then the leaves parted and he was outside, his lips pressed against the glass, his eyes darting about as he searched the room. The wand began to buzz again, almost jumping off the little table. The Woodpecker Man pointed and the window was covered in woodpeckers, their beaks hammering against the glass. Cracks splintered across the surface. A beak broke through, then another. Soon the whole window would shatter.

'Leave us alone!' Sylvie screamed. 'Leave us alone!'

The Woodpecker Man stared at her, shaking his

head, grinning black teeth and pink gums. He leaned back and banged his head hard again the windowpane. A thousand cracks shot across it. He wiggled his long black pointed tongue at her and dangled the triangle in triumph. A woodpecker was wriggling through a hole in the top of the window.

George seized a cushion. 'Get back!' he cried. 'Get back!'

Then, like a splash of cold water on a dream, on the other side of the fence a back door was opened. Someone coughed the night's sleep away. The Woodpecker Man looked round. Down the road came the electric whine of the milk float. The world was awake again. Sylvie's gate rattled, the milkman whistling as he walked down the path towards the kitchen door. Startled, the woodpeckers flew away. The Woodpecker Man banged his head one last time and, spreading his coat out wide, fell, half floating back to the ground. He straightened his hat and hopped away, until all they could see was the red top bobbing down the railway track.

They waited another hour before venturing downstairs. The house was a complete wreck – clothes strewn about, drawers emptied, armchairs overturned. In the kitchen, glass and broken crockery lay all over the floor. Mr Jackson was cowering in his basket. He came up to Sylvie and licked her hand, anxious for reassurance. Suddenly they felt cold. They didn't want to go upstairs again. This house couldn't protect them any more. Sylvie tidied up downstairs as best she could while George made them some hot chocolate. They drank it standing up. They were too scared to sit.

'That's settled it,' George said, his hand wrapped around the warm mug. 'I don't care what your dad's message means. You've got to get help now.' He took a sip, his teeth chattering against the china.

'Uncle Alex will know what to do.' Sylvie picked up the wand and put it in her school bag. 'He might even know what this is all about. And you're coming too,' she added, clipping the lead onto Mr Jackson's collar. 'Just in case they come back.'

Outside, the day seemed unnaturally calm and serene. They walked quickly down to the station, Mr Jackson wedged in between them, his tail slunk between his legs. There were no birds singing, no dogs barking, no sounds of life at all. It made everything else – the noise of passing cars, distant aeroplanes – seem misplaced. Even the clank of the postman's old bicycle seemed unreal.

Once on the platform, Sylvie stood in her usual spot, George glancing up and down, half expecting the Woodpecker Man to jump out from behind the hedge and snatch the bag out of Sylvie's hands. The train was five minutes late. Sylvie scrambled in and settled down with a sigh of relief. They were nearly there. Just a train and a bus ride, and then she'd seek out Mr Flowerdew. How she wished she'd told him everything yesterday.

She looked around. It was good to see the old familiar faces. The man with rabbit teeth was poking a finger in his ear. The woman with kid gloves was tapping out an idle rhythm on her knitting needles. Further down, the plump solicitor was on a fresh topic.

'. . . and as for our station car park, there are not enough spaces. And they charge too much. And the tickets don't stick on the windscreen. What is one supposed to do? Carry a pot of glue?'

'I spit on mine,' his companion observed, 'but then I have very strong saliva.'

The man with rabbit teeth folded his hands over the top of his stick. 'Morning, young miss. School today?'

Sylvie nodded. 'Last day.'

The woman with kid gloves nodded in the direction of Mr Jackson.

'What's that?'

'That's my dog, Mr Jackson,' Sylvie explained.

'Does he have a ticket?' the woman with kid gloves demanded.

'Not at the moment.'

'Well, he should. He shouldn't be here if he doesn't have a ticket. It's not legal.' She pulled out one of her needles and pointed it towards George.

'Your father seems to have shrunk,' she said. 'He must have been a good deal sicker than you led us to believe.'

'This is my friend George,' Sylvie explained. 'He stayed with us last night.'

'He stayed with them last night,' the man repeated. He had a piece of green leaf stuck between his teeth, which made him look even more rodent-like than usual.

The woman scowled. 'Was that wise, with your father so indisposed? How is he, by the way?'

'He's much better, isn't he, George?'

George nodded.

'But not well enough to travel, I note.'

'Not yet. But he'll be up any day now. He doesn't like staying in bed.'

'Unusual.' The woman nudged Rabbit-teeth with her foot. 'Most men I know are terrible babies when it comes to being ill. And when he's gone you'll be . . . all alone?'

'She'll be staying with me,' George put in.

'He talks!' The woman with kid gloves leaned over and patted George on the knee. 'It's always nice,' she said, 'to stay with a friend. As long as they don't lead you into mischief.'

The train moved off. At the next station the scruffy lad with muddy boots got in, iPod blaring.

'Listen to that din,' the solicitor whined. 'I'm surprised his ears don't drop off.'

'Especially as there's nothing there in between,' his companion observed. His mobile phone rang. 'Yes . . . Yes . . . No idea. I'm on the train.'

The train hooted. Sylvie sat back in her seat, her heart banging in her chest. Fifteen minutes and they'd be safely at school. She eased her hand into her bag and felt the wand wrapped in her handkerchief. She looked out of the train window. Any moment they'd be passing the fox's shelter.

And then it struck her. Actually, her father's drawing of the eye referred to two things. It meant 'don't tell anyone,' but it also meant 'look out for the fox.' 'Eyes and Ears' is what her father had said. 'Always remember. Eyes and Ears are everywhere. Look out for the fox, follow his movements, but don't tell a soul. You never know who's listening.'

She leaned forward, her body suddenly uneasy. The train seemed to be running to a peculiar rhythm, as if the wheels were jumping over rows of pine logs, the pulse shaking her insides. Her head was filled with a fantastic jangling, notes jarring like a smashed piano. Sylvie pressed her face against the windowpane, trying to block out all other thoughts and distractions. Slowly the ledge came into view. And there, sitting upright on it as if he'd never gone away, was the old dog fox.

'Look! George!' she cried, quite forgetting her

father's instructions. 'He's back!'

As she spoke, the train shuddered to a halt, throwing her half out of her seat. Across the track the old fox jumped to his feet. He raised his head and, looking directly at her, began to bark violently.

Sylvie could hardly believe it.

'Me?' she said.

The fox pawed the ground. She tapped her chest.

'Me? Are you sure?'

Though the train had stopped, the pounding in her head was becoming unbearable. It seemed to be filling the whole carriage to bursting point, like air in a balloon. She looked across. The woman with kid gloves had thrown open her canvas bag and was beating out a violent rhythm with her wooden knitting needles on what looked like an egg-shaped drum. Rabbit-teeth was beside her, doing the same with his walking stick, now somehow broken in two. A savage beat seemed to be rising up from the carriage floor, turning Sylvie's bones to jelly, her feet to lead. The woman turned towards her, her face alight with fury.

'Drum her fast,' she cried. 'Don't let her get away!'

The man with rabbit teeth pounded on his drum, his hands a blur. Sylvie felt a wall of sound break over her, choking her ears and eyes and mouth. She could barely breathe. She moved to open the window, but shrank back in terror. Outside, the fox, the ledge, the wood behind – everything had vanished, and in their place stood the great arch of Durdle Door, the foaming sea pouring through in huge churning waves. The train began to shudder as they lashed up against the door. The drumming grew louder. It felt like a hammer was trying to break through her skull.

'George!' she cried out in terror. 'George, what's happening?'

George didn't reply, or perhaps he hadn't heard her. Perhaps she hadn't spoken. She couldn't tell for the roaring in her ears. She looked around her. Everyone in the carriage seemed to have their mouths open, but there was no proper sound coming from them. It was as if a barnyard had been let loose, full of shrieks and bellows. The plump solicitor was cowering in a corner, fingers in his gibbering mouth, while his friend was banging his head against the door. The lad with muddy boots had jumped up on his seat, pointing with terror at the floor. A crash made Sylvie look up. A great wave had smashed against the window, lifting the carriage off the rails, pushing it forward then dragging it back towards the arch. Durdle Door towered above her; beneath it, a vortex of black sea. She tried to get up, but her legs crumpled under her. She was going to drown.

'Mum!' she cried. 'Mum! I love you!'

Suddenly Mr Jackson sprang across the aisle, his bared teeth inches from the drumming woman's face. She dropped her drumsticks as her hands flew up in fright. Rabbit-teeth lurched over, trying to pull him off. The drumming ceased. All at once the water began to recede. Durdle Door faded into the mist. Outside, on the bank opposite, the fox was up on his hind legs, barking ever more furiously. Sylvie leaped up and flung the carriage door open.

'Jump, George!' she cried. 'Before it's too late,' and she yanked him to his feet and, with a great shove, sent them both hurtling out, legs flailing, bags swinging, Mr Jackson flying after them. They sailed through the air, rolling down the grassy bank, tumbling to the bottom in a tangled heap.

As she looked up, a blackbird with a white feather in its tail flew out of the train driver's open window, the driver shooing it away with an angry wave of his arm. Her blackbird! The train began to move off. At the open carriage door, the man with rabbit teeth hovered, unsure whether to jump. The woman with kid gloves pulled him back and slammed the door shut. Sylvie scrambled to her feet.

The foaming sea had completely vanished. There was a ringing in her ears but the air was silent. Sylvie was all right, but inside she was still trembling. That wasn't the real Durdle Door, she knew that now, but it had felt real enough. What had it been? Some sort of hallucination? Is that what the drums had done – summon up the thing that frightened her the most? Was that why everyone looked so terrified? What had they seen? The sea, or fears of their own?

George was sitting up, straightening his glasses. Mr Jackson was balanced awkwardly on his haunches, carefully licking his left front paw.

'George,' she called over, 'are you all right?'

George brushed down his school blazer. 'Me? Oh, fine. Pocket torn, glasses bent, and this . . .' He pulled out his mobile. The back had been wrenched off, the innards hanging loose. '*Voilà! Le portable ruiné.* The rents are going to love this. A sleepover at the Bartrams' and they're going to have to buy me a new uniform, a new pair of glasses and a new mobile. Plus, my host pushes me out of a train. Now that's what they'd call hospitality.'

'George, what else could I do? They were after us. Didn't you hear those drums?'

'I saw some old bat banging away with her knitting needles, if that's what you mean. Not what one looks forward to on a train journey, but nothing to get too stressed by. So that was it, was it? You shoved me out of a train because you didn't like the beat?'

Sylvie stared at him uncomprehendingly. 'You really didn't hear the terrible drumming going on, like your insides were going to fall out? You didn't see anything?'

'See what?'

'Whatever you're frightened of.' Her bottom lip trembled.

George picked up his bag. 'I'm frightened of staying here much longer, that's what. You're dangerous company, Sylvie.' He slung the bag over his shoulder and started to walk along the side of the track.

'Where are you going now?' she called.

He turned defiantly, his face flushed, his trousers green with grass stains. He looked like a little schoolboy after a rough hour in the playground. 'Where do you think? Where we said we'd go. To school. If someone is after us, we've got to get help. Besides, I want my kite back.'

Sylvie clenched her fists. She was angry. 'Will you stop thinking about your kites all the time, George! This is serious. We can't go to school. It's not safe. They'll be lying in wait for us.'

'Who will be?'

Sylvie waved her hands to the heavens. 'I don't know! Everyone! The Woodpecker Man, the man who called that night with the SongGlass, those Drummers. They're on the train every day. They might be the ones that kidnapped Dad.' She patted her rucksack. 'They're all after this wand.'

'Well, give it to them. I'm sick of all this, Sylvie. It's only a stupid bit of metal after all.'

'But my dad, George . . . Something's happened to him, and something's happening to us. I've got to find out what. I've got to find my dad.'

'Great. And how are you going to do that? Ask

the fox, I suppose.'

They stared up at the bank. The old dog fox was standing on the ledge waiting, his bushy tail held aloft. He was thinner than Sylvie had supposed and mottles of dried mud clung to his belly as if he'd been on the move for days on end. But though his body looked worn, his face brimmed with intelligence. He stared at her hard. He was trying to tell her something, she could feel it.

'Yes, that's exactly what I'm going to do. That's why the train stopped.'

George snorted in disbelief. 'Oh, the fox stopped the train. How did he do that? Flag it down with his tail?'

'No. I think my blackbird had something to do with it, though I don't know how. But I just saw him flying out of the train driver's window.'

'Did you?' George seemed surprised.

'Yes.'

'Oh.' He took a step back towards her, his brow furrowed.

'Why, what is it, George?'

'Well, it's a bit unlikely, but you've heard of the dead man's handle?' Sylvie shook her head. 'Well, every train driver has this handle which he has to hold down for the whole journey. It's a safety device in case he suddenly falls ill. Unless he's holding it down, the train won't move. So I suppose it's possible, if this blackbird of yours flew in, he'd fly about, the driver's hands would go up and . . .' He seemed reluctant to finish his sentence.

Sylvie finished it for him. 'And the train would stop! See?'

'But even so, you're not telling me that this fox organized it, are you?'

'Yes, I think he did.'

'Oh don't be ridiculous, Sylvie. He's a wild animal. He can't think.'

'Well, if he's just a wild animal, why hasn't he run away? Why is he still here, waiting? Can't think? I don't think so. Stay here with Mr Jackson. I'm going to find out.'

She climbed up the bank. The fox stood his ground, watching her every move. Once on the ledge, she squatted down on her haunches. She could see his age now. The grey bib on his chest had spread down along his front legs. His coat glowed with a rich and tawny gloss, but down his back ran a vivid white stripe which flared out at the base of his tail. He looked proud, like an ancient Native American warrior, ready for battle. She looked into his intense, pointed face, his black velvet ears pricked, his snout-mouth closed. There was a mystery here, as there had been with that tiger. What had Dad said that day? If animals could talk, we would not understand a word they said? And yet she could hear something, as if an unspoken

message lay buried behind the fox's great yellow eyes. She could feel his stare burning into her, her will melting into his. He wanted her to draw closer, she was sure. His eyes glanced down at her right hand and then went back to her face again. She did nothing, uncertain what he meant. He looked at her hand again, this time accompanied by a slight upward movement of his head. Stretching out her arm, Sylvie held the hand out, as if offering him food.

'Careful,' George warned.

The fox took a step forward and nudged the palm of her hand with his black wet nose, circling it like a palm reader might. His jaws opened wide. With her left hand Sylvie rolled her right shirt sleeve up. She placed her right hand into the depths of his mouth.

'No! No!' George cried. 'Don't do it! Don't do it!'

The fox's two front incisors, as sharp as two finely honed daggers, settled onto the nest of her hand. His jaw came down slowly, holding her hand in a piercing vice, his hot breath trickling over her skin. She winced, but kept it steady, her eyes never leaving his unwavering stare. She had watched him every day, and now she was sure that he had watched her too, waiting for this time. He pressed his teeth together, as if testing the elasticity of her skin. Then his grip loosened with a slight movement of his lower jaw. Sylvie relaxed, not knowing what this ritual meant, but relieved it was over. Without warning, the fox brought the full strength of his jaw to bear, biting cleanly through the skin into her flesh. She screamed but he held fast, his teeth slicing in past the fan of her bones until his jaws closed shut. Pain shot up her arm, lightning bolts that coursed through her body. She screamed again, her eyes burning, her hand thrust into flame. Below, Mr Jackson leaped forward, teeth bared, his lips turned back in a silent snarl. With a twist of his neck, the fox shook her hand free and, throwing back his head, howled triumphantly into the air.

Sylvie jumped up, the pain stabbing at her like a madman's knife. She raised her hand high into the air. Blood ran down the length of her arm, bright red like a cockerel's crown, falling onto the ground in a thin steady stream. The earth began to loosen, turning like a switchback ride, gathering speed. She tried to keep her balance, but there were too many spinning colours for her to know how. All was liquid now, neither earth nor water but something thick and fluid, circling her like a sucking whirlpool. She could hear her mother calling from its whirling maw. From the corner of her eye she saw a wave of darkness rush towards her, its crest folding white. It opened up its arms and she fell into it, a great nothing of endless black.

Chapter 5

'Sylvie! Sylvie! Wake up!'
George shook her. It was no good. She was limp, lifeless, her skin deathly pale. He put his ear to her mouth. That was all right. She was still breathing.

Blood was pouring from the palm of her hand. The wounds were deep and ugly. He could see the puncture marks where the fox's teeth had bitten through. He took out his handkerchief, shook the dust and biscuit crumbs free, and wrapped it round as tightly as he could, tying the knot between Sylvie's thumb and forefinger. Almost immediately a dark crimson rose blossomed in the white folds. Raising her arm, he laid the bandaged hand gently on her rucksack so that the blood would drain away. That should stop the bleeding.

The fox was nowhere to be seen, though he could return at any time. Didn't foxes carry rabies? George studied Sylvie's face for signs of recovery. A faint pulse beat on the side of her neck, but that was all. Was it safe to leave her? What would happen if she woke up and he wasn't there? He shook her gently again.

'Sylvie. Sylvie. Can you hear me? I'm going to get help.'

He stood up cautiously and looked around. There was not a house in sight. The railway track stretched away in either direction, the metallic shine of the rails bare and menacing. Anyone walking along it would be very exposed. But which way should he go? Up to-wards the school stop, or back the way they'd come? The school was probably nearer, he thought. And there was a phone box there, as far as he could remember.

As he knelt down again, looking in his inside pocket for a pen to write Sylvie a note, he heard a scrunch of trodden ballast and the rat-a-tat-tat of a marching drum. A moment of queasiness seemed to waft through him.

Peering up, he could see the top of the rabbit-faced man's head coming a hundred metres away up the track, the woman with the knitting needles hurrying along behind. The Drummers! He ducked back down and, crawling up behind her, grabbed Sylvie under the arms and dragged her through the couch grass and brambles into the little dip at the back of the ledge. Mr Jackson followed, his head half cocked. For the first time George was pleased that he'd lost his voice. He patted Mr Jackson on the head.

'Good boy. You stay there.'

Scuttling along on hands and knees, he crawled back for their rucksacks, sweeping the earth as he retreated for any sign of their presence. Reaching up, he pulled down a leafy branch hanging a metre or so above his head and wedged it between two others so that it made a rudimentary screen. He lay down beside Sylvie, his heart hammering against the ground, one arm draped around Mr Jackson's neck. The dog was quivering, straining at the approaching footsteps.

'Lie still, Mr Jackson,' he whispered. 'Lie still.'

The footsteps stopped. The rabbit man spoke.

'This is where they jumped off. Look, there's the back of someone's mobile.'

'That would be the boy's.' The woman's voice cracked with spite. 'I don't think she has one.' He heard her crunch it under her foot. 'Good. That means they can't phone for help.'

The man climbed up onto the ledge. Peering through the latticework of leaves, George could see an oval-shaped drum slung low around his waist. Rabbit-teeth brushed the ground with his suede shoes.

'See anything?' the woman asked.

'Looks like one of them hurt themselves when they jumped. Blood everywhere. That'll slow them down. There's no sign of them going across that field.

There'd be marks in this dew. They must have gone down the track, back to the station.'

He rapped on his drum. Sylvie's eyes sprang open, staring wide. George clamped his hand over her mouth, a finger to his lips, but it didn't seem to register. It was as if she was looking somewhere else, somewhere he couldn't see.

The woman spoke sharply. 'Come on then. She mustn't get away a third time. The Songman's getting impatient.'

The man jumped down. George listened as the crunching footsteps faded.

Another twenty minutes and Sylvie had come round completely. She sat up, blinking, trying to work out what had happened. She felt odd, displaced.

'How long have I been out?' Her voice sounded thick, croaky, in need of a drink.

'Half an hour? How's the hand?'

'Hand?' Now she remembered. She held it open, touching it gingerly. It didn't seem to hurt at all.

'OK, I think.'

'Nothing broken?'

'I don't think so.'

She pressed her fingers against the ground and drew them back in amazement. It was as if a small electric current had passed through her. She put her hand down again. No, it wasn't exactly like a current, it was more like a stirring under her. She could almost hear it, a low rumbling, like the Furroughla made. Dad had been closer than he thought.

She crawled back out into the open air; George and Mr Jackson followed. She felt rather like the Sleeping Beauty, awakening to a place she had seen long ago. There was the ledge and the grassy bank, and there was the gleaming railway line stretching away towards the little railway station, and the fields opposite with a flock of sheep ambling about, but it had changed, or rather the view of it had. It was as if someone had placed a great weight on the world and pressed down, so that the picture in front of her had been flattened and broadened out. There was an edge to what she could see that had never been there before. It was a bit like watching a film on the wide screen in the cinema: there was a frame of blackness around the picture where she saw nothing, yet what she could see was sharper, more intense, more focused, more real.

She stared ahead. Yes, everything looked the same, and yet it all looked different. The countryside seemed to be crisscrossed with tracks of colour like a road map – blue for motorway, red for A roads – only these seemed to shift and shimmer, almost as if they were moving. Take the railway line, for instance. Previously it had seemed part of the countryside, as natural as the trees and hedges that grew along it, but now it looked almost dangerous. There was a fiery glow to it, and she could hear it crackle, as if it were burning. Then there was the field that she saw every day from the train. Whereas before she was aware only of grass and the trees beyond, now it appeared quite altered, cut this way and that by a network of paths, one straight, like a Roman road, leading directly to the wood, others twisting like cobbled streets in some medieval village. The straight one was coloured tawny red – the fox's path, she guessed – while the others were tinged with shades of brown: rabbits, hares, field mice. Looking towards the wood, she saw the low arch of a bramble bush, the animals' entrance, as clear and as obvious as a man-made tunnel. That was it! The landscape now seemed easy to understand, as if there were signs saying 'tunnel' or 'badger's path'. Without even trying she could see the scrubs of bush where danger might lurk, the low dips where an animal might lie hidden.

Something moved in the grass below. The fox! Yes, there he was, lying further along the bank, watching out across the fields and the railway track, on guard. His head appeared, his black velvety ears swivelling, his black nose twitching. He had heard her wake up.

'Sylvie, are you all right?' George's worried voice broke into her strange new world.

'Me? Yes, it's just . . . everything's a bit different, George.'

'Different? How do you mean?' He looked concerned.

'It's difficult to explain. I can see more, hear more.

I feel kind of weird, as if I belong more, and yet belong less.'

She looked at him, unable to say anything else. They were the same age, but at that moment Sylvie knew two things: one, that because of the bite she was different from him; and two, that she always had been. Not the girl/boy thing. Something else. And yet he had stayed with her.

'It's that blasted fox's fault,' George was saying. 'We'd better get you to a doctor before he attacks you again.'

'Oh, the fox wouldn't do me any harm.'

'No harm! He nearly bit your hand off.'

Sylvie shook her head. 'It's not like that.' She got to her feet. She felt a little unsteady. 'We've been here long enough. Look, he agrees.'

The fox was on his feet. George started forward, ready to chase him away. Sylvie held him back.

'No, George. Trust him.'

She looked into the fox's eyes. Her hand began to throb. She could hear him now, a sort of voice, a mixture of rhythms and sounds that coursed through her body. Words and phrases tumbled into her head – not his words, not hers – but a spring of them that seemed to rise up and splash over her like water from a fountain.

You gloamcub
I teeth you I leg the swoop in silent snout and pad grass

I blood hunger snipe empty air
I leg the ground
I teeth you
You gloamcub
Sylvie gulped.

'I'm sorry?' she said.

The fox stared at her again, his yellow eyes glowing ever wider. She let her mind go, another flood of words pouring over her.

You gloamcub
I teeth you I blood the ground
We pad paw we snout the trotting ground
We leg the mufflesongs

'The mufflesongs?'

The mufflesongs, he repeated. His voice was urgent.

We leg the hopping swoop
We gloam the Allamanda

'The Allamanda,' she repeated out loud. 'I don't understand. What's that?'

'Sylvie,' George butted in, 'you're talking to yourself.'

'No I'm not.' She held up her hand, dismissing him, trying to concentrate on the fox. She closed her eyes, feeling his will upon her again, feeling a little bit of her somehow merging into him. The fox spoke again.

The Allamanda
We gloam the Allamanda

Leg the mufflesongs
Nook the burrowdug

She opened her eyes. She knew what she must do now.

'He wants us to follow him, George, to somewhere safe.' She spoke in a low voice, frightened she might break the spell.

'Oh, you can talk to him now, can you?' he said scornfully.

'Not exactly, no. Hear what he feels, what he's thinking. It's the bite, George. It's done something to me.'

'I'll say.'

They stood there, staring at each other. Sylvie picked up her rucksack and hoisted it onto her shoulders.

'You can think what you like, George, but I can hear him, OK? I'm not making it up. The fox wants me to follow him. What else can I do? Look, when I get there, wherever it is, I'll find a phone, call Uncle Alex, your parents, whoever. But right now, I've no choice. You needn't come if you don't want. The station's not far. Just don't tell anyone yet.'

She walked over and unclipped the lead from Mr Jackson's collar.

George pushed his glasses back up his nose. 'You'll try and get help?'

'As soon as I can.'

'OK. You got me into this, you can get me out. But I warn you, I wasn't built for walking.' He picked up his own rucksack. 'All right,' he said to the fox. 'Lead on.'

They clambered down the bank and followed the fox as he edged through a gap in the fence and trotted across the long grassy meadow that sloped upwards to the cluster of trees. The grass was still wet from the early morning dew and a thin gauze of overnight spiders' webs stretched across the surface, wisps of a ghostly mist caught in their tendrils. The fox's path glowed. As soon as she stepped on it Sylvie could feel it, faint vibrations rippling through her, as if it were almost alive. She moved quickly, the fox's bushy tail sweeping in front of her. George was finding it hard to keep up.

'Did you hear what that Drummer woman said?' he called out when they were about halfway across, his question trying to rein her back. 'About the Songman?'

'No?'

'You must have been out still. She said, "The Songman's getting impatient." Who's the Songman?'

'I've no idea. The Woodpecker Man? The man who called that night?'

'That makes four at least, with the Drummers. How many enemies has your dad made? Well, there's four of us, I suppose, if you count your dog. Where is Mr Jackson?'

They both stopped and looked back. They had

a better view of the railway now, the smudge of the next railway station and the little car park just visible further up the track. The school bus had long gone. Mr Jackson was still by the ledge, sniffing at a blade of grass as if he were on one of his regular walks.

'Come on, Mr Jackson,' Sylvie pleaded. 'No time for—' She stopped abruptly. A flicker of movement caught her eye. A flash of green on the station platform, a bob of crimson red.

'George, look! The Woodpecker Man! See, he was lying in wait for us! Quick, before he spots us!'

They started to run, their rucksacks bouncing on their shoulders. The fox had already reached the copse and was watching them anxiously.

Flit! Flit! She could hear him.

Flit the hopping swoop!

Sylvie could have run faster but George was struggling, his face hot, beetroot red, his little legs stumbling awkwardly, his breath coming in gasps. They were still out in the open, clearly visible for anyone to see.

'Come on, George, hurry,' she urged.

'It's no use, Sylvie. I can't—' He stumbled, clutching his side.

Sylvie grabbed hold of his arm and pulled him up the slope towards the safety of the trees. Looking back, she saw that the station platform was now bare, but there was no sign of the Woodpecker Man coming along the track. Perhaps he hadn't seen them after all.

The trees drew nearer – fifty metres, thirty, George's feet dragging along the ground like leaden boots. He fell to the ground, swallowing great gulps of air.

'Can't breathe,' he gasped. 'My inhaler. I've got to—' He clutched at his chest. Sylvie dropped down beside him, searching frantically through his pockets. String, matches, chewing gum, a penknife, a compass – she chucked them out on the ground in a desperate bid to find it. At last she pressed it into his hand.

'Here you are, George. Take a deep breath.'

She stood over him while he wheezed his way back to recovery. He looked so out of place here, so weak and helpless. If they had to keep on stopping like this, she thought, the Woodpecker Man would catch them in no time.

George was thinking the same thing. 'Do you think he saw us?' he said, worry in his voice.

Sylvie looked back. The field was quite empty, just lazy buttercups beginning to open in the morning air. It all seemed so quiet and peaceful, it was hard to believe what was happening to them.

'I don't think so,' she said. 'But we can't stay here long.'

George tried to reassure her. 'I'll be fine soon. But I'm not the only one. Mr Jackson doesn't look too happy.'

She looked across. Mr Jackson was busy licking his right front paw the way dogs do when something isn't quite right, urgently, repetitively.

'Mr Jackson?' she called. 'Are you all OK?'

The dog lifted his head and looked at her with his trusting brown eyes. Her hand began to throb again.

I goodboyMrJackson I downboysitgood

I seeyoulaterMrJackson

Who'salovelyboythen

Sylvie gasped in astonishment.

'George. I can hear Mr Jackson too!'

She squatted down next to him, waves of understanding washing over her. There was the old familiar smell of him, like chocolate biscuits, but now she could sense other things. He was a domestic animal, used to baskets and firesides and regular meals. Jumping from trains, consorting with foxes was not what he was used to. And yet he wanted to be here, she could feel it; wanted to be with her, wanted to play his part in finding her dad.

Isnufflegood I gofetch

MrJacksongofetchmorningDad

'Yes,' she said, almost in tears. 'We'll all go fetch morning Dad.'

She took hold of his paw. He was tense, trusting. Holding it up to the light, Sylvie could see a sliver of glass wedged between the front pads. Mr Jackson drew it back gently.

MrJacksonjabgash MrJacksonpaddyyelp

SylviebettertakehimtotheV-E-T

It'llbeoversoon

'There, there,' she reassured Mr Jackson, stroking him gently. 'That's right. George, we have to get this out. My right hand's a bit stiff. Can you do it?'

George clambered to his feet, his breathing calmer but his face still flushed.

'Good job I don't cut my nails,' he said, trying to sound as calm as possible. 'Tell him to keep still.' Adjusting his glasses, he gripped Mr Jackson's foot. 'I've always thought I'd make a good doctor. The sight of blood doesn't worry me at all. Unless of course it's my own. Hold him steady now. That's it. I've got it. Now, if I just ease it out . . .'

Carefully he pulled the splinter out. It was long and thin and must have hurt a good deal. Mr Jackson wriggled free and began to lick his wound clean.

IpaddypadMrJackson Ipapwag
MrJacksonreadyfortheoff

'Yes,' said Sylvie in reply. 'I think we all are.'

The fox was brushing his tail impatiently over the ground. They started to follow him again, skirting round the edge of the copse, up towards the rise of the hill, and then along a flat ridge. He was taking them a long way from the railway track now, into the heart of the country. Beyond the copse they paused and looked out across a wide sweep of almost uninhabited land. They could see sheep grazing, and a thin spiral of smoke rising up like a twisting wraith from a genie's bottle and, many miles away, falling over the brightly lit land like a great shadow, the dark green of the sprawling woodland.

They trudged on, the land still and quiet, as if it was sleeping. All they could hear was the sound of their own footsteps and Mr Jackson panting alongside. Now the sun was climbing higher, gathering strength. They could feel the heat on their legs and faces and the backs of their necks. They grew hot and sweaty, a thick thirst on their mouths and lips. Their rucksacks began to dig into their shoulders, their legs slow and heavy, the forest still miles away.

'Is that where we're heading?' George asked. 'Only I wouldn't mind a drink.'

Ten minutes later they were following an over-grown bridle path towards a stone bridge, high hedges on one side, old pastureland on the other.

Sylvie sniffed the air. 'Water,' she said.

The path ahead was dry and dusty, like their throats, but alongside, half hidden by long grass, ran a stream, its steep banks home to an old badgers' sett. George threw off his rucksack and scrambled down. Squatting on a flat stone, he began scooping up the water in the cup of his hand. Mr Jackson fell in by his side, Sylvie squashing in beside him. She drank deeply, without thinking, then suddenly caught sight of herself in the stream's reflection, half scooping the water like George, half slurping it with her tongue like Mr

Jackson. It seemed natural somehow, lapping at it like an animal. The water was not particularly cold, but after walking for hours in the sun it seemed wonderfully refreshing. She could taste some of its qualities too: the chalk from the soil, the hint of wild garlic that grew along the bank, an ore of some sort that lingered in her mouth – copper? iron? She could sense other components which she could not name but which ran through the liquid like different notes in a chord. Next to her, Mr Jackson was gulping greedily.

MrJacksonthirstyboy MrJacksonslopslip

The fox edged his way down towards the water cautiously. He was as parched as the rest of them, but unused to such companions. As he drew close, Mr Jackson turned, his back bristling with anger, lips curled in a silent snarl.

Fartdog Sylviefang

Fartdog badboy fartdog rankbottom

MrJacksonbrittleandspit

MrJacksonfartdogfang havehimforbreakfast

'No,' Sylvie said. 'You can't do that. And if it came to it, I think he'd have you.' She put her hand on his head, letting her feelings flow through. Mr Jackson glowered, suspicion in his eyes, then reluctantly moved over. The fox came down and drank steadily alongside him.

George sat back on his heels. 'This Woodpecker Man – what do you think he needs the wand for?'

'I don't know.' She felt for it, wrapped safe in her rucksack. Though she didn't want to, somehow she couldn't help herself: she eased it out and unwrapped it. There it lay, dull, lifeless, malevolent. 'What could it do though? It's only a bit of metal, after all.'

'Well,' said George, taking it from her, weighing it in his hand, 'whatever it is, it won't be pleasant, that's for sure. Here, you'd better put it back.'

George held out his hand; Sylvie held out hers, but she wasn't concentrating. She'd heard the plaintive bleat of a sheep calling not far away, followed by a cow mooing, and they had surprised her. It had been so quiet up till now. But George thought she was ready and let go. The wand slipped from their grasp and bounced twice on the stone before disappearing into the stream.

'Now you've done it,' said George.

'Me? It wasn't me who dropped it.'

George took off his socks and shoes, rolled up his trouser legs and lowered himself in. Though the water was clear, all he could see was a muddle of weed and stones.

'Can you see anything from where you are?' he shouted. Sylvie shielded her eyes and peered in. Up in the trees, a brace of pigeons began cooing to one another. The world seemed to be coming alive again. Intrigued, she looked up. Through the gap in the arch she could see four lines of black-necked swans, flying low towards them, and, following in their wake, a silver hot-air balloon.

'Look!' she cried. 'It's the same one we saw yesterday at school. And look – they're pulling it along! You were right. The balloon was going the wrong way.'

A plume of flame shot up into the balloon's neck; a second later she heard the roar. Sylvie narrowed her eyes. Around the edge of her vision everything went black, but the balloon sprang into perfect focus. She could make out two people in the basket. One could barely be seen, the top of his head peeping over the basket. The other wore a green jacket and a crimson top hat, and the sun threw shadows on his watchful, pointed face.

'It's the Woodpecker Man! Quick, George, under the bridge!'

She grabbed hold of Mr Jackson's collar and dragged him over to the shelter of the arch. George splashed and stumbled down the stream, crouching down by the edge of the bank. They huddled together under the stone, listening.

'What about the wand?' whispered George, his teeth chattering.

'I don't know. Maybe he's too far up.' She peered out. 'George, look! You've left your shoes and rucksack on the rock. If he sees them . . . Hold onto Mr Jackson.'

'Sylvie, don't—' He put his hand out to stop

her, but it was too late.

Bending double, she darted back, weaving in and out of the long grass, using her hands and feet as one, as if she were, yes, an animal, the ground beneath her sure, her eyes sharp, her ears pricked. Her skin was tingling, alive to danger. Quickly she was upon them and, gathering them up, she turned. Above, the sky was clear, the bridge obscuring her from the Woodpecker Man's sight.

George was gesticulating frantically. 'Hurry, hurry,' he was mouthing.

She started to scuttle back, his rucksack and shoes awkward in her arms, her eyes fixed on the sky. She could hear the balloon's fiery roar now, and the rush of animal cries, feel the taste of something burning in the air, a kind of fear sparking like electricity. Then two swans flying side by side came into view over the brim of the bridge. Then another two. She was caught out in the open. She dropped to the ground, curling up in a tight ball, like a boulder, spikes of grass sticking to her face. She lay still, not daring to move, conscious only of her breath and the hammer of her heart.

George looked on, petrified. The balloon drew closer. On the four sides of the basket perched a flock of green woodpeckers, their wings flapping, their sinister beaks tapping impatiently on the edge. The Woodpecker Man was leaning out, sweeping the great triangle back and forth, still searching. Next to him, someone was furiously throwing glass bottles into the air. As they smacked onto the ground, a host of animal cries broke free: the whinny of a horse, the call of a cuckoo, the grunt of a wild pig.

The Woodpecker Man reached down and sent a bottle of his own high into the sky. A woodpecker darted up and pierced it with his beak. The caw of a crow burst into the air. He threw another: the *kraak* of a jay flew past. Cackling with glee, the Woodpecker Man began hurling bottles out in great handfuls, the sky streaked with stabs of green as his birds homed in on their targets. A bottle smashed next to Sylvie's head, a heron's croak deafening her. Her hand began to throb violently, fresh dark blood seeping out through the handkerchief. She twitched suddenly, as if someone had run a feather up her spine. And then she heard him, the fox, a mixture of fight and fear in his voice.

Blood you! Blood the mufflesong!
Teeth the hopping swoop!
Flit! Flit!

She turned her head. He was out in the open, racing along the path towards the disused badgers' sett, the balloon now directly overhead. The Woodpecker Man gave a high-pitched screech and aimed a bottle straight at him. It broke over the fox's back, glass shattering over his coat as he tried to scramble to safety. A savage fox's howl broke loose from the smashed bottle. The fox leaped up, snapping, biting the air, a snarl bursting from his throat, but stopped mid way, as if a plug had been pulled. He reared up on his hind legs, mouth wide open, teeth bared, his throat straining, but nothing came out. His voice had gone.

A clipped little voice came floating down: 'That's right, foxy. Your singing days are over. Jumping's all you're good for now. The Songman's seen to that.' It grew impatient. 'Come on. Can't you get your birds to fly a bit faster? It'll be getting dark soon.'

The Woodpecker Man clapped his hands. The swans pulled harder, their black necks stretched out, their wings falling in time with his beat. The balloon sailed past. Sylvie waited until it was safe, then crept back under the bridge. George was standing quite still, unable to understand what he had seen.

'Did you hear that?' he said. '"The Songman's seen to that"?'

'Yes, and did you see what happened?' Sylvie said. 'Did you see what that bottle did to our fox?'

George nodded, pointing. The old fox was back on the path, his tail dropped to the ground, his body slung low, his yellow eyes boring into Sylvie.

I muffle teethed swoop gulled
The air is empty fritful
We leg the hopping swoop

'Is he all right?' asked George.

'No. He's lost his voice. Every time one of these bottles breaks open, an animal's song comes out which steals the animal's own voice.' Sylvie turned, suddenly alert. 'Is that what happened to you, Mr Jackson? Has this Songman stolen your song too?'

Mr Jackson had come up beside her, trembling slightly. He looked troubled and fearful. His pleading eyes locked into hers. It was like standing on the edge of a cliff, her head giddy from looking down. She fell into his words.

MrJackson nobarkingatthemoonagain ohbequiet ohbequiet
MrJacksonslinktail
IbadboyMrJackson badboy

He looked so sad and miserable, unable to bark, unable to warn and protect her; to do those things he thought were his right, his duty. Faithful Mr Jackson.

She bent down, whispering into his ear.

'You're not a bad boy, Mr Jackson. Mr Jackson's a good boy. You've lost your voice, that's all. This Songman's stolen it. He's stolen the birds' songs, he's stolen your song, he's stolen our fox's, and he's kidnapped my dad. He's the bad boy, not you. Mr Jackson, Sylviedog goodboy.'

George looked on, perturbed. 'But why?' he said, his voice plaintive, uncertain. 'What's this all about?'

Before Sylvie could answer, she spotted an unbroken bottle drifting downstream. She waited until it swirled past, then lifted it out.

'They're just like the one that man had when he called that night. SongGlasses, he called them.' There was a label on the front, the neat black handwriting slightly smudged. 'Badger,' she read, turning it in her hands. 'Look! See what's stamped on the glass underneath? *Courtesy of the Songman.*'

George examined it slowly. 'It looks harmless enough. A wand and now one of these singing bottles. We're getting quite a collection.'

Sylvie held her hand out. 'Give it here. I'll wrap it in grass, keep it safe. We don't want to break it. And we've still got to find the wand.'

They resumed their search, George wading back into the water, Sylvie standing on the bank.

'One thing I don't understand . . .' George said, wiping his glasses clean. 'Last night all the Woodpecker Man had to do was hold up his triangle and he could tell where the wand was right away. Today he passes right over it, and nothing.'

'Perhaps all the animal songs drowned out its signal.'

'Maybe, though last night it acted more like a magnet than anything else. Perhaps it doesn't like water. Ah, got it!' He plunged his hand in and brought out the wand. 'So the Woodpecker Man's not the Songman. Perhaps the Songman's the bloke who called on you that night.'

'No, he was the other one in the balloon. I recognized his voice.'

Sylvie helped George up onto the bank. She wrapped the wand back in her handkerchief, then straightened up, tucking it with the glass bottle safely in her rucksack. It was time to get moving again. The day was passing.

'Well,' said George, putting his socks and shoes back on. 'School's done and dusted now. I hope Miss Coates has put my kite somewhere safe.'

Chapter 6

Miss Coates stood looking out of the window. School was over for another year. Outside, the children were running around, saying goodbye to each other, a year's classwork and the summer games kits being loaded into the backs of family cars. The classroom walls were bare. All that remained was Sylvie Bartram's drawing of an oak tree and George's famous kite, the one he'd nearly lost. Neither of them had bothered to turn up for the last day. No card, no present, not even a goodbye. She'd been surprised, a little hurt, but now, seeing the kite hanging from the wall, its wings outstretched, its head drooping slightly as if it too were sad to be so neglected, Miss Coates thought how unlike George it was to leave one of his beloved kites here – they meant so much to him. And Sylvie had promised to learn that poem. She remem-

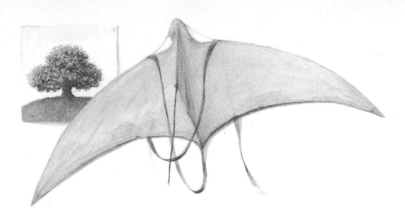

bered the girl's face yesterday afternoon, pinched and worried.

'George wouldn't have left his kite here,' she said out loud. 'And Sylvie wouldn't have broken her promise. Something's up, I just know it.'

Taking Sylvie's picture and George's kite down from the wall, Miss Coates gathered up her goodbye presents, dumped them into the back of her car and drove off. She took the roads a little quicker than usual, but, as she told herself, she had a good excuse.

When she got there, Sylvie's house looked silent, empty. She strode up the path and knocked on the front door. She waited. There was no reply. She knocked again. Not a sound. Bending down, she peered through the letter box and called out.

'Sylvie? Sylvie Bartram, are you there?'

She could see the hall and the little table where the telephone stood. Everything seemed in order, but then she noticed a trail of bright green feathers leading up the stairs, the banisters and wallpaper all scratched and chipped, as if someone had taken a small chisel to them. What on earth had been going on? Upstairs a floorboard creaked.

'Sylvie? Mr Bartram? Hello? Can anyone hear me?' Still that uneasy silence.

Going round the side, she discovered that someone had placed a sheet of cardboard over a windowpane in the kitchen door; shards of glass lay on the concrete step. In the garden, the border had been trampled flat, flowers squashed into the soil; part of the ivy had broken away from the house and hung like a damaged sail torn from its mast.

Pressing her face against the kitchen window, Miss Coates looked in. A pile of broken crockery lay in a little heap by the door, a broom leant carelessly against a chair. Facing her she could see the kitchen dresser, its drawers half open, its jumbled contents spilling out, ransacked. On the table in the centre of the room lay the remains of a meal: two plates, two mugs, a half-eaten packet of biscuits and a carton of milk. There was another mug on the work surface to the right, beside an electric kettle and a jar of instant coffee. A thin spiral of steam rose from the kettle's spout. It had just been used! Sylvie was there, hiding from her. In-censed, she marched back to the front door.

'Sylvie!' she shouted. 'I know you're in there. Open this door at once. I'm not going until you do.' She rattled the letter box and banged her fist on the frosted glass.

The door swung open. 'Yes? Can I help you?'

A cold, hard voice. A stiff-looking woman stood in the hallway, her hair pulled back in a grey bun, a long grey dress hanging from a long grey neck. On the front of her dress hung a pocket, out of which stuck a pair of knitting needles.

'I was looking for Sylvie,' Miss Coates said, momentarily unnerved.

'Were you?' The woman was almost interested. 'And?'

'She wasn't at school today. I'm her form teacher. I wondered what had happened to her.'

'Ah.' The woman pursed her lips. 'The fact is, she's not very well.'

'I'm sorry to hear that. Nothing serious, I hope.'

'Tummy bug. Up all night. She's asleep now.' The woman folded her arms. It was clear she had no intention of inviting Miss Coates in.

'Right. And you are . . . ?'

'Mildred!' a high-pitched squawk called down from upstairs. 'Come and look at this!' The woman scowled.

'Mildred Drummer. I'm Sylvie's aunt.'

'Pleased to meet you.' Miss Coates held out her hand. Mildred Drummer's grip was unforgiving, like a steel trap.

'My name's Miss Coates,' she said. 'Perhaps Sylvie's mentioned me?'

'Miss Coates. Yes, of course. She's enormously fond of you.'

The woman fixed her with an alarming grin. Miss Coates flushed with uncertain pleasure. Sylvie Bartram, enormously fond of her? Her words came out in a fluster:

'It's just that I was worried when she didn't turn up to school this morning. She and her friend, George Sarazin, were the only ones absent. He was staying here last night, I believe.'

'Yes, and I'm afraid he's got it too. Something they must have eaten.' The woman fingered her knitting needles nervously.

Miss Coates stood her ground. There was something not right here. She pointed to the hall.

'You seem to have had a little disturbance here. The kitchen too. I couldn't help noticing when I went round the back.'

Mildred raised her eyebrows. 'Oh, that. My parrot escaped. You haven't seen it, have you, flying about? Green and red, answers to the name of Archie?'

'No.'

'Well, it's probably flown home. Now, if you'll excuse me, I must get back to the sickbay.'

She stood there, waiting for her unwanted visitor to leave. Miss Coates hovered for a moment, uncertain what to do, then began to walk back down the path.

'Wait!' the woman called out. 'Did Sylvie leave

anything behind at school by any chance?'

Miss Coates stopped in her tracks. 'As a matter of fact she did. I brought it with me.'

'Well, if you would be so kind . . .'

Miss Coates went back to her car and returned with the rolled-up painting. Mildred Drummer let the sheet unravel. The oak tree had been painted in the flush of spring. It stood outstretched on the top of a bare hill, its radiant half-moon shape bursting with life. Though Miss Coates had seen the picture every day for a whole term, looking at it now, she suddenly realized that woven into the latticework of branches was the letter S, almost human in its elongated shape, with little budding oak leaves for the feet and a tangle of twigs for hair. It was almost as if Sylvie had wanted to be part of the tree herself.

'Is this all?' Mildred's voice sounded full of disappointment. 'Nothing else? No music, no essays on her father's work, no diary?' She rolled the picture up under her arm.

Miss Coates frowned. She was beginning to dislike this woman. 'Children don't keep diaries at school, Ms Drummer.'

'I don't see why not. It's as good a place to keep a diary as any. Away from prying eyes.'

'Yes, but most people write their diaries in the evening, when the day is over.'

'You may be right.' Mildred thrust her face

forward, her inquisitive eyes bearing down, her long nose half raised like a beak ready to strike. 'Does Sylvie keep a diary?'

Miss Coates drew her breath. She wasn't going to let this woman intimidate her. From up above came the other voice again: 'Mildred, you must come and look at this toothpaste thingy.' A man came clattering down the stairs, a walking stick in his hand, something strange strapped around his back. When he saw Miss Coates, he stopped in his tracks.

'Oh,' he said, taken aback. 'You didn't tell me we had visitors.' Protruding teeth puckered his lower lip. Mildred Drummer's face was set in a tight smile.

'This is Sylvie's teacher, brother dear. I was just telling her that our favourite niece has been in bed all day. With a tummy upset.'

'Niece? Oh yes.' The man stood awkwardly. 'She's not very well at all. There's a lot of it about. Lucky we're here while her mum's away.'

Miss Coates nodded, then froze. Sylvie didn't have a mum. Everybody knew that. Suddenly she realized that this couple didn't know Sylvie at all. What was going on?

Mildred Drummer glanced at her brother, then back at Miss Coates. He had said the wrong thing. They all knew it.

She opened the door wide. The knitting needles were grasped tight in her hand.

'Of course,' she said sweetly, moving out alongside Miss Coates, 'I'm sure Sylvie wouldn't mind being woken. Why don't you come in for five minutes?' Her hand reached out, trying to guide Miss Coates in.

Miss Coates took a step back. 'No, no.' The words came out in a rush. 'She must get her rest. I'll call back later.' Though she tried to keep her face straight, she could feel her legs shaking.

'But I insist.' An arm snaked out towards Miss Coates's waist. She twisted out of the way and began to hurry down the path.

'Drum her!' the woman screamed. 'Skin her alive!'

Miss Coates broke into a run, but as she did so, the garden seemed to tilt, throwing her off balance. Out of the hedges jumped last year's class, and the class before that – all the classes she'd ever taught, their clothes all ragged and torn, their faces painted; little savages crowding round her, taunting her, laughing at her, waggling their elbows, clucking at her like a flock of demented chickens. They pressed in upon her, jostling and jeering, their breath horribly sweet, their eyes narrow and cruel, their sharp little fingers prodding and poking as if she were an animal in a cage.

'Get off! Get off!' She lashed out, trying to force her way through to her car, pushing and shoving, beating their hands away. The laughter grew more shrill, the chants louder as the mob encircled her. Suddenly

Sylvie was thrusting her way to the front, grotesquely large, her face puffed with hatred.

'Want to hear my poem, miss?' she screamed. 'Want to hear my poem?'

Miss Coates smashed a fist into the girl's face. Blood spurted out. As Sylvie fell back, Miss Coates broke through, dashing across the road to the safety of her car. Hands banged on the roof, rocking the car from side to side. She threw it into gear and tore off down the street.

The man with rabbit teeth threw his drumsticks into the air and, catching them, slotted them together again. Mildred clapped in admiration.

'Nice one, brother dear. She won't give us any more bother. Half an hour and she'll be curled up in the corner of her bedroom, trying to blot it all out. She'll be there for days.'

'What do you think she saw?' Rabbit-teeth asked. 'Spiders? Mice?'

Mildred shook her head. 'No. She got it really bad. She saw the worst thing of all. Herself.' She clapped her brother on the back with the rolled-up picture. 'We'll take this back to the Songman. He's not going to be pleased if we arrive empty-handed again.'

Chapter 7

B y the time Sylvie and George reached the edge of the forest, the light was beginning to fade. They had been travelling nearly all day, the fox moving cautiously, his head constantly angled to the sky, reluctant to venture into the open unless absolutely sure. Many times they had lain hidden in grass, huddling under a clump of bushes, waiting for some unseen presence to pass, dark shadows on their souls. They had walked past deserted hop gardens, their sweet smell choking the still air; through unwanted apple orchards, the felled trees spread out on the ground like dead soldiers on a battlefield; beside fields of ripening flax and corn, the country utterly silent. No crows cawing in the trees, no larks singing in the sky, no lambs bleating, no cows mooing. The land was suspended, a green desert, bereft of life.

Inside the wood, it was like stepping into a room with all the curtains drawn, dark, subdued, mysterious. Broad, ancient trunks of oak and beech towered above them, their leaves and branches a distant fluttering roof. All that remained of the summer's day was the silence that seemed to hang from the trees like unwanted decorations, distorting the forest's shape and spirit. Nothing stirred; the wood was deathly still. Even the moss-covered ground beneath their feet seemed part of the conspiracy, blanketing the sound of their own footsteps.

'Kind of spooky, *n'est-ce pas?*' George whispered. He tried to whistle, but somehow it made the silence even worse.

As if aware of their predicament, the fox quickened his pace, leading them down a broad path towards the wood's very heart. Though it was growing darker all the time, Sylvie discovered that she could see quite well. In fact the darker it became, the clearer the forest appeared to her. There were no colours to speak of, but the trees and the paths weaving in and out of the undergrowth stood out in varied shades of light and dark. Everything seemed to be turned inside out, the dark bits light and the light bits dark, rather like the negative of an old camera film; the stripe on the fox's back shone out like a black line on a white road. Nevertheless it wasn't easy, striding into the gathering gloom, with not a clue where they were going. Neither Sylvie nor George spoke for a while, both concentrating on keeping up with their four-legged leader. Though he tried to walk at their pace, the fox often found himself ahead of them and would trot back, his pointed face half-cocked.

Leg multi multi
Fleet fleet

'Yes, yes,' Sylvie would say out loud. 'We're doing the best we can.'

The path narrowed, climbing between thickets of brush and briar, the ground beneath them steep and slippery.

'How much further, do you think?' George said after stumbling rather badly on a half-buried log. 'Only I can't see very well any more.'

'Take my hand,' Sylvie told him. 'You'll be fine.'

'No, no. I'm all right really,' he told her, falling again. 'It's just . . .'

She said nothing but grabbed his hand, pulling him alongside, fighting through fronds of fern and bracken. Sudden hollows sent them plunging down; clusters of fallen trees, old and rotten, obstructed their way. The fox seemed to be taking them into the forest's deepest, most impenetrable part. Far away from the Drummers and the Woodpecker Man, Sylvie thought. Then, without knowing how, they were up on a steep bank, the fox running along the ridge before disappearing down the other side with a wave of his tawny tail.

Following along, Sylvie realized that he had stopped by an earthy ledge like the one by the railway line. There were curled indentations along it, as if a whole family usually settled there. Below lay a broad track cut deep into the side. There was something familiar about it – the way it was settled in, both part of the forest and yet independent of it. Then suddenly Sylvie knew.

'We're back on the old railway track,' she said. 'I'm sure of it.'

They scrambled down onto the ledge. The fox stood there, looking down. He seemed to be making no attempt to move any further.

'Is this it?' asked George anxiously. 'We've come all this way for this? Where are we?'

Sylvie turned to the fox, the same questions running through her heart. There was so much she wanted to hear. The fox sat back on his haunches, locking into her eyes. She scratched her hand. On it came:

We padpad We seek the burrowdug, the earthcoat
We bidby lagleg
Bide the Allamanda the ragwort road

'We wait?' she said.

The fox nudged the ground with his nose in a long circular motion.

We lagleg Bide the Allamanda

'The Allamanda?' She voiced the word again.

Mr Jackson perked up, wagging his tail.

The Allamanda! The Allamanda! Timefortheoff!

MrJacksonsnufflegoodtheAllamanda MrJacksonwalk-about

Wherethebloodyhellhaveyoubeen?

He stood up, looking up and down the track like he did whenever he went on a journey. Was that it? The Allamanda was some sort of road? Sylvie put her hand to the fox, still questioning.

The Allamanda?

Her hand was aching. She unwound George's handkerchief, the dried blood sticking to her skin. To her surprise, the wound had almost healed. All that remained was the four marks where the teeth had entered, spaced like the points of an uneven rectangle. The fox pressed his muzzle against them, licking the bite marks thoroughly on both sides with the rough wetness of his tongue: healing balm, a seal, a gesture of kinship. His words came freely now.

I pad the Allamanda Liggerlegs padpad the Allamanda
Rootymouths, scurryfurs, sagbellies

He looked in Mr Jackson's direction.

Papdogs all padpad the Allamanda
Gloamcub leg the Allamanda on hawhonks
We leglag

He settled down in a comfortable curl and closed his eyes.

'OK,' she said. 'Leglag. Just as you say.'

George looked worried. 'Sylvie? What are we doing now?'

'We're waiting, George.'

'For what? You said we'd get help, and yet we're as far away from help as ever. What's going on? What are we doing here? All these animal voices that you're hearing – I don't understand. Where's it all coming from?'

Sylvie was unable to speak. She was glad the dark hid her from George's confusion. And yet she did know; knew it from the moment she had opened her eyes on the ledge – the extra sense that the fox had awoken. Unspoken knowledge seemed to be unfolding inside her, like the spreading petals of a flower. She traced the little ridges the fox's teeth had left, suddenly remembering. Her mum! Mum had had similar marks underneath her arm. You could hardly see them when her skin was dry, but after she'd been in the water they'd colour up like a bruise. That was it! That's why her mum had loved water better than land. When taking a bath, she would lie in it for hours, waiting until the water had grown cold. She'd had the mark too! Which meant . . . Sylvie gulped, a lump in her throat. The fox had chosen her, like some sea creature must have chosen Mum.

She stared into the darkness. Her world was turning, moving towards an unknown destination which she knew to be hers. It was out there somewhere, quite close, just so.

She felt strange, light-headed. Her heart was beating fast.

A hand pulled at her.

'Sylvie!' George was wide awake. 'Someone's coming! Can you see who?'

Sylvie rubbed her eyes. The moon was up, shining through the trees. Peering down the track, she could see two ghostly white figures, slow and ambling, strangely long. The fox too was standing on the lip of the ledge, watching their approach with an eager brush of his tail.

'They're not "whos,"' Sylvie said, recognizing the shape of their pointed ears, their long, placid faces. 'They're donkeys, George. A couple of donkeys.'

The donkeys ambled towards them, stopping directly below the ledge. It was difficult to see what colour they were in the pale, greenish moonlight, but their necks were thick, their backs sturdy, the fur worn away where saddles had once been.

'What are they doing here?' George demanded.

The old fox came up and rubbed himself against Sylvie's legs.

Heehonks gloam the Allamanda
Gloamcub strid the heehonks
He looked at George.
Blubbercub strid the heehonk
'You want us to ride them?' Sylvie reached down and scratched the donkeys in turn between the ears. They murmured together in unison.
We heegehaws

We clickity clockity
Hickity hockity
Gollup and stonken
Fillychids monken

'On you get, George,' she instructed. 'We're off again.'

George looked down at the waiting beasts.

'I'm not getting on that,' he objected. 'I've never ridden anything before. It doesn't even have a saddle.'

'She, George. She doesn't even have a saddle.' Sylvie ran her hand down the donkey's back. 'You won't need a saddle. Or reins. Just sit tight and hang onto her mane. She knows where we're going.'

'Well, I don't, and you don't either, do you? All this animal talk you say you can understand, and you're no wiser than me.'

'It'll be somewhere safe, I know that.'

'Safe? Home is safe. A police station is safe. Lost in a forest, miles from anywhere, being chased by Woodpecker Men and Drummers, with only a donkey and a fox for protection, is not safe.'

'My home wasn't safe. The train wasn't safe. What makes you think a police station would be any better? I think being here is the safest place we can be. The fox rescued us from the Drummers, remember? He's taking us somewhere. Maybe to where Dad is – I don't know. But these animals are all we've got.'

Sylvie slid down the bank and onto one donkey's

back. George stayed put, unwilling to follow.

'Come on, George,' she pleaded. 'You know you can't stay here. You've got to come. I need you anyway. I couldn't have gone through all this without you.'

'Couldn't you?'

'Course I couldn't. Hiding me from the Drummers, finding the wand, standing by me when the Woodpecker Man came – you were brilliant.'

George sniffed. 'I wouldn't say brilliant, exactly. A marvel on two legs perhaps.' He looked towards the waiting animal. 'How do I get on then?'

'Just copy me and swing your leg over. Settle in, get comfortable.'

George wriggled his way down and settled gingerly onto the donkey's back, his legs dangling down uncertainly.

'OK?' Sylvie asked gently. Her donkey began to paw the ground.

'OK.' George patted his donkey's side. Her coat was coarse and thick. 'She's quite hard, isn't she?' he announced. 'Strong, I suppose.' He grabbed hold of her mane and gave it a gentle tug. 'How do I get her to start?'

As if in answer to his question, the donkeys moved out into the middle of the broad path. Sylvie and George peered ahead. Where were they going? And what lay at the end of it? The track was dark and cavernous, stretching away into a long black nothing. Not a thing moved, not a branch creaked, not a leaf rustled, not a blade of grass stirred. Even the sky seemed stilled, the moon's pale light covering the land as if a thick clear liquid had been poured over it. In front of them the fox stood motionless, Mr Jackson by his side. There was a tautness in the air, like the moment before a thunderstorm, or when snow is about to fall, a sense of something about to happen. Sylvie felt that if she reached out, she could almost squeeze it with her hand. The back of her neck tingled. She turned. Behind them, out of the darkness, a lone barn owl came flying down the track, her silvery white wings beating in long ghostly flaps.

The fox looked back at Sylvie.

The Allamanda! The Allamanda!

Mr Jackson wagged his tail.

The Allamanda! The Allamanda!

Timefortheoff! Timefortheoff!

The donkeys shuffled their feet.

We trickity trockity

Dickity dockity

Flicker and flacker

Allamanda clacker

Sylvie shivered with excitement. The Allamanda! She felt strong but scared.

'OK, George?' she asked, keeping her voice as light as possible.

George gulped. 'OK.'

As the owl passed overhead, a line of tiny flickering lights glowing blue and green lit the floor of the track. What had looked vast and empty now lay before them like a glittering runway, a shimmering carpet ready to carry them they knew not where. Sylvie's hand began to throb. She could hear a jumble of voices far away, as if a whole crowd of animals were calling out in anticipation. The Allamanda! The Allamanda!

The donkeys lifted their heads, nostrils snorting, shivers running down their hides. A tremble seemed to flow down the track, the lights rippling as it ran. The donkeys brayed once and lurched forward. Sylvie grabbed the wiry mane, her knees gripping as the animal broke into a determined canter. The Allamanda! This was it!

Almost immediately they seemed to be travelling at a fantastic speed. It was almost as if the ground were moving under them, with them. Sylvie could feel them being swept along at a much faster pace than the donkeys seemed to be running, and yet she could feel them galloping along, ears flattened, neck lowered, hooves thudding on the ground. Mr Jackson and the old fox were at her side, their mouths hanging open, their feet pounding in rhythm. Mr Jackson seemed ten years younger, no longer the dog content to curl up by the fire but something wilder, freer. Was this where he went on his walkabouts? On the Allamanda? She could hear him urging himself on.

MrJackson, MrJackson, MrJackson strid
MrJackson, MrJackson, snacklespit and brid
Bit back tongue
Blood teeth snipe
MrJackson, MrJackson, nighty padpaw night

The donkeys charged on, the twinkling lights winking as they passed, the Allamanda curling before their feet. To begin with, all Sylvie was conscious of was their own movement, the fox and Mr Jackson on one side, George bouncing up and down on the other, but as she grew accustomed to the pinpricked light, she began to see other passengers on the Allamanda, eyes glowing, some going their way, others scurrying in the opposite direction: yellow eyes, brown eyes, eyes flecked with green and black; the dark forms of badgers and otters and jumping weasels; mice and mink and the occasional worried-looking sheep. A jumble of rabbits caught up with them, pushing and shoving, noses to the ground; a little later, flowing past them like a shaken carpet, a party of tumbling rats. Foxes and goats came and went, and once a solitary tortoise. Even he seemed to be running, his little legs whisking back and forth under the dull gleam of his shell.

On they thundered, through an abandoned railway

station, with its rusting wagons and tilted signal box, under cathedral arches of giant beech, along murky, silent ponds and fields of muted colour. Occasional glimpses of a twinkling land lay far below them, as if they were floating on a plane, sailing on bumpy clouds through the inky air. Then, suddenly, the forest was behind them and they were running down onto the vale; the dense trees gave way to hurried hedgerows and dark green fields, empty barns and sleeping farm-houses just a footfall away.

The country whistled by. They were travelling south, south-east, towards the marshes and the sea. George could hardly believe what he was doing, what he was seeing. It was fun at first, hanging onto the donkey's mane, watching this mad world flash past him between a pair of moth-eaten ears. It was like being in a dream, a crazy dream, and he in the centre of it, oddly suspended, as if it didn't belong to him, couldn't belong to him. He was an ordinary boy, for heaven's sake, with model planes and a mobile phone and a nice comfy bed. This kind of thing didn't happen to ordinary boys. This kind of thing didn't happen to anybody. And yet it wasn't a dream. It was real. The night was real, the donkey was real, and after a while he realized that he was real too.

An unpleasant sensation began to creep up on him – as if his bones were coming loose. Although he tried to find the donkey's rhythm, every time her back went up, he went down, and every time she went down, he went up. The more he tried to match her movements, the worse it became. Down up, down up, bump, bump, bump, his insides shaken like a fizzy can of Coke. It was worse than riding a bicycle over cobblestones.

'Can we stop for a moment?' he cried out. 'I think I've just swallowed my liver.'

Either Sylvie didn't hear or she took no notice. It grew worse. Down up, down up, bump, bump, bump, bump, his bottom banging against the donkey's back, his teeth rattling, his spine shaken this way and that like a dog's stick. He could hardly keep his eyes open. So after a while he didn't. It wasn't as if he had to look where he was going. He had about as much say in the matter as a badly tied parcel.

And then something rather peculiar happened. Sylvie's father had once taken him down to the music shed to work the pedals of the Furroughla. It was a strange machine, with an odd groaning noise that seem to come from the deep, but try as he might, George couldn't get the sound to come out properly. 'It's very important you pedal at the right time,' Sylvie's father had told him. 'You know what it's like when you're about to sneeze and it all builds up inside. Well, that's how the Furroughla feels. She just wants to burp. You have to wait for the right moment and then pedal like mad. Don't listen. Just feel. Then you'll hear it.' And

George had stopped listening and just felt, and after a while he could sense it wanting to burp, and he waited and waited until it all pressed up below, ready to pop, and then he pedalled as hard as he could and the Furroughla wallowed and burped like a slap of wet mud.

Now, with his eyes closed, remembering Daniel's words, he began to feel again. For a time there was nothing, but then slowly, through the dark, a sort of sound-shape took form, made of the donkey's breath and the fall of her galloping hooves. It was a kind of song she was chasing – a poem, the verses repeated over and over again – getting closer and closer to the very heart of it. And though he didn't understand it, and couldn't really hear it, George began to feel it slowly taking shape in front of him. He kicked the donkey's flanks, gaining ground. He opened his eyes. There it was in front of him, nameless, boundless, a dark shape roaring in his head. And then he too was upon it, and he was riding the poem with her, all its verses and rhymes; and though he did not know the words or what they meant, he could hear the sound of them running through his blood.

'I don't believe it!' he cried out. 'I got rhythm! I got rhythm!'

He laughed and threw his hands in the air, rodeo style.

Sylvie grinned back. The Allamanda was busier than ever: lines of animals running quietly, without

fuss, without argument, some overtaking, some dodg-
ing oncoming traffic, occasionally glancing across at
their fellow travellers or simply staring ahead, eyes
fixed on the journey, feet pounding. She remembered
what the fox had told her. The Allamanda was for
all the animals. They could all use it, from the biggest
to the smallest, the fiercest to the most timid, and
while they were on it, they were safe from each other.
She saw a rabbit run alongside a fox; she saw a weasel
swerve to avoid a party of field mice. She understood
how the Allamanda worked now. The more it was
used, the quicker it moved, the rhythm of feet stirring
the earth below: the legs that trotted, the legs that
galloped, the legs that waddled or scurried on tiny
dancing steps; the paws and hooves and claws all added
to the running of the earth. This was the animals'
line, for their use only, crisscrossing the land in veiled
threads – old railway lines, worn bridle paths, hidden
tracks that rose out of the grass; the animals running
in secret, on their secret journeys, to do their secret
work. Now, out in the open country, Sylvie could see
the lights of the Allamanda all over the land, across
the fields, up over the distant slopes, the animals' eyes
glowing in the moonlight like miniature headlamps,
the whole countryside alive with their movement.
The Allamanda was like a living thing itself; the beat
was its heart, the ripples its blood, the tracks its veins,
and, like all living creatures, it loved its own strength,

its magical power. You ran on the Allamanda and the Allamanda ran with you. Oh, the Allamanda! The Allamanda!

They had reached another, smaller wood, more dense, the path narrower, suddenly quiet, hemmed in on all sides by tall arching trees, when Sylvie felt a thump on her back, as if someone had thrown a stone. Something whizzed past her ear, then another. All at once the air was thick with flitting shadows. There was a flurry of blows all around them. George cried out in pain. She looked back.

Flying two metres above the ground, their pointed beaks glinting in the moonlight, came a wave of dark green woodpeckers sweeping along the path after them, and in their midst, coat-tails flying, long legs pounding, arms moving back and forward like steam-driven pistons, ran the Woodpecker Man, the red of his top hat glowing like burning coal.

'George,' Sylvie screamed, 'he's after us again!'

She dug her heels in, slapping the donkey's flank with her free hand as another bird smacked into her. The donkey flattened her ears as she tried to outrun him, but the Woodpecker Man surged forward in long murderous leaps, his legs gobbling up the ground. Quickly he began to gain on them, his eyes never leaving his quarry, his green coat flapping, woodpeckers darting ahead, clearing the path, whooping with glee.

'Faster, faster!' Sylvie cried, and the donkeys

plunged forward, clods of mud flying from their hooves, their breath coming fast, but it was no use. On and on the Woodpecker Man came, nearer and nearer, his feet thudding, his legs driving up and down relentlessly. Now he was only metres away, almost between the two donkeys. They could hear the pant of his breath, feel the glint in his eyes. He was the nightmare under the bed, the stalker lurking in the shadows, the face behind the mask. Under his hat, his skin glowed a malevolent red. He licked his fingers and stretched out his hooked hands, ready to grab them both by the neck.

'He's going to get us!' George screamed. 'Do something!'

In desperation Sylvie reached back, and fumbling in her rucksack, drew out the wand. It was warm to the touch and glowed. The Woodpecker Man lunged across, fingers scrabbling in the air. In that instant she hurled it as high as she could, seeing it twist over, end on end. The Woodpecker Man spun on his heels in a cloud of dust and, whisking his hat off, caught it as it fell back to earth.

'Keep it! It's yours!' Sylvie cried over her shoulder. 'Leave us alone!'

They galloped on. George looked back, relieved. At first he could see nothing, but then, out of the swirling dark, came the birds. 'Look out!' he cried. 'He's not giving up!'

The Woodpecker Man jammed his top hat back on his head and, digging his boots in, set off in pursuit once more. George began slapping his donkey with his open hand, urging her on. Sylvie did the same. Again the donkeys tried to outrun their pursuer, but they were tiring, their lungs heaving. Again the Woodpecker Man began to gain ground, never tiring, never faltering. What did he want? Why was he chasing them still? Hadn't they given him what he wanted? Oh, if only George hadn't picked up the wand; if only they'd thrown it out of the window, or not jumped from the train. If only, if only . . . Fifty metres, thirty . . . soon only twenty metres separated them, and the gap was closing fast. They could see his face in the moonlight. It was shiny and hard and cruel, the thrill of the chase replaced by something darker.

'What do you want?' Sylvie cried out loud, echoing their thoughts. 'What do you want?'

As if in reply, he pointed at her, suddenly leaping forward. Then he was alongside her, his face broken by a black-toothed grin, his tongue wriggling in his mouth like a slippery eel. His breath was hot and smelled like a drain. A sing-song cackle bubbled on his lips. He raised his hat to her, his hair alive with slithering white worms, then snaked a long hand around her waist, his hooked fingers scrabbling into her. He began to lift her off the donkey.

'Help!'

George reached across, trying to hold onto her, slipping from his ride as he lost his balance. He fell to the ground, crying out in pain, as they thundered past. Sylvie tried to hold on, but it was no use. With one violent pull, the Woodpecker Man lifted her clean off, tufts of donkey-hair loose in her hand, her legs kicking wildly, her arms flailing against his face and chest. He laughed, a cracked, spiteful gurgling thing, and, tightening his grip, tucked her under his arm like a bundle of sticks.

'Let me go! Let me go!' she screamed, but he only squeezed her harder. She could barely breathe; blood rushed to her head. He turned and, with a high-pitched screech, began to run off in the opposite direction. All she could see was the black earth beneath her, her rucksack banging on the back of her head as he tore along the Allamanda, his woodpeckers flying low alongside.

Then she heard it – a faint noise following them down the track, a gathering of speed like the wheels of a distant train. The rumble grew louder, vibrations coming up through the ground. The Woodpecker Man heard it too and put on a spurt of speed. Sylvie began to wriggle and kick, jamming her elbow into his stomach, pulling at his slimy hair. The sound began to fill the air – not a train, not churning wheels, but a hundred paws pummelling the ground. The Wood-pecker Man spun round, babbling in dismay. Bounding towards them, yellow eyes flashing, came a wave of foxes – fifty, sixty of them – leaping down the Allamanda, teeth bared, tails aloft.

The Woodpecker Man threw up his hands, shrieking commands. Sylvie dropped to the ground, diving for the shelter of the bank. The woodpeckers rose into the air, beaks poised as they swooped down onto their onrushing foe. Now a deadly fight took place, fur and feather meeting in silent battle, the birds wheeling and jabbing, the foxes jumping and biting, tearing at the birds with their bared teeth. The woodpeckers fought hard, dive-bombing, spearing the foxes in the back, clawing at their eyes, stabbing their soft underbellies with their razor-sharp beaks, but for every fox they wounded another took his place. Bird after bird flew in, only to be torn and crushed and tossed aside. Soon the ground was littered with them, and still the foxes came, drawing nearer to the Woodpecker Man. To begin with he stood defiant, calling his birds down, but gradually they began to lose ground and he retreated down the track, the foxes edging towards him, snapping at his feet. His birds were outnumbered. He called once more and then, with a shake of his fist, turned on his heel and fled, his battered birds following in his wake. Dead woodpeckers lay all about, their wings ripped off, their bodies broken. Three foxes lay mortally wounded, pierced through the eyes to the brain, while others lay licking their gaping injuries, their fur matted with dark blood. Mr Jackson was sitting by the track side, calmly chewing a dead bird.

'Sylvie!'

George was hobbling back up the path, followed by the two donkeys. He ran up to her. 'That was a close call. You OK?'

She put her hands to her face, trying to hold in the fright.

'He came back for me. He was after me. Oh, George!'

She broke down in sobs.

'It's all right,' he said. 'It's all right.' He hugged her, trying to comfort her. 'You're safe now. I'm here. So is Mr Jackson. So is the fox. You should have seen him, leading the charge. He won't leave you. None of us will.'

'But you said—'

'I know what I said. That was before this. This was really heavy.' He looked around. 'These fellows died for you. I don't know what's going on, Sylvie, but I know we're in it, both of us, whether we like it or not. Maybe we can get help. Maybe we can't. But first we've got to get to where your fox wants us, yes?'

'Yes,' she said, suddenly anxious. 'Where is he? He wasn't hurt, was he?'

She looked round. The old fox was standing at the head of his band of followers. They had something to tell her. The fox took a step forward. Her hand ached.

We hawk the gloamcub We hawk the blubbercub
We teeth the mufflesong We blood the hopping swoops
We pad Gloamcub pad blubbercub
We pad the burrowdug pad the yortlehayve
Gloamcub blood the mufflesong
Then rootymouths scurryfurs sagbellies papdogs yortle
Yortle earthsongs

Sylvie recited it back as best she could.

'I'm none the wiser,' said George. 'But I think we should get out of here before he comes back.'

They looked back down the empty track. Was he still there, watching them, waiting behind the curtain of dark? Sylvie grabbed her donkey's mane and swung herself up.

'Come on then,' she called down to the fox. 'Let's get going.'

Chapter 8

They travelled on as quickly as they could, the foxes surrounding them in a sea of tawny brown to ensure the Woodpecker Man couldn't attack again. Dawn was breaking. Animals were leaving the Allamanda, the pace slowing down. Soon the everyday world would wake and the Allamanda would lie quiet once more.

One by one their escort peeled off, until only the old fox remained. Then, as suddenly as they had dropped onto it, they left the Allamanda, breaking away onto a towpath running alongside a dirty green canal. A straight and narrow road ran parallel to it; to their left, on the other side of the road, loomed the rise and fall of the vale, with its covering of rich pasture land and folded hills; to their right, on the far side of the canal, stretched the dank expanse of shrouded marsh, wreaths of mist rising like ghosts twisting up from the ground. A tang of salt hung in the air.

'We're not far from the sea,' said George. 'I think I recognize this road. Look, there's a town back up there. Why don't we make for that?'

The fox took no notice and continued to lead them in the opposite direction, nosing in and out of the undergrowth, sniffing back and forth, as if on familiar territory. Behind them the washed lights of the hill-top town began to fade as the new day took hold. They passed a huddle of houses: a bedroom light came on, a back door was opened, a voice called out, 'Pippin! Pippin!' to a night-prowling cat. The world seemed so ordinary and yet so unreal. They didn't seem to belong in it any more.

The land to their left flattened out. The canal lay inert alongside them, as if in a deep sleep. After a while the fox came to a halt and, checking that the coast was clear, ventured out onto the empty road. He ran across, joining a narrow, barely used path that seemed to lead inland. He turned and, with a scratch of his paw, beckoned them over.

Fleet, fleet, she heard him call.

Wearily they followed. They were completely exhausted. They'd had barely any sleep for the last twenty-four hours. George lay slumped across his donkey's neck.

'Please let us be there soon,' he groaned. 'I don't think I can take any more.'

They trudged on, through an old meadow sprinkled with marsh marigolds, and into a deserted farmyard, where snapdragons grew through the scalloped blades of an abandoned plough. A ruined barn stood to one side, its rotten doors hanging off rusty hinges. Ahead of them, at the end of the track, rose a solitary hill, a cluster of yellow gorse bushes nestling in a cleft at its base. The fox bounded on ahead and, with a shake of his tail, disappeared into the thicket.

'Where's he gone now?' George complained. 'Surely he doesn't expect us to follow him through that?'

But Sylvie wasn't listening. She was staring up at the hill in front of them. It was a perfect hill, perfectly rounded, perfectly green, the grass smooth like velvet. And on top of the perfect hill, at the centre of its perfect dome, stood an oak tree, its tall, proud, perfect trunk holding aloft its perfect clover-leaf canopy. It was her tree, the tree of her dreams, the tree she had drawn so many times, the tree which had been calling to her since the year began. And now it stood before her, waiting for her as it had always been waiting for her, even before she was born.

She slid off the donkey and, with George trailing behind, followed the fox. There was a narrow gap in the bushes, and looking down she saw the marks of a faint track weaving through the thick tangle. She pushed her way in, spiky barbs snagging her clothes, catching at her hair, ducking in and out until she had forced her way through. In front of her, perfectly hidden from the road, was the entrance to a cave.

'Look what I've found, George,' she called out. 'Come and look.'

She stepped inside. It was more like a cavern than a cave: a huge dome of rock towered above her as if the inside of the hill had been scooped out with a giant spoon. At the back, a pool of light shone down, where a chimney of stone broke through to the surface.

The old fox was standing in the centre of the mud-packed floor, and behind him, sitting back on their haunches, two vixens waited, a pair of young cubs playing at their feet. The smaller of the vixens was almost completely grey; the larger darker, with a tawny saddle mark across her back. As soon as Sylvie approached, they scolded the youngsters into silence. So not all the animals had lost their voices.

The borrowdug, the old fox said, rolling his head around.

Burrowdug earthcoat the mufflesong

He nudged one of the cubs forward.

Sprigs
Sprigs cudbark skipsqueak flitterchit
I pad sprigs
Hawk the burrowdug earthcoat sprigs

Earthcoat the mufflesongs
Gloamcub pad the earthcoat
Gloamcub bide the burrowdug blubbercub bide the
burrowdug
Hid the frit mufflefree

'Wow. This is some foxes' pad.' George had fought his way in, Mr Jackson by his side.

'It's our pad too,' Sylvie told him. 'We're staying here.'

'Here?' George's protesting voice echoed round the walls. 'For how long? I mean, it's all well and good for a fox, but what about food and water? Not to mention an interior-sprung mattress. Remember them?'

'George,' she reminded him gently, 'this is where he wants to be. So this is where we have to be.'

'You sure? I mean, that town's not far away. We could get help there.'

'Who from? The police? Ask them to find Mr Jackson's voice?'

'Tell them about the kidnapping.'

'They wouldn't believe us! They'd think we were just two kids making excuses for bunking off the last day at school. There's different worlds involved here. It's beyond ordinary, everyday things like the police.'

'So you say. A bit of ordinary might be just what we need.'

'OK. OK. Perhaps we can find someone. Uncle Alex lives somewhere down here.'

'Now you're talking. It's not that I don't want to help, Sylvie. It's just . . .' His lip started to quiver. 'I'll go and check outside.'

He plunged out, only to reappear almost immediately. 'The Woodpecker Man,' he said breathlessly. 'In the balloon.'

Sylvie ran back out. Peering through the bushes, she could see the balloon coming from the east, the silver dome dazzling as the black-necked swans pulled it away from the morning sun. The Woodpecker Man's red hat was clearly visible. So too was a hand, shielding the eyes, searching the land below. They shrank back, frightened.

'He's still looking for us.' George's voice cracked with alarm. As he spoke, a large rabbit appeared, three youngsters darting through their legs into the cavern, followed by a scuttling squirrel. Charging round the hill came a young deer, and following on her hooves a white-breasted stoat.

'They can't all stay in there, surely,' George said. 'All hell will break loose.'

They went back inside. The animals were standing around uneasily, eyeing each other, keeping their distance. The foxes were up on their feet, eyes fixed on the newcomers; the young rabbits crouched in terror, desperately trying to hide. Their mother stared back, nibbled her babies' ears and, scratching out a nest, settled them down. The foxes went back to washing themselves. The stoat took no notice.

'Don't you see, George?' Sylvie whispered. 'This is a haven, a sanctuary for all the animals. It's a bit like the Allamanda, I suppose. While they're in it, all normal activity is suspended. I don't think the songs can reach through the rock, so they're safe here. That's why the fox brought us here. We're safe here too.'

Eventually the balloon passed by. Some of the more courageous animals ventured back outside. Others stayed put. Sylvie folded her jacket over her rucksack and made her way slowly up the hill, towards her tree. It was a tall, handsome being, over twenty metres high. She recognized the sturdy spread of its base, its timeless symmetry, the way it stood, yes, just so. Standing in its leafy shade, she saw the marks and characteristics she had dreamed in so many dreams. Up there, to her left, was the twisted stump where lightning had struck and, on the same side, the hollow where owls had once nested. Further up, past the squirrels' nest, tucked in the fork of a branch almost out of sight, was the odd scoop of criss-crossed wood that formed a little hollow in which she had always sat; forming a ladder up to it was the secret S of her name, woven in its twisting arms.

She laid her hand on the oak's gnarled trunk. It felt more like the skin of an elephant than bark. It was old and warm, pitted by the seasons. To her astonishment, she could feel a pulse moving beneath it, slow and regular, like a heartbeat. A treebeat, she thought. She pressed her ear to it: a hollow gurgling echoed up from the deep, a thirst being quenched. Trees drank and breathed and had a pulse, just like her. Did they have a song too?

She stepped back, a little scared, her fingertips tingling. She brushed her hands together and swung up, every hold as familiar to her as the garden path back home. She climbed carefully, gripping firmly, testing each branch before resting her weight upon it. On she went, hand over hand, until she was about halfway up, the wind a little fresher, the hill suddenly far below. Higher and higher she climbed, the spindly branches bending to her weight, the ground dizzy beneath her, swaying to and fro. Then came the S, the branches twisting back on each other, the limbs smooth and slippery, the footholds narrow, awkward, barely there. She seemed to be climbing on tiptoes and fingertips, more like a fly than a human, with almost nothing to hold onto but her will and her trust in the tree. Then she was there, the strange little cradle of branches all welded together, holding her so high, so precariously, yet so securely. She settled down, her legs dangling, her right hand looped round the last feathery branch. The ground seemed far away, crystal clear, shining like glass. To the left, some ten miles distant, lay the hilltop town, its red tiled roofs hiding the narrow streets, hiding human activity. It looked like a picture in a book rather than something real. To her right, almost at an equal distance, she could see the smudge of trees that hid the zoo. In between lay the great marsh, its muted colours of green and grey sunk into the ground, and beyond it, the grey, glittering, empty sea. She squinted. The sea wasn't quite empty. There was something else there. Was it moving, or was that just the motion of the trees? She looked again, her vision black around the edges, the view narrowing but blurred like a fogged-up telescope. There seemed to be a shape there. Now she remembered: the abandoned lighthouse near the zoo.

The more she stared at it, the hazier it seemed. There was no light sweeping from it, no foghorn

warning of the mist that seemed to swirl about its base, but she could sense something coming from it, like a call in her head, a voice, a song. Was this why the fox had brought her here – not simply to the sanctuary, and her tree, but for the lighthouse? She screwed up her eyes, trying to concentrate, but as she did so, it seemed to fade.

To the west a reflection caught her eye, a glint of something flashing in the sun. The Woodpecker Man in his balloon, tacking back east! In the grass below, a hare poked up her head, ears cautious, nose inquisitive. She too caught sight of the balloon and lolloped up towards the hill on wary back legs. Halfway, she looked up to where Sylvie lay, hidden by a veil of green. Sylvie held up her aching hand, pressing it hard. The hare's words came flooding in.

Haram-harum. Harum-harum. Harums rivetful. We BOING!runriver, werubnub, weribbyhop. We WHOOP! riddle and rolt, yortle the roon and the rubbysun. Harums eavedrum the boxgrass, nest BUCKJUMP! in Harum earfields. Harums snibble-and-VOLT!

Harums yortle. Harums LIGGER-LIGGER!

Yortles JUMP!-rooked SPRANG!-grabbled. Yortles muffled. Harums scambol-funked, skip-frizzled.

Haram twitch and box. Harum skipdig BOING! BOING! BOING!

Harum eavedrum a burrowdug

B

U

R

R

O

W

D

U

G

?

The hare's questioning eyes darted back and forth. Sylvie willed a response.

Burrowdug

The hare bounded in. Sylvie climbed down as fast as she could. George was waiting anxiously at the entrance to the cave.

'Did you see it?' she asked breathlessly.

'Yes. Seems like the fox was right after all. We'd better stay put.' He pointed back to the hare, sitting nervously behind him. 'I see you've found a new friend.'

They found a number of new friends that morning: a grunting black pig, a pair of ducks, a young lamb and her voiceless mother, and lastly three chickens, a vain-looking cockerel strutting in after them.

'Eggs!' exclaimed George and, darting out, picked a handful of grass for them to lie on. 'If we found an old can or something, we could boil them. The eggs, I mean,' he added hastily. 'Not the birds.'

All day long the balloon tacked back and forth across the sky, heading east before returning an hour or so later. All around, the countryside seemed under constant observation, red-headed woodpeckers flying urgent swoop-hopping missions, the still of the afternoon broken by the Songman's deadly songs. The animals listened apprehensively as they heard the faint calls of their own kind piercing the quiet, but however near they fell, the potency of the SongGlasses could not penetrate the thick walls.

It was not easy for them, being so close. They were not used to each other's company, but as in times of drought or fire, they tried to suspend their uneasy differences as best they could. They had to learn to stay together. It was too dangerous not to. No one ventured outside; no one called back in reply or outright defiance. They knew the danger. Too much was at stake. They spread out, finding their own hollow, their own outcrop of stone, making themselves as comfortable as they could; the two donkeys stood on either side of the entrance like a pair of shabbily dressed bouncers.

We stoddy and stanker
Floddy and flanker
Hum and honken
Burrowdug plonken

Eventually the day drew to a close. The balloon sailed back for the last time, the setting sun turning it into a blood-orange chariot pulled by birds of burning gold, their fiery wings aflame, the silent earth below under its complete command. One by one the animals left, to eat, drink, do what they had to do under the cover of the dark. By dawn they would return again. Only the fox and Mr Jackson remained. They were on a different journey now.

As dusk fell, Sylvie and George went out on a scavenging expedition. They were hungry and very thirsty. In the abandoned farmyard George found a rusty, but still watertight, biscuit tin, while Sylvie rescued two plastic milk crates she found in the deserted barn. Round the back of the hill they discovered a field full of barely ripe sweetcorn. Drinking their fill from the stream by the road, they filled the tin with enough water to cook with, and made their careful way back.

Using stones dug out of the floor, George made a little fireplace under the chimney and, using some dry grass and small twigs, lit a fire. Smoke billowed out into the cavern, smarting their eyes, before it found the natural draught, the spiral rising up in a steady stream. Soon the water was boiling, four pale corn cobs cooking sedately over the flames. Sylvie and George pulled the upturned milk crates near and spread out their hands near the flames, their faces bright and red and smeared with the dirt of their long journey. Flickering shadows danced madly up and down the wall. Mr Jackson ambled over, stretched out and sighed. This was almost like home. But the fox was uneasy. Fire meant only one thing to him. Danger.

'Come on,' Sylvie called out, patting the ground next to her. 'You're quite safe.'

He shrank back, hugging the far wall, ready to dart out. Mr Jackson looked on contemptuously.

Fartdog frit theniceandcosy

Fartdogwildedim

'Mr Jackson,' Sylvie scolded. 'That's no way to talk.'

The old dog understood Sylvie's tone well enough. He got up and, walking over, rubbed his body against the fox's, letting the warmth from the fire travel through.

Niceandcosy skyballsprig niceandcosy cracklespit
Niceandcosy snuggleMrJackson snuggleSylvie
Niceandcosy snuggleFartdog

Mr Jackson slowly pushed the fox forward, reassuring him with every reluctant step. The fox stared hard at the blaze, trying to understand its voice, but it was difficult. He had known only lightning strikes and hayfields bursting into flame. It was not easy for him to understand. But gradually the warmth began to intrigue him. He knew the benefits of warmth, knew the fiery ball in the sky that provided it. Mr Jackson was right. Fire was like a baby sun, crackling and spitting, unruly like all infants. He drew closer, the flames flickering in his intelligent eyes, his red coat glowing like the embers. He turned his body this way and that, his bushy tail sweeping near.

'Careful,' Sylvie warned. 'Don't get too close.'

Don'tgettooclose don'tgettooclose, echoed Mr Jackson.

He stretched out once more, his head half raised, seeing what the old fox would do. The fox circled once, checking as he always did for unseen dangers, hidden threats. He was a fox, and this was how he survived. Satisfied, he placed his nose against Mr Jackson's and lay down beside him, two animals together, one wild, one domestic, joined in common cause.

The corn cobs were soon cooked. There was no butter to spread over them, no forks to hold them with, no plates to place them on, but they managed all the same. Mr Jackson looked on hopefully. He'd eaten two of the dead woodpeckers, but a bit of extra food never came amiss.

'What I don't understand,' said George, his mouth half full, 'is why the Woodpecker Man is still after you. I mean, he's got his manky wand back. What more does he want?'

'It's not just him, George. It's this Songman. He's the one who sent the Drummers – probably sent the Woodpecker Man too, and the man at the door.'

'But why? It can't be the SongGlass we lifted from the stream, can it? Perhaps we didn't examine it properly. Fish it out.'

Sylvie went over to where the rucksacks were stacked and began to rummage about. As she pulled out the bottle, she noticed something else, shoved into the outside pocket.

'George! Look!' She drew out the blue file. 'Dad's music folder! He gave it to me the morning he disappeared. He couldn't carry all his stuff to the station, so I helped him out. I've had it all this time!'

In the folder she found three sheets of paper, covered in Daniel's handwriting.

'Listen.' And she started to read.

This is the testament of Daniel Bartram.

In a few hours I shall take the following pages up to London, where I shall place it under lock and key, away from prying eyes. It may well be that no one will read these pages for years – decades – maybe even centuries to come. I fear the world is not ready for them yet.

Yesterday evening, with my daughter Sylvie in attendance, and by freakish accident, I created a field of unparalleled musical energy, which both thrilled and appalled me. While experimenting with my own invented instruments, a note was released – a note of stupendous power, one which could lead to the unravelling of myriad unknown secrets – secrets I have been searching for all my life. In the attached pages I have written down the exact positions of each instrument involved, the harmonies that were played, and the degree of adjustments that were made at the critical time. However, I write them down reluctantly, and with many misgivings. Like the scientists at Los Alamos who set loose the atom bomb upon the earth nearly seventy years ago, I too fear the force that I might have unleashed. Like them, I feel that my discovery could be used for great good – but also, alas, for great evil. That is the conundrum of all power.

Nevertheless I have written down what I witnessed, meticulously and without guile. Under the right conditions, if the instructions are followed to the letter, it would be simple enough to reproduce what nearly tore my small studio apart. However, I may destroy these notes still, and then all that would remain would be this solitary page, to be believed or not as the reader saw fit. I am undecided as yet. I seek a wiser man than me for advice. Yet it is hard to dispense with knowledge and discovery because of one's lack of faith in one's fellow men. If I do destroy these pages, believe me: my instruments did this thing, the Furroughla, the Shinglechord, the Featherblow and the Clattercloud. Together they opened a door into another world – a world which lies just beyond ours; a world of different sights and different sounds and different perceptions, but which is as bound to our earth as the sea and sky and the land before us.

Daniel Bartram

Sylvie rifled through the other pages. They were all there.

'This is what the Songman's after, see! Not me, these!' She pointed excitedly. 'Look, he's even included the picture the Harmonograph drew that evening. See that funny shape in the middle?'

Sylvie bit her thumb. Seeing her father's familiar hand only served to remind her why she was here: to find him. But rather than getting nearer, he seemed further away than ever. Where was he now, at this minute? Awake, asleep, staring at some blank wall in some dank cellar? Was he thinking of her like she was thinking of him? If only she could hear him like she could hear the fox, or Mr Jackson.

George pushed his glasses up his nose and squinted at the picture carefully.

'I see what he means about force,' he declared. 'That looks exactly like a mushroom cloud – you know, the thing you get in nuclear explosions.'

Sylvie nodded. 'No wonder he didn't want anyone to know. But somehow the Songman must have found out. He wants this note for himself. That's why he kidnapped Dad. He thought he had the papers on him that morning. Only he didn't. I did.'

'Yes, but what does he want it for?'

'I don't know. Something bad. Something to do with his SongGlasses? The two must be connected somehow.'

They stared at the papers. The fire flickered invitingly.

'Perhaps you should destroy them like your dad said,' George suggested, nodding to the flames. 'Then we can all go home.'

'George, I can't. Dad wanted to keep them if he could. Anyway, we can't go home. We've got to get the animals' songs back. We've got to find my dad.'

'Well, you can't keep lugging them around in your

rucksack. It's not safe. What are you going to do? Bury them?'

'No.' She thought for a moment. 'I know!' She dragged a protesting Mr Jackson over and took off his collar. 'See this pouch inside? My mum made it.'

She pulled out Mr Jackson's letter and, kissing it once, put it in her jacket pocket. Folding her father's sheets of paper into tight, thin bands, she tucked them into the pouch.

'There,' she said, putting the collar back on Mr Jackson. 'They're quite safe there. No one knows about that 'cept me and Dad.'

'And me. And the fox. And of course Mr Jackson himself.'

Mr Jackson wagged his tail. Collar adjustments usually meant one thing.

timeforyourconstituonalMrJackson timeforyourconstitutional

Sylvie patted him affectionately. He'd come a long way, Mr Jackson, without a word of complaint.

'I guess it is too. What do you say, George – a turn up the hill?'

They wandered up the grassy path, Mr Jackson snuffling ahead. The donkeys were at the top of the hill, enjoying the evening air having eaten their fill, their pointed ears silhouetted against the skyline.

We mustle and mistle
Thustle and thistle

Munch and monken
On hawland lonken

Sylvie and George lay back in the long grass. The stars were out; the moon was coming up over the hill, its pale light throwing a ghostly wash over the marsh beyond.

'So what now?' George asked. 'Any ideas?'

'I do, as a matter of fact. But you won't like it.'

'So what's new? Come on, out with it.'

'We follow the Woodpecker Man; follow the balloon.'

George sat up, startled. 'Are you out of your mind? We've just spent two days running away from him.'

'I know that, George, but we can't stay here for ever. If we follow him at sunset, when it's getting dark, chances are he won't see us. We don't have the wand, so that won't give us away. Then we can see where he goes. Maybe he'll lead us to where Dad is, where the Songman is.'

'And then what?'

'Well, maybe then we can get help.'

'Hmm. Dark, you say.'

'Yes. We can follow him on the donkeys. There's some sacking in that barn – we could even muffle their hooves. What do you think?'

'I think you're trouble, Sylvie Bartram. What the rents would call a bad influence.' George's voice quavered as he suddenly thought of them. 'You know, when I don't think about them, it's all right, but I do miss them, the rents. They'll be sick with worry, wondering what's happened to me. I'd kind of like them to be here now.'

'I know, George.'

'But the funny thing is, if they were here, I wouldn't be, if you see what I mean. I wouldn't be on this adventure, helping you.' He lowered his voice. 'I've never been on an adventure before. That's what we're on, isn't it, an adventure?'

'I suppose.'

'I can almost feel it. It's like I'm on a ship, moving.' George fell silent.

Mr Jackson came alongside and settled down at Sylvie's feet.

NightynightMrJackson nightynight

He tucked his head between his paws and sighed. Then came something else. She could scarcely believe it. Mr Jackson was singing to himself, singing the letter song, only the words weren't quite the same.

I'm gonna sit down tight and bite myself a sweater
And take the lead it came from you
I'm gonna bite birds, oh so sweet
They're gonna knock me off my RABBIT!

His legs started to twitch.

Sylvie stared out into the dark. People had it all wrong. It wasn't dark at all, the night. It simply had a different glow to it, that was all. It rose up from the ground, a wash of blue and green, as if everything was under water, flooded by a thick luminous fluid. The marsh looked like a sea itself, dark, restless, unfathomable. She thought of her mum, her wet black hair flat down her back, diving down into the night's inner depths, coming up laughing. She could imagine herself doing the same, swimming in the dark pool before her.

Her hand began to ache. She sat up. Down below all the animals stood, spread out at the bottom of the hill, the old dog fox in the middle. He took a pace forward and turned his back to her. At once the cockerel threw back his head and, shaking his jowls, began to crow at the moon. Then the donkeys brayed and the foxes howled, animal upon animal breaking into their own songs – the clucking hens, the grunting pig, the chit-chat squirrels – a midnight chorus rising up from all the animals hiding in the sanctuary. And as they called, they began to dance, leaping and twisting around the base of the hill, jumping and prancing, the hare on his hind legs boxing the night air, the pig spinning on his trotters, the lamb twirling his tail, gambolling in and out of his mother's legs. Round and round they went, weaving in and out of each other's ballet, dancing and singing for Sylvie; all save the fox, who stood silent, voiceless, watching with her as they skipped by. And as if in response, there rose a yawling howl from the east, long and far away. It sounded like a lament from the depths of some ruined castle, or the cry of someone lost, forgotten, trapped. Trapped like an animal in the zoo. Sylvie gazed into the dark. Wasn't the zoo where Dad had said the animals had started to lose their voices?

The animals heard the song too, and called back, ever louder, voices winging back and forth across the great emptiness. They were in the heart of it now, Sylvie knew: knew by the silence weighing on the land; knew by the dancing animals and the simple fact of this great tree; knew above all by the long mournful cry that seemed to come from another realm. George was right. She could feel herself moving too. Something had happened to her, something which had changed her for ever. There were many things she did not fully understand, but she felt at home here, as if this place, this adventure, had been waiting for her all her life.

Chapter 9

The next day went slowly. They ate a hard-boiled egg each for breakfast, one brown, one white. More animals found their way to the sanctuary: a mink who smelled of stale fish, three pointy-eared field mice, a disreputable-looking goat, who coughed all the time. The Woodpecker Man ploughed back and forth in the balloon, spreading the Songman's songs of silence ever wider. The world seemed to be closing down around them.

By late afternoon they had it all in hand. George had checked he had everything he thought they might need: his compass, his box of matches, the remains of his kite, a couple more eggs, and the SongGlass, just in case. They were both on edge, apprehensive. George kept packing and repacking the bag, trying to calm his nerves. Mr Jackson was getting worked up too. He could tell when some sort of outing was in the offing. He kept nudging Sylvie's pocket where she kept his lead.

Wherethebloodyhellishe? MrJacksonreadyfortheoff.

'Pretty soon, Mr Jackson. Pretty soon.' Sylvie looked across at George, who was unfastening his rucksack for the fifth time. 'Why don't you and Mr Jackson go down to the barn with the donkeys? We want to be ready when the balloon appears. I'll go up the tree and keep watch.'

They gathered their things, the eyes of every animal on them as they left. Most of them were there, still unwilling to venture outside in daylight, although the old fox had left – to fetch more members of his family, they assumed. Sylvie watched as George picked his way down the track, Mr Jackson trotting ahead, then made her way up the hill. She knew the climb intimately now, and climbed the oak with ease, without thought. She settled back. It had become quite crowded in the sanctuary, taking on a particular smell of its own. It was good to be up here, in the fresh air. She felt quite safe. The thick foliage kept her well hidden.

Above, the leaves rustled pleasantly as something fluttered through the branches. She looked up. A sheet of paper floated down, gliding through the latticework into her hand. One side was blank but the other had a picture on it, upside down. She turned it the right way up. It took her a few seconds to work out what it was, then she blinked in disbelief. It was her drawing – the drawing on the classroom wall of this very tree. The drawing she had left behind. What on earth . . . ?

A violent tremor shook the earth. The tree rocked back and forth, nearly shaking her out of the branches. There was a great hollow clang, like a hammer beating against a sheet of metal. Soaring up over the other side of the hill came the balloon, the Woodpecker Man straddling the lip of the basket, triangle in one hand, wand in the other. He banged it again from side to side, the clamour crashing to the ground. Great cracks appeared in the hill, rocks and earth running down the side like molten lava. Sylvie could hear petrified cries of animals desperate to escape coming from inside.

'Get out of there!' Sylvie yelled. 'Run! Run!'

The Woodpecker Man struck again. Sound waves rippled out like a tsunami. The earth heaved, bucking like a spooked horse, the tree shaking her loose, tipping her out. With a scream, she tumbled down, her body smashing from side to side, her hands clawing, trying to find a grip. Down she fell, bouncing and banging against branch and trunk, blows to the right, blows to the left, on her arms, on her legs, bang, bang, bang, bang, before crashing through, landing smack on her back, the wind knocked clean out of her.

'Help me!' she rasped, her lungs heaving. 'I can't

breathe! I can't breathe!'

Then the fox was at her side. She grabbed hold of him and rolled over onto her hands and knees, fighting for breath.

FLIT! FLIT!

The fox was tugging at her coat. He began pulling her towards the far side of the hill. A branch crashed down close to her head, smothering her in leaves. Crawling through, she followed him down, but then something sprang up out of the long grass and grabbed her head, digging into her eyes and scrabbling at her mouth. It was hot and hairy, and not quite human, a strong little body clambering over her, seeking every part of her out. She tried to throw it off, but it was everywhere – legs, arms, body – chattering obscenely in her ear. The fox leaped up and sank his teeth into its arm. Blood spurted in her face. With an ear-splitting squeal, the thing let go and she rolled down the hill, the fox bounding after her. Pitiful wails pierced the air – the shrill bleat of the lamb seeking its lost mother, the pig bellowing in pain.

'Sylvie! Sylvie!' The voice was urgent, close.

Looking across, she saw George peering out from behind an upturned cattle trough, his face streaked with dirt, one hand looped through Mr Jackson's collar. They were both safe.

Sylvie scrambled over. 'Are you OK?' she panted.

'Yes,' George gulped, wiping his mouth with the

back of his hand, his words tumbling out. 'We got out the back. Those poor animals. We couldn't do anything. Anything.' His voice was full of self-reproach.

Sylvie nodded. 'I know you couldn't, George. But the donkeys?'

'I don't know. They bolted.'

The ground shook again. The hill was swarming with dark, scampering figures. Animals were running everywhere, the air thick with SongGlasses, snatching their songs from them as they tried to escape. Her beloved tree had toppled over. The Woodpecker Man was hopping up and down the uprooted trunk like a demented tap dancer, her painting fluttering in his hand, woodpeckers whirling crazily about his head.

FLIT! FLIT! the fox called again; George echoed his thoughts.

'Come on, Sylvie. Let's get out of here while we can.'

Sliding down into the ditch, they ran along just above the waterline. The ground was wet, slippery, full of thistles and nettles and reeds that cut into their legs like razor blades. Sylvie and the fox worked together, the fox running ahead, Sylvie checking their rear, both aware that every dip, every clump of trees, every square of open sky might suddenly bring danger. The songs grew fainter. They carried on, through fields of sweetcorn and hemp, and then a small copse, listening, watching, fearful of the land, fearful of the sky.

Eventually they found themselves back near the straight road and the still canal. The hill was now miles away to the west. There was a T-junction ahead, and to the right a bridge where the road leading into the marsh crossed over the canal. On the verge, the two donkeys were munching patiently on the grass, acting as if nothing had happened. They looked up in unison, mouths chewing.

We fling and fleeflaw
Sling and sleeslaw
Drong and dringer
Gloamcub bringer

'Quick, George, get them under the bridge. We can all wait there.'

'Wait? Wait for what?'

'The Woodpecker Man. There's no reason to change our plan. He's still got to come this way, and he certainly won't be expecting us now, will he?'

They hurried under the bridge, out of sight. Sylvie sat back on a little stone ledge. George took off his glasses and dipped them in the cloudy water.

'I can't quite believe all this is happening,' he said, rubbing the lenses clean with the tail of his shirt. 'I mean, what are we doing here? We must be crazy.'

'Yes. We must,' Sylvie admitted. 'Crazy.'

They looked at each other and burst out into a nervous laughter. It was crazy, what they were doing. But it was real, and something, they knew now, that only they could do.

'You look terrible by the way,' George added. 'Like you've strangled a couple of chickens. And enjoyed it.'

Sylvie washed her face free of blood and muck. George retied a broken shoelace, checked that the SongGlass was still in one piece and that his matches were still dry. They waited. The day was drawing to an end, the sun sinking behind the hills. A car passed overhead; a man on his bicycle, whistling his way home. Then there was a rush in the air. Across the far field, flying east, came a flock of woodpeckers.

'He's coming,' whispered George. 'Can you hear it?'

Sylvie nodded. The burners flared again. They pressed back into the shadow, hearts fluttering as the balloon appeared, the black-necked swans pulling the basket above the straight road. It was flying lower than usual, more slowly too. The Woodpecker Man was leaning out, still searching for them, scouring the land below with his quick black eyes. Songs broke out on either side – not the usual songs, but cries of wounded animals; cries of agony, cries of terror, cries for help. As he drew nearer, they grew louder and louder, shrieks of torture and pain filling the air. It was all George could do to stop Sylvie running out, begging the Woodpecker Man to stop.

'He's trying to force you out into the open,' he said,

holding her firm. 'Stay strong. It'll pass.'

The balloon swung right, over the canal, out towards the marsh. The cries stopped abruptly. It rose as the burners flared once more, the swans picking up speed. When it was safe, Sylvie and George led the donkeys out onto the road and began to follow. The balloon was a good four hundred metres ahead, the Woodpecker Man's back, the silhouette of his top hat, just visible against the darkening sky. They moved quietly, keeping as close to the protection of the hedge as they could. After about a mile though, the terrain began to open out, the hedges and trees gone, the paths and tracks obliterated, nothing left but the long stretch of dank earth and the low sweep of sky.

It grew darker, the rising moon drifting in and out of dull cloud, but the flare of the burners kept them on course. They rode along through a deserted landscape, the few solitary houses shrouded in shadow, not a soul in sight. It was a friendless, unforgiving place, and they felt small and alone and far from home. On and on they travelled, with nothing but empty road and desolate scrubland before them, the sullen marsh closing in behind them, the balloon leading them further into the unknown. They felt as if they were being drawn towards the edge of the world.

The change came as a welcome relief.

'The sea's not far,' Sylvie whispered, suddenly encouraged. 'I can smell it.'

Above, air vents hissed. The balloon began a slow descent as the Woodpecker Man pulled on the ropes, directing the swans. Sylvie and George brought their charges to a halt. Before them lay a small quayside with a narrow wooden jetty. On either side lay a long straight pebble beach, wooden groynes reaching into the black water like severed fingers. The sea was covered with a light mist that seemed to wash in and out with the motion of the waves. Sylvie could hear it too, above the swish of the tide, murmuring to itself in a thousand secretive whispers. The shifting moonlight made it look as if she were looking upon a watery graveyard, the voices of dead sailors bubbling up from the deep.

'That's where it must be landing,' she whispered. 'Let's take cover over there.' She slid off the donkey's back and made to lead her across to a nearby fisherman's hut.

'But it's not landing,' said George. 'It's heading out to sea. Look!'

It was true. Instead of descending further, the balloon levelled off. As it passed over the shore's edge, the Woodpecker Man raised up the triangle and ran the wand lightly around the perimeter. The mist shimmered and shook, then began to part like a pair of theatre curtains pulled back by an invisible cord. Veil upon veil was lifted, the balloon floating along an avenue of mist, the starry sky above and the moonlit sea below. And at the end of it they saw an island lying on the swollen water like a precious stone set upon folds of black velvet. Dark cliffs rose up from the dark sea, pointed rocks flecked with foam scattered at their feet. Set back from the cliffs, looking like an iced cake, stood a two-storey house, white and perfectly round, lighted windows pressed into its side like silver decorations. But what held their eyes was the tall, tapering lighthouse that rose up from its centre like a giant candle, its luminous white stone topped by a huge glass dome, out of which streamed brilliant white light. Behind it, the mist hung like a ghostly backdrop.

'Wow,' said George. 'Look at that.'

'I don't understand,' Sylvie said. 'I know where we are. That's the lighthouse near the zoo. I saw it only weeks ago. But it's meant to be deserted.'

'Well, it's not now.'

They looked again. The island seemed to be growing in intensity as the balloon approached, the colour of the cliffs shifting from black to grey, the lighthouse glowing ever whiter, as if lit from inside. The whole island was coming to life, awakened. Then the silhouette of a figure appeared inside the dome, hands cupped to his mouth. A long call came winging through the air, high and solid, almost like a bugle, though somehow round in shape, as if it were looping in on itself. All at once the swans began circling round the glass dome; white light fell on the livid red and

green of the Woodpecker Man and his flock of birds.

'That must be him – the Songman!' Sylvie exclaimed. 'See how the swans just did his bidding?'

Round and round they flew, the black of their necks giving them a ghostly appearance, as if their heads had no bodies and their bodies no heads. The Woodpecker Man bowed to the figure inside, his birds weaving their red-capped heads from side to side in dutiful imitation. Then the song seemed to change its shape, pulling itself into a sort of twisting spiral and floating downwards. Gently the swans guided the basket onto a flat rock to the left of the round house. Guy ropes were thrown down. A door opened. Tiny bent figures gambolled out and began to pull down the deflating balloon. As they did so, the song faded and the mist returned. Soon there was nothing left but the sea and the mist lying on the water like a disturbed dream. It was as if nothing had happened.

'Now you see it, now you don't,' said George. 'Serious malarkey.'

Sylvie stared hard into the dark, her horizon flattened, black borders creeping in around the edges of her vision, the night turning inside out like a blurred negative. Yes, she could see something through it – vague dancing shapes like shadows in a snowstorm, the lighthouse bending into a slithery S, the picture breaking up like interference on a television set. She could hear something too, like someone running a stick along a fence only many tones lower.

'It's all to do with the vibrations,' she told him. 'Can't you hear them?'

George shook his head, then held up his hand. The noise of an engine came out of the dark. Across the water a faint light flickered through the fog.

'A boat,' he declared. 'We'd better hide.'

The lights from the boat grew stronger, the *chug-chug-chug* of the motor louder, then dying away as it idled towards the jetty. It was an elegant craft, with dark polished wood and gleaming brass railings, a neat little cabin amidships lit by lanterns, its name emblazoned across in silver-blue letters. On the stern was fixed a large, empty wire cage.

'Do you see what it's called?' Sylvie whispered. '*Chanson*. It must be the Songman's too.'

As the boat approached, a man leaped onto the jetty and tied the boat to one of the posts.

'Rabbit-teeth!' George declared.

The man pushed out a gangplank and, returning to the boat, opened the door to the wire cage. Back on the jetty, he began pacing up and down, checking his watch every now and again.

'He's waiting for someone,' Sylvie whispered.

Minutes passed. Five, ten, fifteen, twenty. Rabbit-teeth was becoming impatient. He tapped his foot; he tapped his watch; he fussed about with the ropes. The mist washed in and out, whispering voices hovering at the water's edge, the Songman's secret safe. Although she could see nothing, Sylvie could feel something. Was that where her dad was held – on that island? If only she could get across. Then she noticed: lashed to the rails on *Chanson's* starboard side, just behind the wheelhouse, was a small rowing boat, its canvas top flapping in the light breeze.

'See that?' whispered Sylvie. 'If we could get past Rabbit-teeth, we could climb in; get onto the island.'

'Get to the island? Are you mad? How do we get back?'

'Same way of course.' She stared into the foggy deep. 'I've got to, George. What if Dad's there? If we use the SongGlass to distract his attention, we could get on board, no trouble.'

'I like this "we" business. What say do I have?'

'What say do you want?'

George muttered something about the unfairness of life, and Sylvie Bartram in particular. Sylvie felt in his rucksack and unwrapped the SongGlass. The raised letters stamped on the bottom rubbed against her fingers: Courtesy of the Songman. It seemed entirely right that they should use one of his own devices to sneak aboard his boat.

'OK. When I give the signal, throw it as far as you can. Just hang on a sec.' She knelt down and reached out for the fox. He was there, as he had always been.

'I can't say it,' she said, whispering the words to herself. 'I don't know how to, but feel it, if you can.' She pressed the palm of her hand tight over his muzzle, letting the words tumble out of her. 'You've done your bit, old fox. Now it's our turn. Look after your family. Keep a lookout for us. We'll be back. But over there is not the place for you.'

The fox quivered. He had understood – understood her meaning as she understood his, not word for word, not with exact precision, but well enough. He pushed his nose deeper into her hand.

Gloamcub pad the brittersplash
I bide the gritground bide the gloamcub
He licked her hand carefully.
Gloamcub warytread
Stealth the hopping swoop, the mufflesong
Gloamcub scamperlick swiftback

'As soon as I can,' she whispered. 'OK, George, when you're ready.'

George drew back his arm and hurled the Song-Glass into the dark. The bark of a badger hit the air.

'Who goes there?' Rabbit-teeth jumped up and blundered off into the dark.

Quickly they scuttled up along the jetty and down the gangplank. Once on deck they dashed past the wheelhouse. It was neat and orderly inside, with little wooden seats, dials and gauges and a floating compass set above the wooden wheel. A set of wooden steps led to a slatted door and the cabin below. On the door was nailed a poster.

'Look, George! It's the same poster I have at home. Dad's pop concert, see? *Also Appearing: The Orchestra of Light, Conductor: Walter Klopstock.'*

Sylvie looked at it hard. She had forgotten all about it. What did a pop concert matter now?

George tugged at her sleeve. 'Come on, we can't hang about gawping. We've got to get under cover.'

They ran over to the rowing boat, the deck creaking under their hurried steps. Sylvie pulled back the canvas. There was a seat in the middle and benches all the way round. George heaved himself up over the rail. Together they hauled up a wriggling Mr Jackson, Sylvie swinging over after him, her coat catching on one of the hooks that held the canvas in place. She yanked it free and pulled the cover back over their heads. It was dark and damp. Mr Jackson was scrabbling at something with his paws.

'Be quiet,' Sylvie scolded. 'Be quiet.'

They could hear Rabbit-teeth coming back.

'Blasted badger,' he was muttering. 'We'll learn him. Ah . . . about time.'

Sylvie peered out. A van was heading towards them, headlights bouncing down the bumpy track. As it drew up, the door opened. Mildred Drummer jumped down, pulling her drum out after her.

'You're late,' Rabbit-teeth called out, pointing at his watch. 'I don't like hanging around here. Someone might think I'm a smuggler. Ha ha.'

'I had to drive half across Kent to catch this lot,' she grumbled. 'Come on, help me out with them.'

Rabbit-teeth ambled across and pulled open the rear doors. 'How many have you got?' he said, peering in.

'Thirteen.'

'Not bad. He'll be needing them. The others are plumb worn out. Come on, let's be having you. What's your name then?'

Grabbing a rope, he pulled out a bedraggled-looking Welsh border collie. More dogs followed – Alsatians, Labradors, two black poodles, any number of mongrels and lastly a Bedlington terrier. Though they sniffed the ground, raised their faces to their new masters, even wagged their tails in the hope of eliciting some sign of friendship, no sound came from them – no whimper, no bark, no murmur of protest. They had been silenced, just like Mr Jackson. Herding them together, Mildred and her brother dragged them down the gangplank towards the cage. Mildred stood by the door, unclipping their name tags, before Rabbit-teeth pushed them in. When he saw where he was going, the Bedlington terrier started to pull violently at his rope.

'Run away, would you?' Rabbit-teeth snarled. 'Plenty of time for that. Now get in there.' And kicking him hard, he slammed the door shut.

Laughing, he went back to the wheelhouse.

The engine spluttered, then sprang into life. The boat reversed, water churning under its propeller. Mildred Drummer was up on the prow, the wind pulling at her hair, her egg-shaped drum slung round her waist. As the boat turned to face the wind, she raised her drumsticks and rapidly began to beat one side of her drum. Almost at once a rattle skittered along the water's surface, not as powerful as the beat created by the Woodpecker Man's triangle, but enough to ease the mist aside as they chugged across. Though the moon still illuminated a silvery path, light no longer shone down from the dome. It stood dark and empty, full of foreboding.

Sylvie felt a hand squeeze her arm. George was by her side, watching too. There was no going back now.

Chapter 10

The trip took longer than Sylvie expected, the engine working hard against the strong swell that swirled underneath. Gradually the island became more defined. It was higher than it had appeared from the shore; larger too, the cliffs dark and inhospitable, the house set upon a broad expanse of rock, surrounded by scrub. Though the windows on the ground floor had been lit before, now all were shrouded in shadow, like the lighthouse rising above it. They could see how huge it was, bursting through the flat roof of the round house like an enormous rocket waiting for lift-off.

The boat was making for a small opening in the cliffs. A group of cormorants stood on the jagged edges, flapping their wings as if signalling its presence.

As they drifted through, they found themselves in a tiny harbour, set in such a way that, once in, the boat was completely protected from the sea outside. Steep steps cut into the rock that led to the top.

Rabbit-teeth switched off the engine and quickly tied the boat to iron hoops set in the landing stage. Flinging her drum round the back of her neck, Mildred Drummer opened the cage and dragged out the frightened dogs. Sylvie and George watched as the two of them led their captives, tails between their legs, up the steps. Soon their footsteps faded into the dark.

They squeezed out onto the deck of the boat. Mr Jackson sniffed at the cage where the dogs had been. The boat rocked slightly as the swell of water lapped against the steps. All was quiet. The moon shifted in and out of the clouds. One moment they could see their way clearly, the next it was as black as ink. Only Sylvie could see ahead.

'Hang on to my blazer,' she whispered. 'You don't want to fall in.'

Cautiously they climbed to the top, Mr Jackson leading the way, the stone slippery and wet under their feet. Peeking up, their heads level with the ground, they could make out a broad gravel path leading to an oak door set in the round house above a flight of steps. A similar path skirted round the whole building. To their right, some distance away, stood the

Woodpecker Man's wicker basket, folds of the balloon hanging limply over the side. All around lay bare rock, scattered with clumps of coarse grass.

'We've got to get inside,' whispered Sylvie. 'I don't like the look of that door. Let's see if we can find a way round the back.'

Ducking down, they ran across, the wind whipping at their coats, salt spray wet on their faces. It had been a warm evening on land, but here, surrounded by the cold sea, the night deepening, the temperature had dropped. They could hear the water all around them, huge and restless, a dozing giant only half awake. They felt like insects – small, helpless; at any moment some irresistible force could swipe them away.

When they reached the building, Sylvie looked back towards the shore. For a moment she thought she saw a distant light, high up and far away – a farmhouse perhaps, someone making a bedtime drink or watching a show on television. The shoreline was flat and empty, nothing more than a fuzzy pencil line on a blank sheet of grey paper. Was their fox standing on the beach looking out towards them? She clenched her hand, hoping to hear him, but nothing came. Then the mist swirled round once more. She shrank away, as if afraid it might engulf her, her back pressed against the stone.

'George,' she said, surprised, 'feel that. It's warm.'

George placed his hand on the wall. 'More than I

am,' he said. 'Let's find some shelter before we freeze to death.'

They moved along cautiously, hugging the wall, bending low under the windows. As they came round to the side facing the open sea, light began to bleed out over the ground. Rather than continuing round, they crept out into the scrub, following the edge of the darkness, to take a better look. Before them lay a floodlit paved area, about the size of Sylvie's garden. A pair of tall rubber swing doors led into the round house itself, while opposite, on the other side of the yard, stood a row of storehouses. In front was parked a large-wheeled wagon loaded with hessian sacks. It was not unlike a railway wagon, only smaller and without sides. From the depths of one of the sheds came the sound of heaving, nostrils heavy with breath.

'I hope that's not where the dogs are,' whispered George. 'That Alsatian didn't look too friendly.'

As he spoke, they were astonished to see, lumbering out, a massive black-haired gorilla, a bulging sack tucked under each of his muscle-bound arms. He stood in the doorway for a moment, looking around anxiously, as if sensing something he could not see. He sniffed the air, his thick brow furrowed, his toes curled round the lip of the door jamb, his tree-trunk legs half bent, ready to spring forward. His nose was broad, his cheeks worn and wrinkled. He looked old and tired – tired of living, tired of life. Unable to see anything amiss, he shuffled across and threw the sacks onto the wagon. Suddenly the rubber doors swung open, and another younger-looking gorilla came through, pushing an empty wagon. Manoeuvring it next to the shed, he too began to load up.

'If we could hide in amongst that lot, we could get in without being seen,' whispered Sylvie. She put her hand to Mr Jackson's face and let the silent words tumble: 'Mr Jackson, will you be all right? Otherwise we'll have to leave you here.'

Mr Jackson wagged his tail.

I goodboyMrJackson IbequietMrJackson Fluttertrotthewispywalk

At first it didn't seem possible. When the older gorilla was inside the shed, the younger was outside, loading up his wagon. But the younger one worked faster than the other, and soon their actions began to overlap.

'OK. The moment they go in together, we go. OK?'

George nodded. They waited. The two gorillas emerged, threw down their sacks and shambled back inside.

'Now,' said Sylvie and, running across, they jumped onto the first wagon, Mr Jackson wriggling in beside them. He was getting to like all this hiding.

'Feels like sand,' George whispered, prodding the sack in front of him. 'What does he need sand for?'

Sylvie put her finger to her lips. The older gorilla was returning. A sack thudded above her head, then another. Then the gorilla stopped and sniffed again. He could sense something wasn't quite right.

'Come on, you! Chop, chop, we're waiting.'

Rabbit-teeth's voice rang out. Scratching his head, the gorilla moved round to the back and began to push the wagon across the yard. Sylvie and George pressed themselves into the sacks, Sylvie pushing Mr Jackson's head firmly into her lap as they rolled past the watching Drummer. Then the doors opened. They were in.

They were moving along a broad tunnel that soon began to descend. Lighted flares showed the way down. The wheels started to rattle as the wagon picked up speed; behind them they could hear the gorilla's breath as he strained to keep it from careering out of control. Down they rolled, the clatter echoing round the passageway.

The tunnel flattened out. The gorilla began to push his wagon towards another pair of swing doors, similar in size to the ones they had first come through, though made of a thick semi-transparent plastic. The air grew hot and hazy, thick with the smell of burning electricity. The gorilla gave one last heave and banged his way through.

The moment they were inside, the heat hit them full in the face. All around they could hear the sounds of activity: fires roaring, steam hissing, metal clanking, men chattering, moving about. The gorilla pushed the wagon into a wide unloading bay, which was divided into sections. Each sector had a sign hanging above it. *Magnesium*, read the first. Then came *Soda*, *Lime*, *Silica*, *Bladderwort* and lastly *Sand*. Bringing the wagon to a halt, the gorilla started to unload, throwing the sacks onto a stack behind him.

'We'd better drop off when his back is turned,' whispered Sylvie. George nodded. They both held their breath, waiting. He was very close. Suddenly the sack in front of Sylvie was lifted away, and there he was, light shining full on his inquisitive black face. He froze, staring at her. Sylvie stared back. The gorilla's eyes darted back and forth, suspicious, flecked with fear. Here was something out of the norm, something unexpected, something that might get him into trouble. Sylvie pressed her scar, hoping to hear him, but nothing came. He half turned, his hand poised, ready to raise the alarm.

'No!'

Sylvie put her finger to her lips, shaking her head vigorously. He stopped, curious now. He put the sack to one side, his eyes never leaving hers. She smiled and tapped her chest with her open hand.

'You again! He's going to have to have words with you.'

Rabbit-teeth was standing by the swing doors. Sylvie looked to where the Drummer's voice came from, shook her head and frowned, her fist clenched. The gorilla watched her expressions intently. She beat her chest once more and, reaching out, lightly tapped his. His hair was fine, almost like silk. He looked down at her tiny hand, then back to her face again, questions in his eyes.

'Did you hear me! Get a move on!'

Rabbit-teeth's voice was harsh. Sylvie's eyes darted across. Instinctively, her lips parted in a silent snarl. From the gorilla came a deep intake of breath, and then he too bared his teeth in agreement. She had spoken to him! Almost subconsciously she had spoken gorilla! Their eyes locked again. Although they were looking at each other over a great gulf, she could feel the animal in her infecting her flesh. Every look, every gesture, every movement of her limbs carried a weight they'd never had before. This was the world of beasts and birds, where nothing was without meaning. Sylvie tapped his chest once more, her mouth oddly puckered, her eyebrows arched, and in reply he clenched his great ham of a fist and, beating it once against his chest, placed it gently against hers, as lightly as a feather floating to the ground. He couldn't talk – she could sense that now. His inner voice had gone. Was that the inevitable consequence of what the Songman was doing? That with their songs stolen from them, the animals would simply shrivel up inside, nothing left but a dead world where no animal could sing or hear its inner voice, the animal kingdom reduced to a life of silent slavery?

Sylvie held out her hand, her eyes looking meaningfully at it. The gorilla wrinkled his nose and laid two huge fingers in her palm. She grasped them gently. How strong they were, how warm and full of trust! She lifted them up and pressed them against her neck so that he might feel the vibrations.

'I can sing,' she whispered. 'And one day, you will sing again too. I promise.' And with that she reached up and touched his throat too.

The gorilla understood. He took her hand and placed it against his lips.

'Are you deaf, you great ape?'

Brisk footsteps rang across the floor. Quickly the gorilla pushed the sack back into place, sheltering Sylvie from view.

'Stop that dawdling – we haven't got all night.' Rabbit-teeth poked him with a drumstick. Carefully avoiding the sacks that hid Sylvie, the gorilla resumed his work. Rabbit-teeth marched off, shouting orders to someone else. The moment the coast was clear, Sylvie and George slipped off the wagon and hid behind the growing mountain of sacks.

They were in a foundry, lit by an intense, vibrant light. Opposite their hiding place, twelve dogs were running in huge iron wheels, their pink tongues hanging out, their eyes glazed. Electricity sparked in great crackling arcs from coils of copper wire that hung overhead. On the wall behind, luminous dials quivered.

'Looks like some sort of generating plant,' whispered George. 'Those poor dogs turn the wheels, the wheels generate electricity, like turbines.'

Sylvie winced, the wound in her hand sending sharp shooting pains up her arm. She looked up. One of the dogs, a black Labrador cross, was looking at her. The words spun in her head.

WeJimbo WeNelson WeLoladaddy'sgirl

WeMonster   WeChuffy   WeArchdukeFerdinandofPrussia

ITilliethegreedyguts   Tilliethewonderthief   Tilliestealthefoodoffyourplate

Weboodle-bagged collar-nobbled

Loladaddy'sgirl   basket-snatched   Nelson   grippedwalky-walky

ArchdukeFerdinand fetchstick-grabbled

We paddypaddy the running-ground Wepaddypaddy the goodmorning

We paddypaddy the night-night sleep-tight

We padworn we slakedrooped

Tilliewoebedog Tilliepadpine hungryhome

Tilliegoodgirl

Comeonlet'sgohomenow let'sgohome

Tillie looked at Sylvie with sad longing eyes.

Sylvie put her hand to her mouth. 'One day,' she promised silently. 'One day soon.' The dog dipped her head and went on running.

At the back of the foundry, set behind massive iron doors, burned a huge furnace, white-hot coals roaring greedily as it sucked in more air. In front of it, a gang of strange goggle-wearing men, small and bent, were pulling out a blackened melting pot the size of a water butt, molten liquid bubbling from the dip of its thick, blackened lip. They looked like mad racing drivers from a bygone age.

The man with rabbit teeth now stood alongside them, his face bright red from the heat. Mildred waited next to him, a clipboard in her hand. As the melting pot emerged, he hooked it up onto a long chain. The little men ran around excitedly underneath as it moved along, showers of iridescent metal spilling down the sides. Sylvie noticed that one of them had a bloody bandage around his arm.

'They're not men,' Sylvie exclaimed, remembering the creature that had attacked her on the hill. 'They're chimpanzees!'

In the centre of the room was a small structure about the size of a photo booth; a window was set directly above a little rubber-lined aperture. As the melting pot was lowered down in front of it, the man with rabbit-teeth took out a hunting horn and blew on it sharply. All at once the activity stopped. Every chimpanzee turned to look up to small door high in the wall at the top of a metal staircase. The door opened and a man stepped out. Pressing his thumbs under his chin, he uttered a sharp chattering sound that ricocheted across the foundry. As one, the chimpanzees bowed their heads.

Sylvie gripped George by the arm. 'That must be him! The Songman!'

He was dressed in a suit of shimmering silver-grey. Light seemed to glide off it. He was tall, with long arms hanging by his side, his fingers running up and down as if he were playing an imaginary flute. On his head he wore a white skullcap, while a white mask covered both his nose and his mouth, as if to protect him from the dust and dirt below. In his hand he carried another mask, this one black. It looked like an old-fashioned gas mask, only with a long rubber tube capped by a metal spike where the gas filter would have been. As he made his way down the steps, the chimpanzees clustered round, stretching out their little hands, vying for attention. Waving them away, he strode over to where the dogs were running. He walked elegantly, purposefully, his hands swinging from side to side, his head erect. The dogs looked at him expectantly out of the corner of their eyes, but he took no notice, merely barking to them in rapid urgent snaps. They began to run faster, their eyes starting out of their heads. The dials flickered, the gauges rose, the coils hummed. The Songman waited for ten minutes, watching the instruments intently, then barked again. The dogs stopped, panting furiously. Satisfied, he walked over to the booth. With his back turned to them, he took off the white mask, replaced it with the black one and stepped into the booth. Once seated, he threaded the metal-spiked tube through the rubber-lined hole and clapped his hands. The chimps ran over, each taking something resembling a billiard cue from a stack beside the booth, before standing in line in front of the molten liquid.

'They're blowpipes, for making glass,' said George, his voice drowned by the noise. 'I've seen this done before, in Venice. You stick the pipe into the mixture and blow, and out of the other end comes a bottle. That must be how he makes those SongGlasses.'

The first chimp dipped his blowpipe into the molten liquid, then lifted it out again and began to blow. As the bottle blossomed into shape, a second chimp jammed the metal-spiked tube into the quivering glass. The Songman began to sing. Sylvie recognized the song immediately: a nightingale. It sounded so close, so true, it was as if it were singing in a bush right behind her. When the song was finished, the chimp sealed the bottle with a pair of pincers, before lifting it off the pipe and plunging it into a vat of cold water. The process had taken little more than two minutes.

Then came a short pause. Diagrams were consulted. Moulds were brought forth and placed in front of the booth, then the dogs were urged forward once more. Another melting pot was hauled out and set down by the moulds. Again the Songman took up his position as streams of liquid rainbows poured into the unseen shapes. But as the first mould began to bubble and the metal spike was inserted, the Songman sang not one but three songs: the trumpet of an elephant, the growl of a bear and the howl of a cheetah, all sung into the hollow of the glass before it was sealed and plunged into the waiting water. There was a lull as he waited for it to cool: he strode up and down, agitated, while the chimpanzees hung back, apprehensive of his mood, and the Drummers muttered to themselves. Then, with the Songman standing over him, the man with rabbit teeth prised the mould apart and lifted out a glass violin, sparkling in the golden light. The Songman clapped his hands in delight and went back to the booth. Next came a trumpet, then the slide and horn of a trombone, all with different songs inside. For some he could cup his hands; for others he pressed his throat with his knuckles or puffed out his cheeks as if blowing a trumpet. There seemed to be no song he could not sing, no song that he couldn't trap inside those magical-looking instruments. By the end of the night, half a dozen instruments lay on the table, every one laden with his deadly songs.

'Looks like he's making a whole orchestra,' observed Sylvie. 'But why?'

The horn blew twice. The night's work was done. The furnace was damped down, the moulds dragged away. The Songman stepped out of the booth and, running up the metal stairway, threw boiled sweets down onto the floor before disappearing through the door. The chimps scrambled over each other, tearing off the wrappers with their bony brown fingers before popping them into their mouths and trooping out through the swing doors. Mildred Drummer unlocked the iron wheels and led the dogs out, their bodies limp with exhaustion. The gorillas returned. Rabbit-teeth stood, arms akimbo, as they loaded the packed crates onto the wagons and trundled back up the tunnel. The lights went out. All that remained was the glow from the furnace doors.

'We'd better get out too,' Sylvie urged. 'We could try that door up there.'

'OK, but we'd better wait a while,' George advised. 'They're still about. Listen.' Rearranging the sacks, he made himself comfortable.

'Don't close your eyes, George,' Sylvie warned. 'We mustn't fall asleep.'

'Fat chance,' he said.

*   *   *

Sylvie woke. George was lying next to her, fast asleep, Mr Jackson snoring by his side. She rubbed her eyes, trying to remember all that had happened, where she was, what they had done. Of course! The Songman! The island! Where Dad might be.

Her foot was cramped. She got up, stretching, her ears popping as she yawned. She could hear the distant cry of seagulls. They'd slept all night! The foundry appeared very different from the evening before. Then it had been full of activity, bursting with a kind of dark energy. Now it stood bare and lifeless. It was hard to believe it was the same place.

A movement caught her eye: something weaving along the floor towards her. The mist again! Only it wasn't a mist; it was more like a sound, a vibration, slithering along in an elongated S shape, rising and falling, like a hooded snake in a snake-charmer's basket. She rubbed her eyes. No, there was nothing there – but as she said this to herself, she felt it gliding over her feet, wrapping itself around her ankles, slowly writhing up her. Round her legs, across her stomach, over her back and chest, under her arms it rose, muscular, invisible; her body constricted as it squeezed her tight. Then it wound itself around her neck and through her hair, before leaping off into the air, whirling round her head like a humming top. And for the first time Sylvie could hear it. A song. A lovely song!

She gulped. All at once her body was set free as the

tune wheeled round and round, weaving patterns in the air; her hand stretched out as if she could catch them and put them in her pocket. And out of the patterns, sunk into the tune, she could hear words – melodious words, beguiling words, reassuring words, which seemed to slip through her fingers, dance on her lips. 'I am the Songman,' it sang, 'and this is your Song. I sing it to you. Can you hear it, Sylvie? Can you feel it? Come closer and it will be yours, yours alone. The most wonderful Song you will ever hear.'

Sylvie looked around, but there was only George, oblivious to what she could hear. She knew she should wake him, but the Song told her not to. Why should George hear it? Why should anyone?

Now the Song seemed to fall away, slithering back along the floor, turning, beckoning, calling out to her. Past the booth, up the metal stairway it floated, then slipped under the door, its murmur just discernible. Of course. That was where the Songman had appeared. Was he there behind it now?

'I'll just take a quick look,' she whispered.

Taking care not to disturb George and Mr Jackson, she ran out onto the foundry floor and up the metal steps. She placed her ear against the door. She could hear it again on the other side, waiting for her. It was a lovely tune. If only she could just hold it, keep it.

She stepped through the door and into a narrow passageway, curved and lined with rough stone. Her

Song lay a few metres ahead. It seemed pleased that she had followed it and spun round her head once, twice, before moving off again. There were doors and windows on the wall to her left: doors to open, windows to peek through – she could see dogs chained up in their pens, chimps fast asleep on their beds of straw. But the Song was impatient and would not let her tarry. On they went, up another flight of stairs, another corridor, until they came to another door marked ROUNDHOUSE. ANIMALS NO ADMITTANCE. The Song drifted underneath. What choice did she have?

She was standing in a hall. To her immediate left was the studded oak door she and George had seen the night before; to her right, a broad wooden staircase which led up to the first floor, and, running round the building, a gallery. The Song spun round her feet, skipping up the stairs, disappearing down the passageway. She could hear it floating down the corridor like a fluttering ribbon. All she had to do was follow.

Once up the stairs, she turned left, moving along the polished wooden floor in a slow dreamy circle. The Song had changed now. It was no longer moving; rather, it was in one fixed place, growing stronger with every step she took, pulling her towards it like a magnet. There were doors on the left-hand side, leading to rooms facing the sea, she supposed, but her Song led her past them all. The wall to her right rose implacably. Halfway round she came to a low, nail-studded door, embedded in whitewashed stone. Behind it, the Song pulsed like a beating heart.

She raised the latch and pushed, stepping into the well of the lighthouse tower. Narrow stone steps spiralled up into the cavernous hollow, a glass railing embedded in the smooth white wall. The Song floated down like a writhing mist, wrapping itself about her once again, pulling her upwards. She hesitated. There was no balustrade on the open side, nothing but the huge space and the sudden drop. Then she heard the words again.

'I am the Songman, Sylvie. This is your Song. Come closer and it will be yours.'

She had no choice.

She gripped the handrail and took the first step. Then the next. She kept her eyes on the glass rail and the wedges of stone slotted into the wall, not daring to look across. A current of cold air began to blow her hair in her eyes. It would be so easy to falter and fall. She tried to put it out of her mind, concentrating on the Song as it led her ever upwards.

Then it struck her. It wasn't just the Song that she would find. The man who was singing it, the Songman, stood at the top of this tower, waiting for her. Perhaps Dad was there too! She'd almost forgotten about him! How could that be? Shivers ran down her spine, the palms of her hand suddenly sweaty. Perhaps it was Dad who had written this Song. Didn't he know more about her than anyone else? Who else could have composed something so beautiful, so particular, so her. Could Dad be the Songman? What sense did that make? Round and round she went, higher and higher, one foot after the other, the Song growing stronger, her mind reeling with tumbling thoughts.

And then she reached the top. She stood on a little landing, a closed door in front of her. She took a step forward, her hand on the latch. The Song and the Songman were on the other side.

She raised the latch.

The door opened.

The Song vanished, a puff of nothing.

The sudden light made her wince, the white circular room dazzling under the huge glass dome, which rested like a bell jar on the outer stone wall. Standing in the centre, his back to her, stood the Songman, his hands held out, praising the heavens. His head turned slightly on hearing the door. He brought his hands to his mouth, kissed them as if in prayer. He twisted his right heel, preparing to face her. On his foot was a shoe of impeccable grey leather.

Something stirred inside her – a memory, something simple, something funny, something horribly wrong. Her life began to churn inside her – all the things she had known, all the people she had trusted turned awry. The Songman spun round, bright sunlight falling on his face, his silvery suit shimmering like dappled water, and as he turned, she knew; knew who he was, who he had always been, catching her in his arms, singing her lullabies.

'Uncle Alex? You're the Songman?' She could barely get the words out.

Alex Flowerdew smiled at her coldly, patting his hair, usually so unkempt but now as smooth and white as rare porcelain. 'Ah, Sylvie.' He gestured with his hand. 'Come in. I've been expecting you.' He held a button in his hand. 'From your school blazer, I believe. You must have snagged it on the *Chanson*. As soon as I saw it I knew it must be yours. Who else from the school would be playing the dutiful daughter coming to her father's rescue? So I sang your Song. I know you quite well, don't you think?'

His voice sounded different from the Uncle Alex she knew, as if every syllable he spoke had a note behind it, accompanying his words. They sounded hollow, like the sounds she made rubbing a wet finger over one of Dad's wine glasses.

She stepped in, her eyes adjusting to the light. There was a low couch round the circumference of the room. Sprawled upon it lay the Woodpecker Man, half asleep, his red hat balanced on his lap. Sensing her presence, he sat up, suddenly wide awake, pulling his coat-tails free, jet-black eyes glittering. He looked ready to fly across the room. The Songman saw the expression on her face.

'You haven't been formerly introduced, have you? Sylvie, meet the Woodpecker. He's very keen to get to know you better, as I am sure you know.'

Staring, the Woodpecker Man blew on his fingers, then swept the ground with his hat in mock greeting, beetles falling from the sleeve of his coat.

'But' – she looked around, bewildered – 'I don't understand? What's this all about?'

'Songs,' the Songman replied. 'It's all about songs. It always was. Even your father agrees on that.'

'Dad,' she said, her heart quickening, her voice rising. 'Where is he? What have you done with him?'

'All in good time. Daniel is quite safe.'

'I want to see him.'

'Later.' He stretched an arm out. 'So what do you think of my little hideaway? You didn't imagine, did you, seeing me teaching little oiks like your friend George, that I was preparing all this?'

She looked around. Apart from the twelve two-metre-high candles that were ranged around the edge, there was only one thing in the room: a Harmonograph.

The Songman immediately noted her reaction. 'You recognize it? Apart from your father, I think I am the only man in England who possesses such a machine. After his "accident" that night, the pen started to dance across the paper like one of those action paintings. Oh, I should have been there with him. Then none of this unpleasantness would have been necessary.'

'Unpleasantness? What do you mean? Is Dad all right? If you've—' She stopped, the words burning up inside her.

'Calm down. I haven't done anything, yet. He's under lock and key. As, by now, is your friend George.'

'George! He's safe? And what about Mr Jackson?'

'Is he here too?' He brushed the lapel of his jacket, as if he had just discovered unwanted dog hairs upon it. 'Good. I need more dogs. The furnace eats electricity.'

'You can't do that! They're so cruel, those wheels.'

'Ah. So that's where you were hiding. You saw the SongGlasses being made, I suppose.'

Sylvie nodded.

'It's a little laborious, having to sing a single song into a single glass for whatever type of animal is within reach, but effective nevertheless. I sing the song of the fox, and all foxes within hearing distance, hang their heads. Soon, however, I expect to speed things up dramatically. Mr Jackson is welcome to help. He's a dog, to be put to use, like all other animals.'

'But he's too old,' she protested. 'He's part of the family.'

'The family!' The Songman's voice was scornful. 'What good are family dogs, lying around all day, eating, sleeping, fouling the pathways, barking aimlessly in back gardens.'

'They give us love and affection,' Sylvie argued. 'What more can you ask?'

'Obedience? Silence? My songs do both. They remove animals' incessant chatter, they bring them under my control. That's the thrill of it, Sylvie. I can sing their songs better than they can!' He put his hands together. 'So, just tell me where they are.'

'Where what are?' She tried to keep her face straight, a look of innocent puzzlement. She knew she hadn't succeeded.

'The diagrams, Sylvie; the notes your father made on how his instruments delivered that extraordinary note. I know you have them – or rather, I know you have hidden them. Just tell us where.'

'I don't know what you're talking about.'

'Yes you do.' He placed a long finger under her chin and lifted her face to his. 'You've had them all along, though it took a little time for me to work it out. When Daniel rang me that night and told me he was going to take the papers to London the next day, lock them away, maybe even destroy them, I had no choice. I had to act. So we took him. But he didn't have them. And they weren't in the house. They were with you. They still are. So where are they?' He folded his arms, waiting.

'We burned them in the wood,' she said. A momentary look of panic crossed his face. The Woodpecker Man shook his head.

'The Woodpecker says no. He would have smelled the fire, poked among the ashes.' He leaned forward, his face frozen hard. 'What do you want me to do, Sylvie?' he challenged, gesturing behind him. 'Hand you over to him, you and Mr Jackson? What sport he'd have.'

'Uncle Alex!'

'I am not your Uncle Alex.' He straightened up, his dignity insulted. 'I am the Songman. This is the SongHouse, not your home. Don't lie to me, Sylvie. I haven't the time. You have the papers, I know you have. Just tell me where.'

'Why? What do you want them for?'

The Songman raised his hands to the ceiling. 'It's very simple. All I want is the Note. The One Note.'

'And for that you kidnapped Dad, stole his instruments?'

'He brought it on himself. He should share his knowledge, not keep it to himself. I need it.' He brought his face close to hers. All these years she had looked and seen a kind, trusting face. Now she saw someone different: the nose, the eyes, the mouth, all the same, but the spirit behind had changed them. He was right. He wasn't Uncle Alex any more. He was the

Songman, a different being entirely. Is this what being adult was? Being different things to different people, a life of masks?

'Don't make this hard for me,' he was saying. 'Tell me what I want to know and you can see your father straight away. You can both go home, enjoy the holidays. Wouldn't you like that?'

She shook her head stubbornly. 'I want to see Dad,' she repeated.

'Tell me first.'

'I can't. He told me not to.' Sylvie was close to tears.

'Can't? You mean won't. Didn't Miss Coates teach you the difference?' He gripped her hard, his fingers digging into her shoulder-blades. 'For the last time, where are they? Tell me.'

'No. Let go! You're hurting me.'

'I'm hurting you?' His face turned pale with anger. 'I'm hurting you? After all these years of being a family friend, singing you to sleep, helping your father, encouraging him every step of the way, I'm hurting you?' He turned to the Woodpecker Man. 'Take her, she's yours.' He pointed a long finger at her. 'You won't like yourself much after he's finished with you. He goes for the eyes first.'

He sang, a screeching, hopping call. The Woodpecker Man leaped across the room and grabbed hold of her arms. He began to drag her towards the door.

'No! No!' Sylvie struggled wildly, her hands flailing at his grinning face. 'Help me! Help me! Please!' She held out an imploring hand.

The Songman stared at her impassively for a moment. Then something registered, his brow narrowing.

'Stop! Wait!'

He ran across, seizing her wrist.

'What's this?' he demanded, forcing her right palm open. The weal looked red and angry.

'Just a bite,' she said.

'I can see that. Let go, you.' He pushed the Woodpecker Man aside, holding her hand steady, examining the wound.

'When did you get this?' he queried.

'A few days ago.' Sylvie looked away, embarrassed. Back on the couch, the Woodpecker Man had brought out a handful of live spiders from one of his pockets, and was dropping them, one by one, into his mouth, seemingly oblivious to her presence. Wriggling legs protruded between his lips.

'What was it? Not that dog of yours.'

'A fox.'

'A fox!' The Songman took a deep breath, digesting the thought. 'Yes, the four teeth, so carefully placed, without any tear or any bone damage. You must have held your hand very still for this, hmmm?' He stared at it intently. 'And is it true' – his voice suddenly gentle

– 'you can hear inside them – the dogs, the rats, the owls?'

Sylvie blushed.

'Come, come, Sylvie, don't go all coy on me. I want to know. Is it true?'

'Yes.'

'Yes. You don't know how lucky you are. Saved from the Woodpecker Man by the Mark.'

'The Mark?'

'I have only heard speak of it. Never seen it. May I . . . touch it?'

The Songman traced the faded outline with a finger, genuinely moved. A shiver of apprehension ran through her. 'Wonderful, wonderful,' he murmured. He spun on his heel, his face alight with excitement, eyes flashing round the room.

'Do you know what this means? What you and I could do together? Can you imagine the worlds we could explore – worlds that have remained hidden for hundreds and thousands of years? Me with the animals' songs at my command, you with their languages. Everything would change, Sylvie. Everything!' He held her away from him, his face utterly changed, thrilled, delighted, running with thought. 'Would you like to hear your Song again?'

'Not particularly,' Sylvie lied, her heart hammering.

'I'm going to sing it anyway. It's a very special song. Listen.'

He opened his mouth. The Song flew around the room, settling on her like a summer's rain. It was a song of her lost mother and of the lost tree and how they had both folded their arms about her. It made her feel whole, at peace. She wanted to bathe in it, let it flow over her for ever and ever. It was wonderful, sublime; hers. The Woodpecker Man batted it away from his face as if it were an angry insect.

'Wasn't that beautiful?' the Songman whispered.

She could barely reply. 'Yes,' she said, her heart sinking.

'Wasn't it better than any animal's song? Better than the fox's, better than Mr Jackson's? Tell me where the papers are, and you can hear your Song any time you want. All you have to do is ask.' And he sang the Song again.

Sylvie tried to fight it off, but it was no use. It warmed her like the rays of the sun. She wanted to hear it every day, every hour, every minute. It was too beautiful to bear.

'Stop!' she cried. 'Stop it!' The Song ceased. The world grew cold again.

'Just as you wish. I see you appreciate the menace of excess. That is good. That is all I want to do with my Songs. Eradicate superfluous noise. Nothing is more beautiful than my voice. You can see that now. Nothing else matches its power, its reach, its beauty. Why should anything else sing when they can hear me?'

'Because they want to.'

'For now they do. But after they have heard me? Count yourself lucky, Sylvie. You are one of the first humans to hear their own Song. In time I could give everyone such a Song. It's just with human beings, there's usually a little more to sing.' He paused for breath, his eyes shining with excitement.

'Come. Step outside. See the world as I see it.'

He ducked down the little steps under the low stone wall and, opening the heavy oak door, stepped up onto the balcony that ran around the glass vault, the glass railings glinting in the rising sun. Sylvie followed. Below, the water foamed green and white, the current around the old lighthouse fierce and strong. There was nothing to be heard but the wash of the sea and the low whistle of the wind. Down below, the *Chanson* was moored securely in her little granite harbour. Across the water Sylvie could see the flat expanse of marshland, and beyond, a smudge of huddled trees and the zoo. She thought of the tiger lying there, his head to the ground, listening.

'I love it here,' said the Songman. 'The emptiness of it, the quiet. That's what I want – to bring an understanding to the world of how and what they should hear, how valuable silence is, how the world should be a vessel waiting to be filled with something glorious. Doesn't the lark sound more wonderful after the quiet of the dawn? Isn't one sheep bleating on a lonely moor more powerful than a great herd of them bellowing away? That's why I silence them – to make them more beautiful, more precious. If I wanted to, I could release them all. One song is all it would take.'

'You could do that?'

'Songs are like everything else, Sylvie, broken down into components, elements, atoms, molecules – call them what you will. There are those which are the same for every animal. Do you know, you've given me an idea. If I achieve my destiny, and I will, despite your father's obstructions, once a year I will let all the animals sing to their heart's content for just for one day. SongDay, I shall call it.' He turned and smiled. 'You see? We're working together already. You deserve a reward. Come with me.'

For the next two hours the Songman took her round the SongHouse: down the one hundred and thirty-three steps that ran inside the tower, on to the elegant first floor, with rooms shaped like half-moons overlooking the sea; over to the Song Library, where all the animals' songs were stored in alphabetical order, and finally to the SongDome, deep underground, where he sang her Song again and she heard it bounce from surface to surface, before falling silently to the floor. It was, she thought, the most beautiful sound she had ever heard. It seemed to speak not simply to her, but about her – all the things she could do, the unknown wonders that the Mark had laid before her.

The Songman knew what she was thinking. 'Your father has a talent,' he said. 'But you have a greater one.' He placed his hands on her shoulders. 'Oh, Sylvie. Don't be my enemy. You are loyal to your father and I commend you for that, but do not turn aside from me. Join me or suffer the consequences. I will have the Note. You will not be able to resist. I know the power of your Song, my voice. Think for a moment. Try to understand what lies within your grasp. Will you do that?' He straightened up. 'That's enough for one day. I shall talk to you tomorrow. And the day after. And the day after that.'

'Can I see Dad now?' she said.

'Of course. Just tell me where his papers are, and you can be with him the very next minute.'

Sylvie shook her stubborn head.

'Then I cannot.' The Songman opened the door. 'I have work to do. Until tomorrow.'

Back in the SongHouse, the Woodpecker Man sat stroking one of his birds. He scowled angrily as the Songman returned.

'Try and curb your frustration,' the Songman told him. 'Your time may come. But she has the Mark and it would be a pity to waste it. We must play her carefully, take her to the very brink, then pull her back just in time. Give me seven days. The Song should break her by then. And if that fails, then do what you will – George, the dog, it doesn't matter, as long as she tells us where Daniel's papers are.'

Down below, Mildred Drummer led Sylvie through a maze of corridors and stone-cut steps to another nail-studded door. On the other side George sat on the edge of a narrow bed, his head between his hands, Mr Jackson sitting despondently by his side.

'Sylvie,' he cried, springing to his feet. 'Where did you get to? We woke up with her standing over us. We should never have come here.' His eyes were red with dried tears. Poor George, suddenly all alone. No wonder he looked frightened.

The door closed on them, bolts shot home. Mr Jackson was jumping up and down, his tail thrashing madly.

MrJacksonMrJackson! MrJacksonwaggerwagger!
MrJacksonjubybliss timetogohomenow timetogohome

'Not yet, Mr Jackson.' Sylvie tickled him gently. Her voice was grave, troubled. 'I met the Songman, George. You'll never guess who he is.' She cleared her throat. There seemed to be something stuck there.

'Flowerdew!' he exclaimed as she told him. 'But – but he can't even do up his shoelaces.'

'That's what he wanted everyone to think.' She coughed again, her voice not quite right.

'Still . . .' George ruffled Mr Jackson's neck. 'He hasn't found—'

Sylvie put her fingers to his lips.

'Do you know what he wants them for?' She shook her head.

'He just says he wants to listen to the Note, but there's more to it than that.'

'What about your dad? Have you seen him?'

'No. But he's definitely here. So where are we?'

'Some sort of old storeroom. Basement, I guess, judging by that window. Stand on the bed and you'll see – it's almost level with the ground. Despite the bars, it opens, so we won't suffocate. You can just make out the shore too. That little door there leads to a loo and a basin. When Mr Jackson needs to go, you just bang on the door and that Drummer woman takes us out onto the rock. There's no way we can swim across the water. The current is far too strong. We'd need wings.'

'Good place to talk though, without anyone listening. Anything else?'

'I haven't really looked.'

There wasn't much. Two beds, two chairs and a rickety table; wedged at the back, up on its end, stood an old dinghy, the bottom badly holed, a canvas sail hanging forlornly from a broken mast. Propped up next to it stood a clatter of fishing rods, and from hooks in the wall hung a row of battered drums, their skins cracked.

George untied one of the fishing hooks and

scratched a line on the wall. 'Day one,' he said gloom-ily. 'I wonder how many more.'

'No idea, but he needs the Note soon, I got that much. Maybe I can find out why. He's got this mad idea that I should join him.'

'Join him! What makes him think you'd do that?'

'Search me, but . . .'

'But what?'

'Nothing.' Sylvie sat back, afraid. She could feel the Song crawling inside her, like a creature woken after a long sleep. From across the water came a long call, like a hollow horn, soft and yet strong, powerful, unending. It rose from the earth up to the sky. It was sung under the sun, but it was a song of the dark. It came from the marsh, but belonged to the forest. The tiger!

'Hear that?' said George. 'The Songman hasn't silenced them all. Not yet.'

But Sylvie didn't reply. She was thinking of the days ahead.

Chapter 11

The next morning Mildred Drummer took Sylvie back up to the SongTower. The Songman was standing in the hard light, his hands behind his back; the Woodpecker Man was seated behind him, his top hat wedged between his knees, a green woodpecker squatting upon it. He stared at her as she entered, stroking the bird's scarlet plumage, whispering into its ear.

'So,' said the Songman. 'You slept well?'

'Not very,' Sylvie stammered, uneasy at the Woodpecker Man's presence. 'The furnace – it's very noisy.'

'It won't be for much longer. Just a few instruments to be made before the–' He stopped himself abruptly. 'I have a question for you. What do you want more? To see your father or to hear your Song?'

'To see Dad of course,' she replied without hesitation, irritated that he should ask such a question.

'Will you tell me where the papers are?'

'No.'

The Songman opened his hands. 'Then I am afraid you cannot. Instead I shall sing your Song,' and he stroked his throat and sang her Song. Although she tried not to show it, Sylvie drank it down like a thirsty child. It tasted so good.

'Now go and call your father's name,' the Songman told her, glancing back at the Woodpecker Man. 'Stand at the top of the steps and call him as loud as you can. See if he hears you. You can see him if he does.'

Sylvie ran to the steps and looked down into the deep, empty hollow. 'Dad! Dad!' she shouted. 'It's me, Sylvie!' Her voice boomed back up to her in great loud bounds.

'See?' said the Songman, coming up beside her. 'He cannot hear you. You did not call loud enough. Maybe tomorrow. If you tell me where the papers are, you can see him without calling.'

He sent her away, the Woodpecker Man's cackle ringing in her ears.

Back in the cell, George was relieved to see her. It scared him to be left alone, even with Mr Jackson for company.

'What did he do?' he asked.

Sylvie cleared her throat, a flicker of suspicion rushing through her. It was her Song, not his. There was no need to tell George everything. 'Nothing much. Just made me shout for my dad.' She rubbed her neck. Her throat felt dry.

'That's psychological,' George suggested. 'He's playing with your head.'

Sylvie suppressed the flash of irritation coursing through her. George thought he knew everything.

'Yes, George, I know. Don't worry about it.' She cleared her throat again.

'You OK?' he asked.

'Just a frog in my throat,' she said. 'Nothing more.'

At noon they were allowed to take Mr Jackson outside. In daylight they could see what a fortress the island was – the sheerness of the cliffs, the sea pounding against the rocks below, how strong, how secure the lighthouse appeared. Overlooking the harbour a foghorn sat on top of the cliff, directed towards the shoreline. George put his hand on it. He couldn't hear anything but it seemed to tremble.

'See how he sends the vibrations out,' George said.

'Oh, you believe it now?'

'Eyes and Ears, Sylvie,' George reminded her. 'Eyes and Ears.'

The mist wasn't as thick, looking landwards, but

there was enough. For all its compact solidity the island felt alien, as if it wasn't anchored to the real world, but part of an invented, imagined one, the world the Songman wanted.

'What do we do now?' George said, watching Mr Jackson rooting amongst the rocks.

Sylvie didn't reply straight away. Out across the water the current seemed to be swirling around the island, as if they were stuck in the middle of a whirl-pool. Was that a seal's head she could see, swimming there? She placed her fingers round her neck. It felt cold inside.

'We wait,' she said, her voice uncertain, quavering. 'What else can we do?'

The following day the same thing happened. Sylvie was taken up to the SongTower again. The Woodpecker Man sat in the same place, his top hat between his knees, his black eyes sparkling with dark malevolence. And again the Songman asked the same question.

'What do you want more, Sylvie? To see your father or to hear your Song?'

'To see Dad,' she replied, knowing how the Songman would respond.

'And will you tell me where his papers are?'

'I've told you already. No.'

The Songman raised his hands. 'Then you cannot. Instead I will sing your Song,' and he sang it, and despite herself, she gulped it down like a greedy baby at a feeding bottle. It was so warm, so sweet. When it was over, she swallowed hard, her mouth dry. She wanted to ask for more. The Songman shook his head, as if he knew what she was thinking.

'Go to the SongTower steps,' he told her. 'Call for your father. If he hears you, you may see him.'

And Sylvie stood at the top of the steps and shouted, 'Dad! Dad! It's me, Sylvie!' The echo bounced back, though it seemed to her that it was not quite as loud as before. She turned, looking back anxiously. She hadn't done it right.

'You'll have to do better than that,' the Songman admonished above the Woodpecker Man's crowing, and again he sent her away.

Back in the cell, George asked his question too.

'I don't want to talk about it,' she croaked. 'I need some water. This throat of mine . . .' She went to the mirror and opened her mouth wide. It didn't look inflamed. It didn't feel inflamed. And yet . . . She touched it gingerly. It felt as if a layer of cotton wool were stuck halfway down. She coughed hard, trying to force it out, retching into her hand. There was nothing there.

'When Mildred comes to let Mr Jackson out,' she rasped, 'can you ask her for some cough drops? I think I'm coming down with something.'

Outside, the island was swathed in white. Mr Jackson ran in and out of the swirl.

'It's a little closer than yesterday,' George observed. 'Looks more real too. I suppose they do have real mists here too.'

They gazed out into it. To Sylvie it looked like her voice felt, thick and yet thin, insubstantial, evasive, there and not there. George stuck his hands in his pockets, feeling for his inhaler. He hadn't needed to use it in days.

'I don't understand,' he said. 'He's gone to all this trouble to get you, and he just asks you a couple of questions every morning? And all you have to do is say no? He must be up to something.'

'Well, tell me when you find out,' she said, the words coming out low and hoarse. 'I'm going back inside. This weather isn't doing my throat any good.'

The cough drops didn't work either. Sylvie sucked through a whole packet and still her throat felt strange, as if its batteries were running down. George tried to cheer her up with a game of noughts and crosses with the pencil and paper Mildred Drummer had given them, but it did little to raise her spirits. The remainder of the day passed in restive silence, Mr Jackson pawing at the door, Sylvie fidgety, uneasy, unwilling to talk. George was almost pleased when night came, and he fell asleep to the sound of the furnace roaring in the depths below. It sounded almost normal.

On the fourth and fifth days the pattern was repeated. Each time, the Songman asked Sylvie the same question, and each time she gave the same answer. And each time the Songman would sing her Song, and she would close her eyes, carried somewhere far away on its power and beauty. And then he would send her out to stand at the top of the Song Tower steps, and each time she looked down into the empty void and called for her dad. And each time, although she shouted as loud as she could, the echo that came back was fainter than the day before, and the Songman would scold her for not doing her best, the Woodpecker Man laughing at her, rubbing his hands in glee. And each time

George would see her return, her eyes a little heavier, her skin a little paler, the light within her flickering.

On the sixth day he could keep quiet no longer.

'Sylvie,' he said, sitting her down at the table, 'tell me the truth. What's going on up there?'

Sylvie shrugged her shoulders. She'd almost given up talking. It was easier that way.

'I've already told you,' she croaked. 'He asks me if I will give him Dad's papers. I say no.'

'That's all? He just asks you, and you say no?'

'Yes,' she whispered.

'That's all he does?'

'Yes? Why do you go on at me?'

George stared at her closely, trying to read her face. 'You're not telling me everything, Sylvie.'

'I am,' she protested, her voice cracking with the strain. 'I go up. I say no. I shout for my dad. I come back.'

'There's something else. What is it?'

'Nothing! I'm only there for ten minutes. What else could there be? Leave me alone, George. Leave me alone.'

She turned away, her precious Song burning in her head. If only she could block out all this meaningless chatter. It was all she wanted to do really – hear her Song. What was so wrong with that?

Mr Jackson laid his head on George's knee.

MrJacksonSylviedog Sylviesongmuffling

Leaveitaloneyoudisgustingcreature leave it alone

He raised a troubled face. George could see him, see his saddened eyes, his furrowed face. But he couldn't hear him.

And on the seventh day . . .

Mildred took Sylvie to the tower. Once, she'd been told the number of steps, but she couldn't remember much any more. Once, she'd had a friend called George, but all he wanted to do was prise the secret of her Song from her. Once . . . she tried to remember what it was, why she was here. Her dad – yes, that was it. Her dad.

The Songman was standing where he always stood, the Woodpecker Man sitting where he always sat, looking at her like he always looked at her. Something to peck at. Though he still frightened her, she was glad he was there. It meant only one thing.

The Songman unfolded his hands. He had lovely hands.

'Well, Sylvie,' he said gently, 'what do you want more? To see your father or hear your Song?'

And for the first time she hesitated, a pleasant little worm creeping into her head. Why shouldn't she hear her Song first? It would put her in a good mood. It would only take a minute. She could see Dad afterwards.

'I want to see Dad,' she said, her voice struggling to

be heard, 'but perhaps before that . . .'

'Of course!' The Songman smiled, glancing at the Woodpecker Man, then bent close and sang her Song softly into her ear. She could feel herself swooning as it rushed in, floating up inside her like a wonderful dream from which she need never wake.

'Go and call him now,' the Songman instructed, and she ran out, her legs unsteady, holding onto the railing, giddy with pleasure.

'Dad! Dad!' she called. 'It's me, Sylvie.' She rocked back and forth, waiting for the echo, but although she waited and waited, this time it didn't come back at all. She tried again. 'Dad! Dad! It's me, Sylvie,' but still there was nothing; nothing but a ghostly wind swirling up from the dark depths.

She ran back into the room where the Songman stood, one hand on the Harmonograph. The Woodpecker Man clapped his hands in derisory applause.

'The echo,' she whispered, holding her throat. 'I can't hear it.'

'How can you hear an echo when there is no voice?'

'No voice?'

'Yes.' The Songman looked out across the water. There was nothing there but the sea. Nothing. 'What father would want to hear that?'

'Please, I'll try again.'

The Songman caught her as she tried to run back.

'No. What's the use? He won't hear you.' He bent down, his face next to hers, his eyes piercing, his lips barely moving, his voice like a sharp needle, etching thoughts in her head. 'You don't want him to hear you, do you?'

'Yes I do!' she protested. She could feel her world slipping away under her feet.

'No you don't. If you did, you'd call louder. But you don't. You whine and dribble, then run to me, complaining about the echo. The truth is, Sylvie, your father is nothing to you now. You've lost interest in him. And you know why? Because you've found someone else who can give you what you need, who can take you under their wing, sing you your Song, show you your path through life. Come. It's time to go.'

'Go? Go where?' Sylvie's eyes darted from side to side, frightened at the thought of leaving.

'To the zoo of course. Isn't that where all good families go?'

George watched with alarm as the balloon left for the shore. Sylvie had never been away this long before, and now she was leaving the island without him. Was she coming back or what? It was difficult to know what she was doing, she was behaving so strangely – almost as if he wasn't there. Once they'd been in this together, but now . . .

'I've got to find a way out of here, Mr Jackson,'

he said out loud, trying to keep his voice as calm as possible. 'Maybe if I could fix the boat, we could pick the lock or something, drag it out after dark.'

No chance. There was a huge hole in the bottom. He'd never be able to mend that. He examined it again, attracted to the thick canvas sail twisted round the mast and the spare ropes that lay curled at its foot. Pulling at the loose knot that held the sail in place, he unfurled it and took a closer look. It was old and faded, but still sturdy. Perhaps he could make a kite, fly it up on the ropes, send a message to the shore. At least it would be something. He looked about. The fishing rods standing in the corner could be used as struts. Bouncing on the hard bed, he put his hand underneath. It was as he'd thought: thin slats of wood holding up the mattress. That would give the kite some rigidity. He could tie them all in with the fishing twine, using one of the fishing hooks for a needle. Come to think of it . . . He looked at the sail again, remembering what had happened to Miss Coates. This canvas was ten times the size of that kite. It could carry a lot more than a message. It would take some time to make, but if he was left alone long enough . . .

He spread a couple of sheets of paper out on the floor and started drawing a diagram. Other ideas came to him as the kite began to take shape. The strings around the drums could act as guy ropes, the drums themselves provide weight for a tail. And if he could pry it loose, the dinghy seat could carry someone. Mr Jackson looked over his shoulder, watching the strange squiggles take shape. He was familiar with this sort of behaviour and it made him feel good, looking at it. George reminded him of Daniel, the way he leaned over his drawing as if nothing else mattered, the way he muttered to himself as he worked, paced about the room working things out. As he did at home, he tried to help as best he could. When George hunched himself over the paper, Mr Jackson hunched over with him. When George paced the room, Mr Jackson followed. And when George sat back on his heels, thinking, Mr Jackson sat back too, and thought of his basket and his bowl and the smells under the garden hedge.

'See this, Mr Jackson?' George said when it was finished, tapping the dog's collar. 'This could be as important as what you've got tucked away in there.'

Mr Jackson wagged his tail.

MrJacksonGeorgepalGeorgegothisheadintheclouds-again

The lock rattled. George stood up, stuffing the sheets under the arm of his jacket. The door swung open. Sylvie stood there, her face drawn and bled of colour.

'Sylvie?' he said, relieved to see her, but astonished at her appearance. 'What's happened?'

She stumbled in, unable to speak. What could she tell him – the thing she had seen, and all her own fault? Oh, if only she hadn't goaded him. If only she had kept quiet, gone along with what he'd said. She was full of bad selfish thoughts, that was the trouble. George couldn't even begin to understand.

Before they left the island, the Songman had sung her Song again, and then they were up in the air, sailing across the water in the balloon, her head in a trance, swimming with light. It was lovely up there in the SongBird, away from George and Mr Jackson, and all their petty worries. Up here she was with the Songman, floating, dreaming; her Song was just a cloud away.

Once on shore they had walked quickly to the zoo, the Woodpecker Man following some distance behind. She could feel his eyes on the back of her legs, feel his fingers itching to scrabble in her hair. He made no pretence of disguising it. Whenever she looked back, he was placing his giant feet in her footsteps, parodying the way she walked, grinning.

'Can't you make him stop?' she said, the words barely audible.

The Songman shrugged. 'I can't make him do anything,' he said. 'He's his own master. But for the moment we suit each other's purpose.'

Her words came slowly, each one forced out. 'What is your purpose? What's his? I'd like to know, truly.'

'Mine? In time, Sylvie. In time. His? I've no idea.

Something that bubbles up from the deep. It's best not to ask.'

Even from this distance, the zoo seemed unnaturally quiet. Notices hung from the fence, warning people of an unknown epidemic that had affected all the animals. Two vultures stood guard on either side of the zoo gates. In their shabby black feathers they looked like stooped funeral directors. As the Songman approached, they began clacking their hooked beaks in greeting.

The zoo was deserted. The Songman led Sylvie down the empty paths from one compound to the next: the lions, the giraffes, the elephants, the kangaroos, the imprisoned animals crowding up against their fences, anxious to please him, desperate to hear their songs again.

'You see' – the Songman had gestured with a proud sweep of his hand – 'there is no epidemic. I have simply captured all their songs. There is no one here that won't obey me.'

'The tiger still roars,' she had said. 'I heard him last night.' The Songman had scowled. She should have held her tongue, right there and then. 'And besides,' she had added, feeling wilful argument rise within her, remembering that gorilla, 'not all want to obey you.'

'You doubt my power?'

Sylvie swallowed, forcing the words out. 'You're

not an animal. You don't know how they think. You can't control everything they do.'

'No? Watch.'

They were standing opposite the enclosure where the antelopes were housed. A young female was standing by the fence, her eyes questioning, her nose inquisitive. The Songman tipped his head back and called. The delicate creature pawed the ground, shivers of apprehension rippling over her dappled skin. The Song told her that she should trust him, but instinct told her to be wary. He sang again. She hesitated for a moment, then, on spindly legs, jumped the high fence, skittering on the ground as she landed on the other side. Another, older deer ran up to the fence, as if beseeching her offspring not to be so foolish, to return. Once more the Songman sang. Pleased with herself, the young antelope nestled up to him, her trusting brown eyes looking up into his face. Ruffling the top of her head, he led her a little way down the path until they came to the wolves' quarters. On the other side of a high fence, a steep bank ran down into a rocky pit. A group of four wolves lay at the bottom, despondent and bored. As they approached, the wolves caught the young animal's scent and raised their heads expectantly. The antelope started to tremble.

'I could make her go in there,' the Songman said.

'Why would you want to?' Sylvie asked, frightened of the reply.

'Because it will upset you. Because you will remember.'

He started to sing. The antelope jumped back, her hooves stuttering on the ground as if in protest. She was terrified. He called again. The wolves below seemed to sense his call, and they sat up. The young antelope looked around, terror in her eyes. She stood there, her flanks quivering.

'I believe you,' Sylvie tried to cry. 'Don't! Please don't!'

'Too late. You've cast the die now.'

The antelope stood there, and then, with fear and incomprehension on her face, leaped the high fence. She landed awkwardly on the other side, juddering down the steep bank, coming to a halt five metres away. The wolves were on their feet, sniffing the air, staring hard at their foolhardy intruder. She began to shake violently, her whole body seized with fright. She turned and looked back, her face frozen in a moment of panic and death. Then, as one, the wolves leaped upon her and she fell, her killers busy on her bloody neck.

Sylvie hid her face in her hands, sobbing. 'That was a wicked thing to do,' she said, forcing the words out.

The Songman shrugged his shoulders. 'That was their dinner,' he said. He raised a questioning finger. 'So, will you do as I ask now?'

Sylvie pushed the question away, saving what

little voice she had left.

The Songman pointed to the corpse, the wolves tearing at the flesh, the vultures perching, waiting their turn. 'Not even to save another young innocent's death?'

She hung her head, unable to reply.

'One more demonstration. Less messy this time.'

The tiger was lying quite still, curled up in a dirty corner, a lump of untouched meat by his side, flies buzzing around. Ten metres away lay the gate, which opened up onto the no man's land between him and the path. Sylvie stood there. How long ago was it when she was here with . . . her father? Yes, she and her father came here, so long ago. She tried to picture him, remember his voice, but it was as if he was bathed in fog.

'What are you going to do?' Her thin words were coated in anxiety.

'Teach you a lesson,' the Songman replied. 'Teach you and the tiger a lesson.'

Slipping the bolt back, he stepped inside, onto the parched grass. At the click of the lock, the tiger turned his great head and stared. As the Songman approached, he rose, stretching slowly, thick folds of skin rippling like incoming waves down the run of his back. Even in the shade of his mean enclosure, his colour burned like a forest fire, wild and jagged and unpredictable. Something stirred in Sylvie's memory:

George kicking her legs, the classroom reverberating with twenty-three voices chanting. The tiger took a pace forward. The Songman halted and, looking him full in the face, drew out a SongGlass, raising it high in the air. Though his eyes moved, the tiger remained absolutely still.

'See?' the Songman cried. 'Here is your Song, locked away, ready for use. But for you I will sing it in person. And then you will bow down, as all the other creatures have.'

He threw back his head and sang the tiger's song, a raw, brutal thing, the veins in his neck full to bursting, his mouth stretched wide, his teeth bared to the sky. He swayed as the power of it rose up in his body and ripped into the air. Sylvie stood amazed.

The tiger twisted his head this way and that, as if trying to shake off an invisible enemy. A low growl rose from his throat as he backed away, uncertain of his foe. The Songman moved closer and sang the tiger's song again, one hand reaching out, palm down, as a master might instruct his dog.

'See, Sylvie Bartram!' he cried with glee. 'He is mine already.'

Without warning the tiger hurled himself at the bars of his cage, a savage roar erupting from his throat, his mouth huge and dark. A paw shot out, claws raking the air, ripping into the Songman's coat. The SongGlass smashed to the ground. Roar fought with roar as the tiger reared up, his jaw locked around the bars as he tried to wrench them free.

'You dare attack me!' the Songman screamed. 'You dare!'

The tiger flung himself once again, desperate to break loose. Hate and rage dripped like molten metal from his huge yellow teeth. They stood there, staring at each other, the tiger and the Songman, both taut and breathless, their business unfinished. The Songman threw off his jacket. A streak of blood had seeped through the sleeve of his shirt. His face had turned a deathly white.

'I'll not have any animal defying me, however grand. Do you understand?'

The tiger inclined his head and roared again, long and defiant, never once taking his eyes off his enemy.

'Very well.' The Songman slung his jacket over his shoulders, rubbing his wounded arm. 'Keep your song, if you must. It will be your death sentence. From now on, tigers are an extinct species. And you will lead them into that eternal wilderness. Come, Sylvie, to the SongHouse.' He bent low, his face trembling with anger. 'And if you value your father's life, do not mention this again. Do not mention this to anyone!'

On the way back, all Sylvie could think of was the antelope, her coltish gait, her delicate skin, her terrified, trembling eyes. Oh, if only she hadn't questioned his power! Now, back in the cell, she could hardly believe she had let it happen.

'Well?' said George, still waiting for her to speak.

She looked over at the window, half open. If only she could hear her Song again. Then everything would be all right – this hollow feeling she had inside her would be filled.

'Song,' she said, forming the word with difficulty.

'Song? What song?'

Sylvie's eyes were wide, suddenly realizing what she had said.

'The tiger,' she croaked. 'He can't sing the tiger.'

She slumped on the bed and started to cry. Mr Jackson crawled up beside her and put his head on her lap.

MrJacksonSylviedog what'sthemattertheneh? what'sthematter?

'Nothing,' she said. 'Nothing's the matter. I'm just a bit tired.'

Mr Jackson nudged her again, unwilling to let go.

MrJacksonwho'sacleverboythen Sylvienottickety-boo
Sylviesongmuffled
MrJacksonbettertakehertotheV-E-Tsoon

'Be quiet, Mr Jackson. There's nothing wrong with me. Nothing at all.'

George crossed over and sat on the edge of her bed, Mr Jackson in between them.

'He's right, you know,' he said, looking down.

'What?'

'Mr Jackson,' he said gently. 'He's right.' Sylvie pushed her face into the pillow.

'Oh, you can understand what Mr Jackson says, can you?'

'No, but I can hear your answer, so, by a process known as deduction, I can guess what he's saying. There's nothing wrong with you? There's plenty wrong. What's going on, Sylvie? What's happening to you?'

'It's nothing. It's nothing. Just leave me alone.'

Mr Jackson laid an insistent paw on George's lap.

'Yes, you know what I'm talking about, don't you?' George ruffled the dog's head. Mr Jackson sat back on his haunches and raised his head, exposing his throat. He tried to bark, his gaze fixed on George's questioning eyes.

'What is it?' George asked. 'Trying to tell me something?'

The dog raised his head again, opened his mouth in mime.

'It's no use, Mr Jackson,' George said. 'The Songman's sung you to silence. A mufflesong, I think you call it.'

Mr Jackson started at the word and, turning back, nuzzled his mouth under Sylvie's chin. George didn't understand at first. But then, as the old dog repeated it, again and again, it dawned on him.

'You mean . . . ?' He put his hands on Sylvie's

shoulders, suddenly realizing how thin she was, as if she were wasting away.

'It's the Songman,' he said, the idea dawning on him. 'He's singing to you, isn't he? Isn't he?'

She sat up, her cheeks wet. She grabbed hold of his arm, her eyes unnaturally bright.

'Yes! Yes! Of course he's singing to me, George. He's singing my Song.' Her voice trembled at the very thought of it. 'It's so wonderful. It's like . . .' She looked around, trying to find the words. 'It's like a new world, a promised land that's out there, waiting for me, if only I could hear it more. It's all I want. To hear it more.'

'But what about the animals? What about Mr Jackson, your dad? Don't they matter any more?'

'Of course they matter, but they could have Songs too. Everyone could. He's right. What more could you want?'

'But don't you see what he's doing to you? Have you looked in the mirror lately, listened to yourself? You're fading, Sylvie, fading. It's like every other song he sings. He's stealing your voice, controlling you, every time he sings it. Can't you see that?'

Sylvie shook him off.

'What if he is? I'll still have my Song to listen to. You don't understand, George. You don't have a song of your own. Even if you did, you couldn't appreciate it. You're tone deaf, remember, no use to anybody. I need some air. It's stuffy in here.'

She banged on the door. Mildred Drummer slid back the bolts and let them outside. The memory of her Song made Sylvie feel weak, hardly able to walk. Her legs were made of lead, her arms were dead weights. She was being dragged down. The sea was colourless, drained like her. Nothing seemed alive any more.

'Come on, Sylvie,' George urged. 'A couple of turns round the block, eh? For Mr Jackson's sake.'

Up in the SongTower the Woodpecker Man and the Songman watched as they made their painful away around the island.

'Tomorrow,' the Songman said. 'She's all used up now.'

Sylvie woke hot and feverish, desperate to hear her Song. Only the Song. Dad, George, Mr Jackson – nothing else mattered to her. She sat there, rubbing her knees repeatedly, waiting for the door to open, her mouth dry, her palms sweating. He was late. Why didn't he come? Mr Jackson came bumbling up.

GoodmorningMrJackson   MrJacksonSylviedoggoodboy

Howyoufeeling today?

Timeforyourconstitutional timeforyourconstitutional

'Oh, leave me alone, you stupid dog,' she said, shoving him aside.

She waited for what seemed like hours. Eventually the door swung open. Mildred Drummer stood in the doorway, a daffodil-yellow dress draped over her arm.

'Get this on you,' she commanded. 'You're wanted on the boat.'

'She's not well,' George protested. 'She should stay indoors.'

'Ooh, listen to the doctor,' the woman snapped. 'You keep quiet, otherwise you'll get a dose of his medicine too.'

Outside, sunlight sparkled on the deep green sea. The air was light, cool, the sky cloudless. There was no mist. The pebbled shore looked an age away, a peaceful haven. Six herons stood motionless by the *Chanson*, tall in their grey livery. The wooden boat creaked against the steady waves. The Songman stood waiting. As she approached he took her arm gently.

'See those birds?' he said, leading her down the steps. 'They fish for my dinner: oysters, dabs, softshell crabs. I even have them digging for samphire on the mudflats. They don't like it, but they do my bidding, like everything else. Let's see if we have anything for them.'

He walked across to a wooden box on the side of the narrow quay and opened the lid. Six small mackerel, not yet dead, lay inside, their gills opening and closing in the puddle of salt water that half covered their bodies. He lifted one out, held it in his hand for a moment and dropped it, head first, into the nearest heron's open beak.

'I love the feel of live fish, don't you?' he said, repeating the process to each of the herons in turn. 'So cold, so muscular, so at one with their element.'

The herons ate greedily, then lined up, staring at him expectantly, their heads to one side as if asking a question.

'Not today,' he told them.

Once on board they cast off quickly, leaving the island behind. The day was calm, the sea still and flat. The sun sparkled on the water. It was a shimmering world. The boat smelled heavy with perfume. Sylvie and the Songman sat up at the bow, watching the boat cleave through the sea. Sylvie found it hard to keep still. Usually the Songman sang her Song first thing when they met, but now it seemed the last thing on his mind. Her skin itched, she felt nauseous: she needed to hear it, needed to hear it soon. The Songman cut the engine. Her heart lurched expectantly. Perhaps he'd sing it now!

'I've a hamper here,' he told her. 'A spot of lunch?'

He pulled out a wicker basket and opened the lid. Nestling among damask napkins was a cold chicken, a pie of peaches and apricots, a punnet of wild strawberries, a bowl of Chinese figs and a bottle of white cordial with two wine glasses.

'Eat, why don't you,' the Songman murmured.

He uncorked the bottle and handed Sylvie a glass. It was thick and sweet, and like the Song he sang. She grabbed at the chicken and started tearing off lumps of meat. Pie, fruit, figs – she stuffed them into her mouth in any order. She didn't want any of it, but she couldn't help herself. Anything to stop the gnawing pain inside her. Where was her Song? The Songman looked on with an expression of amused indulgence.

'This is pleasant,' he said lazily, 'to be in the company of my protégée, the future so bright, so welcoming, so very, very quiet.' He held out his hand. All they could hear was the noise of the boat as it idled upon the water.

'You remember your father?'

She nodded. She remembered him.

'Would you like to see him now?'

She closed her eyes, trying to banish the traitorous thought swirling within her. The Songman smiled – such an understanding smile.

'Of course. Look under your seat, Sylvie. You'll find a wooden box there. It's not heavy.'

Sylvie pulled it out.

'Take off the lid,' he instructed.

Sylvie did as she was told. Beneath lay twelve Song-Glasses, sparkling in the sunlight. She felt like dancing with joy.

'There's another twelve underneath,' he told her. 'Twenty-four SongGlasses, each one containing a special Song. You can guess whose.'

Sylvie nodded. She could feel her legs shaking. The Songman leaned forward, his voice as tender as the breeze.

'Think of it, Sylvie. Twenty-four of your very own Songs, there for you to listen to any time you want.'

'Can I hear one now?' she pleaded. They were the first words she had spoken that day.

'If you like,' he said carelessly. 'Just give the top a quick twist. The cleaner the break, the clearer the Song. It gets easier with practice. Go on, try it.'

Sylvie lifted the bottle out of its casing. Her hand was shaking. She licked her lips. Everything she wanted lay inside. She gripped the neck with her right hand and gave a twist. The cap snapped. The Song rushed out into her. Her pulse started to race. Her eyes went bright. She felt dizzy, floating on a sea of flowers. She wanted to ride with her Song for ever, fly away on its melody, never to return.

Something strange bobbed in the water nearby, something dark, staring at her.

'What was that?' she whispered, the spell broken.

'What?' The Songman looked up, distracted.

Sylvie pointed. 'Over there – like a head. It's gone now.' She scanned the water, wishing it would come back.

The Songman brushed it aside, irritated at the intrusion. 'A seal, no doubt. I haven't sung the sea yet.'

'No, a woman's head. I saw her feet flip.'

Together they studied the water.

'Just a trick of the light, probably,' the Songman reassured her. 'No one could swim in these waters and survive. Not unless they were half fish.' He turned back and looked at the bottles. 'Well, aren't they simply the most lovely things you have ever seen?'

Sylvie laid her hand on one, incapable of speech. The Songman closed the lid and pushed the box back under her seat.

'You can have them all tomorrow.'

'Tomorrow?' Panic took hold of her. 'Just one more for now?'

'No.' The Songman raised his hand. 'Not another word, Sylvie. Not another sound. I have tried to bring you with me, offered you companionship, even equality, but you are like your father after all: wilful, stubborn, small-minded, unfit for my world. So now you will return in complete silence. Tomorrow you will tell me where his papers are. If you don't, you will never hear your Song again. I will watch you crumble, dying for your Song, shrivel into dust, barely able to talk, nothing left, nothing but pain and sorrow. Not a word now. Not a single word! Think on it while we return.' He put his lips to her ear, his voice hard, metallic. 'You stand on the very brink of oblivion,' he whispered, 'and I will push you over the edge without a moment's thought.'

Mildred was waiting on the quayside. The Song-man leaped out.

'Put her in solitary,' he barked. 'No George, no dog, nothing.' He turned on his heels and walked away.

She sat alone for the rest of the day, in a bare room with a bare mattress on a bare stone floor, the barred window way out of reach. No food, no water, the silence broken only by the pounding of her broken heart. All she could think of was the wooden box and the SongGlasses. Her Songs were waiting for her, twenty-three of them, lying in untouched, silent rows. She felt her will crumbling. The Songman was right. There was nothing more beautiful than his singing. Why listen to anything else?

She started to bang her fist on the door, but no one came. She tried to call, but nothing came out. She curled up on the mattress and cried, desperate, bitter tears, her stomach knotted, aching with hunger. Would he never come? All she wanted to do was tell him where Dad's papers were. Then she could hear her Song again, and the world would be right.

The light faded. Night came, such a long and lonely night that it seemed it would never end. She paced the walls, counting out the minutes, the hours, trying to recapture the Song in her head, but that only made the gnawing emptiness worse. She slumped down on the floor, wedged herself in a corner, biting her nails, muttering incoherently to herself. She lay huddled there like a cornered animal, shivering hot and cold, her body hardly her own any more, raw with a clawing pain that seemed to tear at her very soul. What did it matter if there were no birds to listen to, no dogs, no tigers? What did it matter if Mr Jackson never barked again, the fox never howled? What did it matter, if there was still her Song? That was all she wanted to hear. That was all she needed to hear. Oh, if she could just hear it now, how wonderful it would be! She could drift away on it, away from this ache and pain. She was gone and she knew it. Only one thing could save her now. Her Song.

And then, when she thought that it would never end, when even her teeth were jangling with shredded nerves, the door was flung open. The Drummers marched in.

'He'll see you now,' Mildred announced.

She jumped up and, pushing past them, began to run down the corridor.

'Come back!' Rabbit-teeth cried, but she took no notice. She knew the way. Up the stairs she stumbled, up to the first floor, and down along the corridor towards the thick nailed door. In a moment she would be running up the stone steps, ready to claim her gift. Soon she would hear her Song again. She was only minutes away!

She had nearly reached the SongTower when she

heard something strange coming from behind one of the oak-panelled doors. It was a tinny sort of noise, disturbingly familiar. Despite herself, she stopped. Was it her Song? No, but it stirred something inside her, something close, something that seemed to creep in between her and the Song she so desperately needed to hear. Inexplicably she could smell the scent of fallen pine needles, twinkling fairy lights blinking on and off in her head. There it was again – the scratch of a silly tune. She could see herself on the floor, wrapping parcels, her mouth full of string, fingers trying to hold crinkly paper down. The tune started again, then stopped; just a few bars: Dee-dee-dee; dee-dee-dee. It tapped into her skull like a woodpecker's beak. Woodpeckers! She trembled, looking around, but the corridor was bare. In a flash she was back on the Allamanda, the Woodpecker Man flying after her, his claw-like hand outstretched, ready to grab her.

That was part of the Song, wasn't it, the part that was hidden, like that poor deer the Songman had killed. All for a song. She shuddered. What was she doing here? Dee-dee-dee; dee-dee-dee. Suddenly she saw a Christmas tree with a fairy at the top and a pile of parcels arranged around the crêpe-wrapped tub, Dad in his dressing gown lighting the fire, Mr Jackson with tinsel wrapped around his collar. She pressed her ear against the door. It came through clearly this time, a short burst of it, like an ice-cream van, cut short.

Dee-dee-dee; dee-dee-dee. Dee-dee-deee-de-dee. She knew it now. Of course! 'Jingle Bells'.

Jingle Bells?
JINGLE BELLS?
JINGLE BELLS?

Dad's joke socks! The ones she'd given him as a Christmas present! Dad was behind that door! Her dad! Her dear dad! Behind that door!

'Dad? Dad?' Her wispy voice strained at the words, as if something long suppressed were trying to break through. She put her mouth to the keyhole, her fingers kneading her throat, trying to work the words out. 'Dad, are you there?'

She began to hammer on the door. A voice broke through on the other side. Such a wonderful familiar voice.

'Sylvie? Sylvie, is that you?' The tune started again as he ran across the room. Dee-dee-dee; dee-dee-dee. Dee-dee-deee-de-deee. How she loved to hear it!

'Sylvie! Sylvie! Oh, my darling girl!'

'Dad! I'm here, Dad. I'm here!' Something broke inside her, her voice cracking open. She doubled up, a jag of pain stabbing into her like a knife, and then it was gone. Something flew from her like a banished shadow. Relief flooded in.

'It's all right!' she cried, a kind of joy bursting into her throat. 'I'm OK. Don't worry. He hasn't got it! He won't get it either. Not from me. Never! Never!'

A hand yanked her back; another wrapped itself around her waist. She was lifted off the floor.

'No you don't! No you don't!' Rabbit-teeth was pulling her down the corridor.

'Sylvie! Sylvie! What's happening?' The door thudded as her father threw himself against the door. 'Let her go, you brutes. Let her go!'

'Love you, Dad! Love you very much.' Was it loud and clear? She did not know, but she was sure he had heard her.

The Drummers dragged her away. She could hear her dad calling her name until the tower door shut behind her, the silence slapping her like a blow to the head. No wonder Dad had never heard her. It was just a trick. She was pushed up the steps. The Songman was sitting on the couch, the wooden box at his feet. He stood up, expectant. Sylvie brushed the hair out of her eyes; the Drummers stood behind her, arms folded.

'You look a little out of sorts,' the Songman observed lightly. 'Anything wrong?'

'Nothing that can't be put right.'

'Exactly.' He nudged the box over with one of his grey leather shoes. 'So. I imagine you need to hear your Song. They are all here, waiting for you. Such lovely songs.'

Sylvie shut her eyes. She could picture her dad

and his shabby ways; his uncoordinated shirts and his horrible ties. She opened her eyes and looked at the Songman with his perfect suit and his perfect hands. There was no comparison really. She swallowed.

'No.'

The Songman bent his head.

'I'm sorry. You'll have to speak up. I couldn't quite hear you.'

'No.' Her voice was a little clearer. She shook her head. 'No,' she stated simply. 'Not today.'

'No?' The Songman turned, puzzled. 'What do you mean, no?'

'I mean, no.' She looked down. There they lay, all twenty-three of them. If only she could hold one! She fought the feeling off. 'I don't care if I never hear it again. There are lots of songs I prefer. "Jingle Bells," for instance.'

'"Jingle Bells"?' He didn't understand.

'Yes. You must know it. It's a Christmas song. One of my favourites. Much nicer than anything you can sing.'

The Songman's face grew dark.

'And if I do this?' He picked up the box and, walking out onto the balcony, held over the side. 'Tell me where the papers are, Sylvie, or say goodbye to them. I need them now. Today.'

Sylvie dashed out after him. She could almost hear her Songs trapped in the glasses, pleading to be released. Her Songs, her lovely Songs. She hung her head, a picture of defeat.

'No, don't do that,' she pleaded, her hands grasping the sides. 'I'll do it.'

Smiling, the Songman let go. Sylvie shut her eyes and swung the box over the railing, flinging it into the air. It plummeted down, catching on the SongHouse roof, twisting and turning before bursting open on the jagged rocks. As they tumbled into the water, the SongGlasses smashed to pieces, her Songs burbling, screaming to be let out. She was drowning her own Song. She would never hear it again.

The Songman watched them sink, his face impassive. 'A clever little trick.' He placed his finger under her chin, like he had on that first day. 'You're stronger than I thought. But you seem to forget. You can destroy as many SongGlasses as you want. I still have this.'

And he stood and sang her Song again. It flew about her head, fluttering against her face, like a bird against a windowpane. She shut her eyes, waiting for the dread moment when it flooded in and took her over, and then she realized: the Song couldn't get in. He couldn't sing her Song any more. She wasn't who he thought she was. She swallowed, her throat a little more open, her lips a little less dry. He could never sing her Song again.

'I'd like to go back to George now,' she said, her

voice trembling with strained calm. 'Mr Jackson needs his morning constitutional.'

The Songman's eyes shook with fury. He seized her, his hands pincers under her arms. For a moment she thought he was going to throw her off too.

'Out!' he shrieked. 'Get her out!'

The Drummers hurried her out of the room. She could hear the crash of the Harmonograph as the Songman kicked it over; glasses and plates hurled against the dome. She flew down the stone steps, the sound of his rage flying along after her. She banged on Dad's door in triumph before being hustled away and thrown unceremoniously back into her old cell. George was fast asleep, Mr Jackson at the foot of his bed. He raised his head, his sad eyes looking at her.

'Oh, Mr Jackson.' She flung her arms about his neck, burying her face in his fur. 'Oh, Mr Jackson. I'm so sorry. I'm so sorry.' Kissing him, she leaned across and shook George hard. 'George! Wake up!'

George rubbed his eyes. 'Sylvie? Sylvie?' He sat up and stared hard into her bright, lively eyes, feeling Mr Jackson's tail beating wildly against the bed. He held out his arms. 'You're back! Oh, Sylvie, you're back!'

'Course I'm back. Get up. I've something to tell you.'

'What?'

'Not here. Wait till we're outside.' She put her mouth to the keyhole.

'Time for Mr Jackson's constitutional,' she shouted, loving the sound of her voice. 'Come on, open up.'

Upstairs the Songman was pacing the floor, picking his way across the broken crockery.

'It's up to the Woodpecker now. All the time I've wasted. I still don't understand. "Jingle Bells"?'

Mildred shook her head. 'You were too nice to her, that's what.'

'She has it. I know she has.' He wrung his hands. 'Are you sure there was nothing on her, nothing that might give us a clue? Her things? Did you go through their things thoroughly?'

'Naturally.'

'And nothing? No map, no scrap of paper?'

'Nothing, except some letter from that stupid dog of hers.'

'Letter?' The Songman was suddenly alert. 'What sort of letter?'

'Just a letter, that's all.'

'Why didn't you show it to me before?'

'I didn't think it was important.'

'Show me now.'

Five minutes later it was in his hand. The Songman unfolded the lined paper and read it out loud:

'My name is Mr Jackson and I'm a bit lost. Here is my address and telephone number. Please get in touch. My family need me.'

He thought for a moment, trying to work it out. 'And this was . . . ?'

'In her pocket.'

'In her pocket. A message from her dog, in case he gets lost, in her pocket.'

His face lit up.

'Of course! Don't you see? Mr Jackson should be carrying it. Not Sylvie. Only he isn't. And why? Because he's carrying something else.'

Sylvie and George were walking around the lighthouse with renewed energy. The *Chanson* lay in the harbour, its canvas covers tied down. The Woodpecker Man's basket stood empty on its flat rock. It hadn't been used for days. George felt elated. Sylvie was back, and full of hope. Mr Jackson was running in and out of their legs, scuffling round the stony soil, running up to lick Sylvie's hand. He looked so happy.

MrJacksonSylviedoggoodboy MrJacksonwaggerbliss
Who'sagoodboythen who'sagoodboy

'It's over,' Sylvie pronounced, her arm draped around her best friend. 'He's kept us all this time, and still he hasn't a clue where Dad's papers are. Whatever it is he plans to do, he can't. We've won.'

George gazed out across the water, thinking of home. They must be out of their minds, his mum and dad.

'He'll have to let us go soon, don't you think?' he said, fighting back a tear. 'I mean, kidnapping is against the law after all.'

They both looked up. There he stood on the Song-Tower balcony, the Songman, defeated.

'You've failed!' George called up. 'Let us go!'

A cry broke the air. Then another. They looked up. High above, the Songman was singing, his head thrown back, his arms spread wide, calling to the air. He sang again, a song of urgency and menace, a shrill, hunting call. Out from the bottom of the basket sprang the Woodpecker Man, top hat glowing, black eyes blazing, a swarm of green woodpeckers streaming out from underneath his coat, swooping down onto Mr Jackson's back, their thick claws digging into him like demon rodeo riders. Mr Jackson began to run in circles, twisting this way and that, bucking and jumping in a frantic attempt to throw them off.

'Help him!' Sylvie cried, running over, but as she ran, more woodpeckers dived in for the attack, slashing at her hair and arms. Mr Jackson was soon covered with them, their frenzied beaks stabbing at his neck and throat, trying to break the collar free. Sylvie whacked the birds aside, desperate to reach him, but on they came, wave after wave, their bodies thudding into her, their wings battering her face, until she was no longer able to see or move. She rolled up into a ball, hands pressed over her ears, her head bursting with screams.

Then they were gone. Sylvie looked up. A lone

woodpecker was flying up to the balcony, Mr Jackson's collar hanging from its beak.

'Mr Jackson!'

Sylvie jumped up. Mr Jackson was lying motionless on the rock. She raced across. Dark blood clotted his fur; his legs splayed out at awkward angles. She knelt down beside him. His body was twitching and his eyes were watery, wandering a little. She took him in her arms and raised his trusting black face close to hers. He gazed into her eyes, his tail wagging feebly, his pink tongue hanging out of his half-open mouth.

IgoodboyMrJackson ISylviedoggoodboyMrJackson

'Yes,' she said, holding him close. 'Yes, of course you are.'

Mr Jackson struggled, trying to get up.

MrJacksonsnufflemorningDad

IgofetchmorningDad morningDadcomebackhere

'No. Lie still, Mr Jackson. Lie still.' Mr Jackson sank back, relieved.

MrJacksonpadworn inyourbasketMrJackson inyourbasket

He paused, his breaths short. George knelt beside him and gently wrapped his shirt around his wounded neck. Mr Jackson turned his grateful face towards him.

MrJacksonnotahundredpercent bettertakehimtotheV-E-T

It'llbeoversoon

His eyes started to swim about, a milky cloud washing over them. He looked around, trying to see where he was.

TimetogohomeMrJackson timetogohome

'Hold on, Mr Jackson,' Sylvie sobbed. 'Hold on.' She held him tight. She could feel a slow quivering inside him, like the end of a story, or a kite fluttering to the ground.

MrJacksonsleepytime nightynightMrJackson

He gulped, casting his eyes lovingly on her face.

I'm gonna sit down tight and bite myself a sweater
And take the lead it came from you

He was singing again, just as he had heard Dad sing so many times to her all those years ago. Had he sung along with him all those nights, in silent, unquestioning devotion? Oh, how she loved him!

I'm gonna bite birds, oh so sweet
They're gonna knock me off my feet
Lots of kisses on the got 'em
I'll be glad I bottom

'Oh, Mr Jackson! Don't go!' Tears streamed down Sylvie's face.

Mr Jackson raised his head and licked at her salty cheeks. His tail thumped.

I'm gonna smile and say I hope you're feeling better
And close 'with love' the way you do,
I'm gonna sit down tight and bite myself a sweater
And take the lead . . .

He gathered his breath one more time and raised his face to hers.

SeeyoulaterMrJackson seeyoulater
Who'salovelyboythen who'salovelyboy
SeeyouinthemormingMrJackson seeyouinthemorning
Therethere therethere
There . . .

She felt it rush out of him, his faithful honesty, his trust, his old familiar blackness, his wispy eyes, his mutty mouth, the lovely feel of him as he bent his love to hers. She felt him glide over her, all the hours and days he had greeted her, the times he had laid his head upon her lap, or simply looked at her with his loving eyes. He was gone, dear Mr Jackson, her very own friend. All the years she couldn't talk to him, and now, when she could, he had gone. He was dead, murdered. He would never come back. She hugged his lifeless body, racked with grief.

GoodbyeMrJackson goodbyeMrJackson
MrJacksonSylviedog MrJacksonSylviedoggoodboy
MrJacksonbestestdoginthewholewideworld

Chapter 12

They buried Mr Jackson the following morning. The Songman gave them permission to sail out on the *Chanson* and bury him at sea. It was a bright sunny morning, the waves dancing with light. Sylvie wrapped him in a blanket from her bed, his broken collar by his side, the note that Mum had written safely back in its leather pouch. *I'm a little bit lost,* it had said. *My family need me.* Oh, how she needed him!

They weighted the body down with stones and placed sprigs of heather on top. They chugged out some distance, Mildred Drummer behind the wheel, unable to look them in the eye. The service was short and simple. Sylvie said her goodbyes, recalling all the lovely times she had spent with Mr Jackson, before streams of tears stopped her. Then she bent down and kissed him for the last time, while George patted the shroud around his head. Then they tipped the plank and watched his body slide into the sea. As he met the water, a cry of anguish came bubbling out of the deep.

'What was that?' said George, alarmed.

'Air, I suppose, from his lungs.'

It was strange. Mr Jackson didn't sink at first. He seemed to float on the surface, as if held by an unseen hand, the current swirling him around the boat in a strange dance of death. She could almost hear him calling: *MrJacksonMrJackson timetogohome timetogohome*, but his voice was different, high and watery, like rising bubbles. She felt like jumping in after him, to go where he was going. Then slowly he began to sink out of sight, and as he did so, a long unearthly howl went up from the shore. Sylvie felt the blood rush to her head.

'Sounds like the tiger knows too,' George observed.

'He does,' she said. 'He knows everything.'

'What do you mean?'

Sylvie wiped the tears from her face.

'I don't know quite. It's just . . .' Suddenly it came to her. 'The tiger, George! We've got to free the tiger. He's the only animal the Songman can't silence, can't control. If we could find out what the Songman's doing, we could stop him.'

'And how are we going to do that, stuck here?'

'I don't know, but there must be a way. There has to be.'

Once off the boat, they were taken back to their cell. For the rest of the day the SongHouse was a hive of frantic activity. The generators hummed, the foundry working at full stretch as a final batch of SongGlasses were made and packed into the SongBird. From the basement window they could see the *Chanson* plying to and from the mainland, its deck piled high with cases of glass instruments, Mildred Drummer at the helm.

They saw the old gorilla too. Sylvie watched him trudging back and forth, carrying crates from the storerooms down to the boat while Rabbit-teeth strode about on deck, shouting orders. The gorilla looked so old, so worn out, Sylvie wanted to call out, hand him something to eat. On one trip, carrying a cello case, he stumbled, the case flying open, the glass cello smashing to pieces on the ground. Bird songs flew out – a whole aviary of them – Rabbit-teeth leaping down, beating the poor animal with a stick.

'Stop it, stop it!' Sylvie cried, but he couldn't hear her through the thick glass.

Later on, the Songman came down to check their progress, picking his way onto the boat with his delicate shoes, inspecting the cases, checking the labels.

He was more tense than Sylvie had ever seen him, anxious, nervy, impatient, worried about the time, the weather. Then she saw him duck into the wheelhouse, lean forward and pull something loose from the door. He looked at it, smiled, and folded it in his pocket. The poster! She could see it herself, read the words as clearly as if it were there in her own hand. Also Appearing: The Orchestra of Light, Conductor: Walter Klopstock.

A light went on in her head.

'What's the date, George?' she said suddenly, turning round.

George counted out on the wall.

'The thirtieth, I think, why?'

'Dad's concert's tomorrow, in Hyde Park – where he was going to play his instruments, remember?'

'So?'

'So!' Things seemed to be tumbling into place in her head, like numbers in a lock, click, click, click.

'George! Listen to this!' She jumped down. 'The Songman steals the animals' voices by singing their Songs into the SongGlasses. When the SongGlasses are broken open and the animals hear his version of their song, they're silenced, to do his will. Dad told him what happened that night of the accident, about the big Note; told him that he'd written down how it was done. We know the Songman needs that Note for something he's got planned. Are you with me so far?'

George nodded.

'We saw him sing songs into those glass instruments. We just heard one break, all those songs released – what were they? Ducks and crows, a whole flock of different birds. Hundreds, thousands of animals' songs are hidden in those glass instruments. Yes?'

'It looks like it, yes.'

'What if . . . ?' She paused, trying to get the words right, her eyes shining with excitement. 'What if he's going to put the two together: attach the songs – the songs that steal the animals' voices – to Dad's Note. All of them, in one go. Think of it as a bit like a nuclear explosion. As the Note sounded, the glass instruments would break. The sound wave carrying the songs would radiate all over the land. The songs would spread out like radioactive fall-out, silencing all the animals as they rained down. He'd control them all. Think of the power he would have. Imagine it: all the dogs in England, hundreds of thousands of them, under his command. What could we do against that? Or an army of a million rats advancing on a town, a city; all the birds in the sky, every single animal in the land, all bent to his will. We'd be powerless. He could do whatever he wanted.'

George whistled. 'And not just here, Sylvie. A note like that could travel hundreds, maybe thousands of miles.'

'And we'll be next, George. You saw what he nearly did to me. It will take him a little longer perhaps, but after the animals are silenced, he'll want to silence us humans too. This concert is just the beginning. We've got to stop him.'

The door was unlocked. They looked up. The Drummers walked in carrying two heavy trays. Behind them, in a dazzling white suit decorated with crotchets and quavers, came the Songman, a chimpanzee at his side carrying a bundle wrapped in his long arms. The Songman looked serene, confident, all trace of anger erased.

'Sylvie,' he announced, 'we are leaving now. Just your father's instruments to ferry across and we will all be gone. You will be quite safe here, though all the exits and entrances to the SongHouse have been secured. My advice is to sit tight. There is enough food for you for two days, by which time I will have returned.'

'What about Dad?' Sylvie demanded. 'Can't I be with him?'

'When I'm back.' He took a step towards her. 'There's still time to change your mind, Sylvie. Look, I have had this made for you, the same cloth as mine.' He chattered his teeth. The chimpanzee took his bundle and let the dress unravel to the floor. 'Just say the word. A new world awaits us.'

'A world of silence. I know what you're doing,

using Dad's note to steal all the animals' songs, to silence them. And then us, I suppose. It's wicked and wrong.'

'Wrong? Wrong to create the world I want, the world my voice deserves?' He looked at her hand. 'There's a place for you in it, even now.'

Sylvie clenched her fist, covering her palm.

'I think you're mad,' she said evenly. 'And that dress is ridiculous. My place is here, with Dad and George and . . . and Mr Jackson.'

The Songman bowed his head for a moment.

'Yes. I am sorry for that. I did not wish him harm. But you put him in my way, Sylvie. You must bear some of the responsibility.'

'Don't you think I don't know that?' Sylvie felt the tears coming back.

'Yes, I think you do. And this?' He took the dress and dropped it on the floor. 'Keep it as a souvenir.'

The Songman turned on his heel and left. Sylvie sat, her head in her hands, sobbing.

'You OK?' George asked gently.

Sylvie nodded, forcing herself out of it. Outside, the old gorilla had begun wheeling Dad's instruments onto the boat. Though they were shrouded in heavy cloth, she could identify each one by its shape. First came the Furroughla, then the Shinglechord. As each one was pushed onto the deck, the Drummers busied themselves tying it down while the gorilla went back to fetch the next one. As he shuffled back for the third time, Sylvie had an idea. Lifting the catch, she drew back the window.

'Pssst.'

The gorilla stopped, looked around, his hands sweeping the ground.

'Psst. Here!'

The gorilla looked down and saw Sylvie's face pressed against the bars. His eyes lit up. He banged his chest, touched his throat. Sylvie beckoned him forward. The gorilla stepped closer, inquisitive.

Reaching out, Sylvie gripped the nearest iron bar and, staring hard at the gorilla, pulled, her voice straining with the effort as she did. Then, shaking her head, her mouth turned down, she pointed, first at him, then at the bars, and began to nod vigorously, smiling. The gorilla looked at her, then looked at the bars.

'That's right,' she said out loud. 'You have a go.'

The gorilla bent down, winding his huge fingers round the bar nearest the stonework. He wrinkled his nose, took a deep breath and pulled. Nothing happened. He shook his head angrily.

'Harder,' Sylvie urged, and gave a grunt, as if she was pulling herself. The gorilla pulled again. Nothing happened. Squatting down, he put both feet against the wall and, with two hands wrapped around two bars, pulled again. There was a wrench and a crack, and he catapulted back with the bars in his hands, rolling head over heels onto the ground.

'Oi! What do you think you're playing at, you gormless monkey? I've never seen such a lazy brute. The moment my back's turned . . .' Rabbit-teeth jumped down from the boat. 'Go on, get the next one,' he shouted. The gorilla sprang up and, tucking the bars under his arm, scampered off.

Sylvie jumped down from the bed.

'See, George,' she whispered as Rabbit-teeth hurried by. 'We can get out easily. Now, if we could get to the boat.'

But it was no use. Every time they looked there was someone there – one of the Drummers, the Wood-pecker Man, even the Songman himself – watching the instruments as they were loaded aboard.

Finally the herons stalked onto the boat. Rabbit-teeth started the engine. The *Chanson* chugged out of the little harbour, the Furroughla, the Shinglechord, the Featherblow and the Clattercloud lashed to the bow – Dad's lovely instru-ments, all that he had worked for, now turned against him. As the Songman climbed into the Song-Bird, the Woodpecker Man raised his red top hat. The burners flared. The balloon rose, clouds of green wood-peckers circling. The black-necked swans took up the ropes and began to pull the balloon slowly across the sea, the Songman singing a song of coming victory. As he crossed the marsh, another song rose to meet him, a roar thrown against his passing. The tiger again.

Sylvie clutched onto George, unknown forces flooding over her. They were alone, locked away on an island of rock. She sank back on the bed, head in hands.

'If only we could have got out of here, we could still have disrupted the concert. Smashed one of Dad's instruments or something. But we'll never get across now. We've lost, George. We've lost.'

'What if we could fly over?' George's voice was calm.

'On a magic carpet, I suppose. It's not a joke, George.'

'Not a magic carpet, no. A kite.' He walked over to the battered boat. 'While you were . . . away, I worked it all out. I think I could make a kite big enough to carry us across.' And he told her how, speaking slowly. Sylvie recognized the tone. It was the same voice he'd used when she'd first met him, solid and thoughtful.

'If it got enough lift,' he continued, 'we'd make it across without much difficulty. There's only one problem. Height. If it's to carry us across the water, it has to reach the strong winds. We haven't enough rope, and unless we find some outside, we'll never get it high enough.' He shook his head. It was the one thing he hadn't been able to work out.

'What if I climbed the SongTower?' The words jumped into Sylvie's mouth before she knew what she was saying. They looked at each other, astonished. 'Why not? I could do it, I'm sure. We can both get up onto the flat roof of the Roundhouse easily enough. There's a drainpipe running up from the ground. Once I'm there, you can strap the kite to my back and I'll climb up the outside of the tower itself. It looks smooth enough from a distance, but close up there's lots of bricks jutting out. They'd be fine as footholds. If I launched the kite from the balcony at the top, you could sit on the seat below, ready to guide it.'

George looked doubtful.

'And what would you do?' he asked.

'I could slide down, then stand behind you, like on swings.'

'You couldn't slide that distance,' George objected. 'You'd upset the equilibrium. But if you held the kite steady as it rose, I would rise up with it. With a guy rope looped through the balcony railing, the kite would act as a kind of pulley, pulling me up against the tower. Then, when I got level with you, you could swing across, let go of the guy rope and away we'd go.

What do you think?'

'What do I think?' Sylvie leaped to her feet, squeezing him in a tight hug. Trust George! 'I think you're a genius, George. How long do you think it will take to get across – twenty minutes?'

'Less, with a strong wind. It'll pick up quite a speed. We'll have to make sure the wind's in the right direction, otherwise we'll be blown out to sea.'

'If we start making it now, we might be ready by dawn.'

They worked steadily through the night, George cutting the canvas, laying out the kite on the floor, Sylvie following his meticulous instructions: first tearing the bed sheets into strips, and then, with the help of the fishing hook and a length of twine, sewing the canvas to the bound rods. Then they attached the wooden slats from the bed, to give the structure enough rigidity. It was hard work – their backs hunched over the floor, their fingers aching with the strain of forcing the needle through the tough material. For George the most difficult part was wrenching off the boat's little wooden seat and attaching it to the two ropes that hung down. There were no holes in the seat, so when the time came he would have to tie them on as best he could.

'Will it hold?' Sylvie asked, doubt in her voice.

George held up the kite. It stood about two metres high and slightly less across. He gave it a proprietorial shake. 'It better,' he replied.

By dawn all was ready. The guy ropes were in place, and George had used the rowlocks from the dinghy as steering handles. Now all they had to do was find out the direction of the wind.

'Well?' Sylvie demanded, anxious to be off. George peered out of the window.

'We can't go yet. See those clouds? The wind is blowing off shore. If we launch it now, we'll be blown out to sea.'

They watched the sky all morning. The wind blew steadily from the shore, chasing their hopes out to sea. The afternoon proved no better. It was almost as if the wind had joined the Songman's conspiracy. Time was running out. And then:

'Sylvie!' George's voice was trembling with nervous excitement. 'The wind's changed. It's coming in from the sea.'

'OK. Let's go. You first. I'll push the kite through. Tie that dress round you. I don't want to climb with it, but it might come in handy if we get there.'

George wound it round his waist, stood on the bed and grabbed hold of the bars. It took a bit of effort on his part, wriggling and squeezing, but with a couple of pushes from Sylvie, he managed it.

'OK,' he whispered. 'Let's have it.'

Sylvie took the struts out of their linen pockets and pushed the rolled-up kite through, then climbed after. Holding it between them, they set off, following the curve of the wall, with only the sound of the sea and the wind for company. When Sylvie reached the drainpipe, she shook it to make sure it was secure.

'I'll go first with the rope. Then I'll pull the kite up and you follow. Use the brackets holding the drainpipe as footholds, OK? But first, see that light there?' She pointed to the first-storey window next to it. 'I think that must be Dad's. I've got to tell him, say goodbye, you know?'

George nodded.

Sylvie grabbed the drainpipe. It was easy. Halfway up she swung her right foot out and, gripping the bar of her dad's window, pulled herself across, her feet resting on the lintel below. Dad was sitting in a chair, his head buried in his hands. He'd always tried to be strong for her, but now she saw how lonely he was, how unhappy, how frail, how like everybody else – subject to fear and despair.

'Dad!' she called quietly. 'Dad!'

He sprang to his feet, startled. 'Sylvie, what on earth . . . ?' One hand gripped the iron bar, the other squeezed through, touching her arm.

'Listen, Dad. Don't talk. We're going, me and George. Going to save the songs.'

'But how?'

'It's George. He's built a kite. We're going to fly across.'

'A kite!' His face froze in horror. 'Are you out of your mind! Come here.' He clasped his fingers around her fist. 'You can't cross the sea in a kite. I won't let you.'

'Yes we can. We have to. And you can't stop me, Dad.'

'But it's too dangerous, Sylvie. You mustn't, do you hear? I'd rather all the songs in the world were stolen than anything should happen to you. Get back inside, please. Your mother would never forgive me.'

'Mum?' Sylvie held up her hand. 'Recognize this?'

Her dad's eyes opened wide.

'When did this happen? Who . . . ?'

'Who do you think? Our friend by the railway line. Trust me, Dad. I can take care of myself. I'll be back, don't worry. See you later.' *Seeyoulater*

'But Sylvie—'

'No more, Dad. It's my turn now. Love you. Love you very much.'

She leaned forward, kissed him and, crossing back onto the drainpipe, climbed up onto the flat roof. The kite followed without a hitch.

'OK, George,' she called down. 'Your turn.'

George put his foot on the first bracket and hauled himself up. He was fine for the first couple of metres, and then he seemed to slow down, fearful of going any further.

'Come on, George, hurry.'

It was the wrong thing to say. George leaned out dangerously, looking for the next hold. He didn't know how to lever himself up or balance. He was swinging on one arm, losing his grip, one leg scrabbling for a hold.

'Hold still, George,' she warned. 'Hold still.'

George grabbed the pipe and hugged himself close. 'I thought you told me to hurry,' he said, not daring to look up. 'Make up your mind.'

'I did, I'm sorry. Take as long as you like. One foot at a time. When one foot feels comfortable and you can see where to put your hand, push with your leg and reach out. It's one movement, George. Push up and reach out. But be sure you know where you're going first. Picture it.'

George shifted. She could hear him panting with nerves. He held still for a moment, gazing at the wall. Sylvie said nothing.

George pushed, he reached out; one movement. He rose a half-metre. A pause and a puff later, he pushed and reached out again. He rose another half-metre. Soon a hand appeared on the ledge, followed by a pair of glasses and a ridiculous grin.

'This climbing lark,' he said, pulling himself over, 'isn't as difficult as it looks.'

Sylvie pointed upwards. 'You want to try the next bit?'

George shook his head and strapped the kite to

Sylvie's back. 'Are you OK?' he asked.

'I'm fine.' She looked up. The SongTower had never appeared so tall. It seemed to reach up into the sky. Blowing on her hands, wiping them dry, checking that her shoes were tightly laced, Sylvie prepared to climb. A slight wind was picking up, the air starting to cool. She was facing the climb of her life.

George hugged her. 'Good luck,' he said, and kissed her on the cheek. She turned and faced the stone.

Sylvie had been right. Although the lighthouse looked smooth from a distance, a sequence of stones, about the width of an adult foot, jutted out in an ever-climbing spiral. The moment she took hold of the first she understood. Of course! They were the other side of the stone staircase, set through to the outer brickwork for extra strength. If she kept her head, she could climb round the SongTower until she reached the top.

She began, her left foot seeking a ledge, her left hand reaching out for the hold two bricks above, her weight transferring onto her left leg as she pushed herself up. Then her right foot came up, her weight moving from her left leg to her right as she prepared to repeat the manoeuvre. It was easier than a tree in some ways, because the distance between the stones was absolutely regular. All she had to worry about was the relentless vertical incline, and the wind that took sudden hold of her. One moment there'd be none at all, and then, as she moved round, it would hit her full in the face, the kite flapping on her back, jeopardizing her balance.

She climbed steadily, though not as quickly as she had hoped. A thin mist was forming. What would happen if she was stranded halfway up, unable to see up or down? Her arms were already getting tired and she had no idea how high she had climbed. She didn't dare look down and she was too close to the wall to see up. How many steps did he say there were? A hundred and fifty something? She wished she'd started counting, then she'd have some idea. Still, if she kept on like this, maybe just a little bit faster—

Her foot slipped. She hung for a moment by one good hand, her face pressed against the wall, her left leg hanging free, her right resting uselessly on a lower ledge, her body too far over for it to take any weight. She knew if she tried to regain her balance that way she would fall head first. Slowly she raised her left leg, searching for the ledge, unable to look. Her fingers were slowly slipping. She couldn't find it. Had she raised her leg too high? Was it further away than she thought? She scraped the wall with the tip of her boot, but still nothing. Her fingers were almost at the very edge. Perhaps she hadn't gone high enough. She raised her leg again, and there it was. She settled her foot upon it, the weight transferred from her grateful fingers. She clung there motionless, regaining her breath. Then she started again. It seemed like she had only just begun.

She counted the steps: 'One, two, three, four . . .' Sweat broke out on her forehead and ran down into her eyes. The muscles in her legs were crying out with pain, her hands raw from the rasp of the stone, the joints in her fingers stiff. Step after step after step after step, one hand reaching up, the other leaving safety behind. Time seemed to hang still. There came a point when Sylvie thought that it would never stop, that she was doomed to end her days climbing this everlasting white tower, that she would fall to the earth still climbing, her scream breaking the awful silence of the Songman's barren world. Poor George, she thought, brought to see her die, when all he had ever wanted was a friend. Poor Dad, to be left alone. But it wasn't so surprising, this end. That's how Mum had died after all, going round and round in a whirlpool, only here it was a whirlpool of stone, not water, that would take her.

And then.

She held. She pushed. She reached out. No stone this time, but the slight overhang of a metal rail, still warm from the summer's day. The balcony. She had reached the top! She swung herself over. Through the glass she could see inside the SongHouse, dark and empty, the broken Harmonograph propped up against the wall. Then she was running round to where George stood far below, looking up anxiously. She waved. He waved back.

Carefully she unfolded the kite, checking the struts were all in place before lowering the ropes over the side: two thick ones for George to tie the seat to, two thinner guy ropes which he would use to steer, and a fifth which she held in a loop. Ten minutes later there came a tug. George had attached the seat and the rowlocks. Together they walked round until they were facing the land, the wind whistling behind them. Bending down, she passed the fifth rope under the railing before wrapping it firmly round her hand. As the kite rose, she would pay out the line. George held the seat ready, his arms folded into the slack of the ropes. Now came the difficult part. Holding the kite high, Sylvie turned it into the wind. It quivered in her hands, the sail billowing with the rush of air. It wanted to fly! She could barely hold it. The ground was so far away. It was madness, what they were doing!

'OK. Now!' George shouted, but before she could respond, the kite was torn from her hands, the rope unravelling fast, whipping through her hands. She was pulled violently against the railing. Below, George was jerked upwards, the seat swinging out violently, away from the lighthouse, then banging back into it. His feet crashed into the wall as he tried to push himself away. Sylvie braced herself, paying out the line as the kite surged away, the ropes to which the seat was attached now some five metres from the balcony. George was rising all the time. Three, six, ten metres, the huge kite soaring, tugging, desperate to break loose.

'Let her go! Let her go!' George was screaming. She looked down. His head was now only three metres away, the ropes leading down to the swing a quivering jump away. She climbed up onto the railing, her legs bending against the strain. Letting go of the rope, she leaped out, grabbing hold of the two ropes, sliding down onto George's back. They were airborne. The kite ballooned out over the sea, but now, feeling her weight, began to dive, the water racing up to meet them. George worked the controls frantically, the kite swerving from side to side as he tacked into the wind. They were on the wing, fast, seven metres above the sea, George twisting and turning, trying to find uplift, skiing on air. Then one final dip and they were up again, soaring skywards like a crazy playground swing, George's legs stuck out in front, Sylvie leaning back, her arms nearly pulled out her sockets.

'Flying tonight!' George yelled at the top of his voice and, tacking to the left, sent the kite into a steep turn. He was doing what he had dreamed of doing, flying through the air, free as a bird. The land loomed up ahead through the mist. Another few minutes and they'd be safe.

There was a rip, the sound of a sheet tearing.

Looking up, Sylvie saw the canvas sail flapping loose at one corner, a seagull flying away. The kite gave a stomach-churning lurch and began to lose height again.

'We're losing height,' George cried. 'I don't think we're going to make it. We're too heavy.'

They plummeted down, George desperately trying to regain momentum. Five metres, three, then only two separated them from the water. Sylvie stared at the deep rolling swell beneath her. How different it looked from a few days before, how huge, how immense, how ready to swallow their hopes.

George looked up at her, a look of horrid fascination on his face. 'By the way,' he shouted, 'I forgot to tell you. I can't swim.'

Instinctively Sylvie let go. As she dropped, the kite surged up again, carrying George towards the shore. She fell in at an angle, the breath knocked out of her as her body slammed into the water. She plunged in, deep and cold, falling, falling, legs kicking, arms flailing, before she felt herself rising. She burst through, gasping for breath, water spluttering out her mouth. Treading water, she tried to get her bearings. She couldn't see the land at all. She spun round. Yes, there it was. Or was it? It was hard to tell.

'Sylvieeee!'

The long thin cry came from the same direction. George! Yes, there he was, trying to keep the kite aloft. He'd nearly reached the shore. If she could swim the half-mile or so, they might still have a chance. She began with steady breast strokes, lifting her head clear at every intake of breath. She tried not to hurry, but it was hard. She desperately wanted to reach the shore, but the more she swam, the further away the shore became. Was that possible? Or was it just the mist coming down, making it hard for her to see?

'George!' she cried. 'Can you hear me?'

Silence. Even the sea had lost its voice. She stopped swimming for a moment and, as her feet dropped, felt the pull of the water dragging them back. So that was it. The current was carrying her out to sea. She'd never reach the shore. The tide was too strong. Better conserve her energy – with a bit of luck she might land up back on the island, where Dad was. Oh, how she wanted to see her dad again. How she wanted to see her dad.

Then, suddenly, she wasn't cold any more. She was warm and comfortable, drifting into a wonderful sunny sleep. She could feel herself swaying to and fro, as if lying in a deep hammock on a dreamy summer's day. She thought she could hear George calling her name, but she turned over, willing his voice away. Looking down, she could see that she was falling, falling weightlessly, not into the dark, but into the heart of a golden light that shimmered far below. She could see splashes of fields down there, green sprawling forests, blue distant hills and dusky flat lands that extended as far as the eye could see. Down and down she sank, the landscape becoming clearer, closer. Now she could see a little garden with neat mown lawns and pretty summer flowers, and over there, fields of yellow sweetcorn beside the dome of a perfect hill. And on top of the hill stood her tree, its foliage wafting from side to side, beckoning her down. At the foot of its trunk sat Mr Jackson, his lovely upturned face waiting patiently for her.

Timetogohomesoon timetogohome.

'I'm coming, Mr Jackson, I'm coming,' she cried, but as the words burbled out of her, something broke through the boughs, something sleek and supple streaming up towards her, moving through the water in bursts of undulating waves. Her hand began to pulse again.

Sylvie! Sylvie

I'm here! I'm here!

Such a low, sweet voice! Then it was upon her, and a strong bare arm wrapped around her; a body pressed against hers, every contour, every fold of flesh somehow familiar. Together they rose, bubbles of unspoken thoughts bursting all around as they broke through the surface. The figure drew her closer. She felt a hand upon her face, fingertips touching her cheek, tracing the line of her nose, wiping the water from her eyes. A head pressed against hers, sleek and wet, with long dark hair running down the length of a strong back.

Sylvie cried out in recognition before she knew what she was saying.

'Mum?' she cried. 'Mum, is that you?' A wave hit her full in the face, salt water choking her. She swallowed, coughing and spluttering. The face turned. Lips pressed against her ear.

'Lie still, my darling.' And then, through the pulse in her hand:

Swarm into my arms, ease my spinning heart

She was spun round, another arm gripping her round the waist, and then she was lying back, her mother's legs kicking beneath her as she pulled her towards the shore. It was her mum! Her mum! How often had she swum like that with her in Lulworth Cove and Oswald's Bay, Mum carrying her far out until Dad called them back, and now she was here again, rising up out of the water, as if she'd never gone away. Sylvie tried to twist her head round, to see her face, to touch her, to hold her.

Still still, the silent voice came.

Let me carry you

Wave you in my arms again
Feel the gloam running wild inside you
Listen to me
Listen

Then she heard a sort of music floating into her, fluttering notes made up of words and feelings that she thought she would never hear again, words that were never expressed but had lived with her always, spoken in looks and gestures and a hundred thousand hugs. Her mum was holding her again. Her mum! Her mum! She was Sylvie Bartram! Sylvie Bartram! No one could change her now.

Then she felt the legs give way and they were standing face to face, waist deep in the swirling water. Sylvie grabbed her arm and made to pull her ashore, but the figure held back.

'I shan't shwo there,' she said. She put her hand to her mouth. 'Can't. I meant can't, can't go there. Forgive me. I am not used to words, the swish of them.'

'Am I dead or something?' Sylvie asked.

'No. Very much aswim.'

'But . . . I don't understand. I thought you'd drowned. We all did.'

Sylvie could see her in the thickening mist. She had changed. Her skin had an almost phosphorescent glow to it, shades of green and blue shifting as the sea splashed over her. And what was she wearing? Sylvie couldn't work it out, where Mum's skin ended and her costume began. Sylvie put her arms around her, hugging her tightly, her face deep in her mum's neck. She felt warm, yet cold too, as if the human part of her lay underneath something else. Her skin was thicker than Sylvie remembered, almost rubbery.

Her mother spoke again, the words coming slowly at first. 'I had no choice, Sylvie. I belong here, in the sea. It was a mistake, the other place.'

'A mistake? Am I a mistake?' Sylvie hugged her ever more tightly, afraid of the answer.

'You? Not you, Sylvie, not you. Oh, if I could, I would, but' – she looked upon the land – 'I can't. Never again. I would die.'

'But . . .' Sylvie was lost for words. 'But now? I mean, what's going on? How did you know I was here?'

'I heard the Song. It sang of you. So I came, in the hope that I might see you, might . . .' Her voice faltered. 'See! I have one here, rescued from the box you threw over. I thought I could listen to it one day.' She pulled the SongGlass out from a scaled fold in her costume. It looked empty, lifeless.

'The Song? It's not my Song any more. I'm older now.'

'No? Then I don't want it. Here, you have it. You might need it where you're going.' Sylvie took it, conscious of the unknown histories between them.

'I've been watching for some time,' her mother said. 'Is Daniel all right?'

'Dad? He's still a prisoner there, on the island. I managed to escape. With my friend George. I have a friend called George now. He flies kites.' Sylvie stopped. This was her mum she was talking to. 'Why did you go, Mum – leave us like that?'

'Oh, Sylvie.' She cupped a handful of water and threw it over her head, licking the drops as they ran down her face. 'There, that is why. There are some of us who live in the water, Sylvie. If it hadn't been for your father, his music, I would never have spent so much time on the land. And then, of course, you came along. I stayed as long as I could, but it isn't good for me, to be out of my element. I could feel myself weakening by the day. I'd outstayed my welcome. I had to go. But we had such a whale, you and I, didn't we? Such a whale. That last day, how could I explain to you both that my time had come? Mr Jackson knew.'

Mr Jackson. Oh, Mr Jackson.

'Mr Jackson. Mum, he—'

'I know, darling.' Her mum looked back to where the sea rolled in. 'You should go in now,' she added. 'You'll catch your death, standing here.'

She wiped her eyes. Sylvie reached out. Tears were rolling down her mother's face.

'Mum?' She fell into her arms. All the times she had dreamed of this, of holding her once again.

'Don't go, Mum. Please.'

Her mum tightened her hug, then broke free.

'I must. And you must too. You have things to do, vital things. We fear the Songman too. Our sea birds no longer sing either. Look!' She pulled back a fold of skin under her arm. There they were, the series of puncture holes – the Mark – but it seemed different now, as if it had grown into something else, almost like a fish's gill. She took Sylvie's hand and pressed the weal against it. Her hand began to throb like never before, waves of energy coursing through her.

'Feel that?' Sylvie nodded. 'I knew it would come to you the moment you were born and I held you in my arms, saw the light of it in your eyes. I told your father, "Watch for the animal that she chooses to watch. Watch for the animal that chooses her. That'll be the one."'

'It was a fox, Mum. I saw him from the train every day.'

'And he saw you.' She put her hands on Sylvie's shoulders, holding her out at arm's length. 'This is my inheritance to you, not the water in which I swim, but the earth upon which you walk. You can see things, hear things, walk and talk among the animals as few others can. Now you must open yourself. Open yourself like a sea anemone, let his Song wash over you.'

'His . . . ?'

'You know who. We can hear his cries, calling across the water. There are such creatures in our world too, you know.' A wave broke over her. She shuddered. 'I must go.'

'But Mum!' Sylvie clung onto her. 'You can't. I've just found you. You're my mum.'

'I know. I know.'

Now they could hear feet running along the shingle of the beach. Sylvie turned to look.

'Go on,' her mother urged. 'We'll meet up one day.'

'When?'

'Sylvie?' George's voice came across the beach towards her.

'When, Mum?' Sylvie turned back. The sea was empty. 'Mum? Mum?' She looked left, right. The waves rolled towards her. 'Mum? Come back, please! Mum! Mum!' She peered into the gloom. Was that a flip of two legs she saw, the wave of a hand?

'Sylvie, is that you?' George blundered out of the murk. Sylvie stood quite still.

'Yes,' she said. 'It's me.'

'Well, don't just stand there, get out. You'll catch your death.'

'Really?'

Sylvie waded ashore.

'Who were you talking to?'

'I'm not sure.' She stared out at the black impenetrable water. Another figure came running – the old fox. He had been waiting for her all this time!

The gloamcub! The gloamcub!

Teeth the hopping swoop the mufflesong!

He rubbed himself against her legs.

'That was something, wasn't it?' George boasted. 'Trouble is, it's all come a bit too late. The concert will have started by now. We've run out of time.'

Sylvie grabbed his arm. 'No we haven't. George, give me that dress. Turn your back while I get changed.'

George waited obediently. Then she stood in front of him, the embroidered notes glowing, her eyes bright with purpose.

'Over the top or what!' she said. 'Come on. We've no time to lose.'

At the zoo's entrance the vultures were nowhere to be seen. Sylvie and George climbed over the gates. Minutes later, they were standing in front of the tiger's compound. It was quiet. The tiger was lying at the back of the cage.

'See that stone over there, George?' Sylvie said. 'See that padlocked box on the other side of the fence? Smash it open, would you? I'm going to set him free. He's going to carry us up to London.'

'Up to London!' George protested. 'Have you gone stark staring bonkers?'

'If I can make him understand, he'll do it.'

'He could eat us too,' George suggested.

Sylvie was insistent. 'Haven't you heard him these past days? Don't you think he doesn't know who his enemy is; why all the other animals are silent? He'll take us. Where we want to go is where he wants to go, where he has to go, to save his kind. Smash the lock, George. It's our only chance. And when you're done, hang onto this.'

Giving him the SongGlass, she slid back the bolt and stepped into no man's land. Raising the stone, George took aim. Three, four blows, and the padlock fell apart. On a hook inside hung the key to the tiger's cage. Sylvie lifted it out. It reminded her of the Wood-pecker Man's wand, the sudden destruction it could cause. She mounted the steps and slotted the key into the door with a trembling hand. The lock was stiff, hard to move, as if trying to warn her of the danger she was walking into. It was madness, what she was doing. Then, with a click, it yielded.

The door swung open on rusty hinges. She took two paces in and then stood perfectly still. She couldn't see the tiger clearly, but she could sense his presence. He was standing there, wary, wondering what it was that had invaded his space. Something strange had entered his world, with breath and warmth and the blood-smell of life about them. He was interested. All he had known was lumps of dead meat prodded through the bars. He edged towards her, alert, ready to spring forward. He was king in his cage, and the price his subjects had to pay was death.

Then he was towering above her, his great head only inches away, his mouth red and quivering, a snarl lying in the back of his throat. His breath was hot. His eyes burned with fury. He circled her once, sniffing the backs of her legs, her knees, her stomach, underneath her arms. Sylvie trembled with fear. She was so small, so frail. He was so huge, so strong. He could rip her open in the blink of an eye.

The tiger drew back, his yellow eyes probing her weaknesses, his mouth half open, his teeth gleaming, his body arched, the muscles down his back rippling with desire. How he wanted to tear her apart, feast on her lungs and liver! How he wanted to kill; to use his teeth, his claws, smell the scent of fresh warm blood! He half turned his head, slowly opening his jaws wide, his fangs poised to strike. Sylvie's hand pulsated violently. She could feel his fury pouring over her, a torrent of hatred, all the years he had been cooped up, unable to run, unable to chase, unable to kill, the aching desire in his imprisoned body eating away at him. Yet she could feel a chink in his wall of rage, a moment's blind questioning, the Mark doing its work, and she turned towards it – a low note within her – as if she were holding her hand into the heart of a furnace, seeking that one spot where he was ice-cold and motionless. She reached out, palm up, as a savage snarl flew from his mouth. His breath stank of rotting meat and blood, his eyes were aflame, one paw raised, vicious claws sliding out like unsheathed scimitars. He threw back his head and roared, and as it hurtled towards her, she grabbed it and held it to her. She could feel his anger tearing towards her, ready to topple her. She steadied herself, bracing her legs against the wake of its power – and then, secure, she let it flood over her.

And in that instant she saw what he saw: an incomprehensible world pressing down upon him, the pain in his limbs, the ache in his heart, his longing for speed and light and blood, with only the sour taste of his own trapped life for company. She moved closer and placed her hand on the tiger's quivering body, ran it down his rolling back, feeling his strength surging down her own arm, the supple bend of her body moving to his, and she grabbed the tiger's mane and twisted his head round so that he faced her again.

And then they came – not tiger words, not her words, but words that set his song off inside her; words that she had never heard or read before, but words that lay within her, like seeds on the ground. Her father was wrong. No, she would never be able to talk to the tiger, but somewhere within her – where, she did not know: her ears? her heart? her blood? – were cells, atoms, chemistries that connected her to this wondrous beast, ripples that woke the words and phrases and sent them surging into her being. She could feel the power behind them, the vast enterprise of his being. She looked upon the tiger and heard the majesty of his voice.

Oh restless fields Oh rolling forests
Oh molten shining paths
Oh groaning mountains Oh trembling deserts
Oh mad infected moon
Swim upon my slumbering form, my vast disdain.
I shudder, shake majestic,
stretch North and South, East and West, contemplate
the wondrous deep, the brazen Death,
the thunderous fury of the dawn

I am sulphur and iron, wreathed in furnace,
enslaved
I drink the dark turrets of dire labours
I am the ark, the hidden beauty
I am fibre, my forehead wroted in blood
I am the flesh of truth, the immortal shape.
Devour my flaming heart, my fiery limbs
I am dark opaqui, the universe, the one the only
I speak it all, the myriad of lights, the limits of
contraction
I howl in sorrow upon the rock
I rage over eternal fields
I dream furious dreams,
devour foul ambition
shake off cold repose

I art terrible
Love my terror, my dark mortality
my oblivious shadow

Look upon me and live

He stood there, eyes burning, nostrils wide, as if breathing into Sylvie's very soul. Yes, that's what it was: she could feel a part of her sucked into him, the mass of his long quivering body, the dome of his great noble head. She raised her hand, grabbed the fur that hung down below his ears, and swung herself up. Now, astride him, she summoned the power of the Mark, let it flow through her legs pressed against his flank, through her arms draped around his neck, through her cheek laid against his. There were worlds they had to save, her world and the tiger's world, and though he wanted no part of her foolish life, he would fight tooth and claw for his. She had looked upon him and lived.

She straightened up and guided him out, down the steps, out of the compound, to where George stood, shrinking in the shadows. She held out her hand.

'Coming?'

George cleared his throat.

'After a donkey,' he said, his voice breaking into an unexpected squeak, 'I expect a tiger's something of a let-down.'

He took Sylvie's hand and hauled himself up.

'Ready?' she demanded. He adjusted his glasses.

'Ready.'

The tiger gave a shudder. He leaped forward. They were off.

Chapter 13

Sylvie sat in front, George's arms wrapped tight round her waist, the tiger eating the ground in huge gobbling leaps. There was no Allamanda now, no glow-worms flickering, just ordinary roads with cars and motorbikes and startled drivers. This was the tiger of that poem all right, the tiger who had kept faith through their adventure. Yes, what the shoulder? What the art? What indeed could twist the sinews of his heart? He was running for his life, chasing what he had always wanted to chase, the very soul of his being. The plunging forest, the leaping gazelle were just a bound away. He was running as he had never run before, letting loose all the years of his captivity, setting his spirit free. Over the ground they bounded, heading towards the city. She knew the way, and though she pressed him with her knees for him to turn right or left, she felt as if he knew the paths anyway. Perhaps he could hear the Songman calling. Perhaps he knew that the city was the place where his battle had to be fought, where he would sing his last song.

First came the villages, the narrow roads, cars swerving into ditches as they raced along, past greens and pubs and leafy lanes. Then they came to a bigger town, with warehouses and factories and super- markets. They galloped through the suburban estates, with their washed cars and manicured lawns and frantic bark-less dogs. They charged through the town centre, where bags were spilled and babies pushed, late-night shoppers screaming, takeaway dinners splattered onto the pavement as people jumped back in fright. Up over a railway bridge they pounded, cars hooting, bicycles wobbling, straight over a richly flowered roundabout, down a slip road and out onto the motorway.

'London,' George screamed in her ear, 'fifty miles! This is serious malarkey!'

The tiger ran on the hard shoulder, overtaking the cars on the inside; startled passengers dropped their phones, their drinks, their mouths, punching but- tons, reporting what they had seen to the police, the radio, a best friend. But there was no stopping him. On and on he ran, like a huge steam engine. He burned, he glowed, his breath rose steaming in the air. Sylvie could feel the fire in his limbs, the boil of his blood, the volcano in his heart. He flowed over the land like white-hot lava, devouring everything in his path.

The motorway melted away. Sodium lights drained the tiger's coat of its vivid colour. They could see the glow of the city now, hear the rumble of its traffic, the beat of its streets. The roads narrowed. Shops and houses pressed in. The traffic slowed, but the tiger did not. He twisted and weaved, charging through traffic lights and along dual carriageways, pounding ever closer to the city centre. Though sirens screamed and lights flashed, they seemed to slip and slide through everything, leaping into the midst of traffic, careering down pavements, weaving from lane to lane. Cars crashed, taxis braked, the tiger's eyes blazing back, defying them all.

They had reached the hub of London, a typical summer's evening, with tourist buses and theatre crowds and office workers on street corners, leisurely drinks in their arms. The tiger sensed it. He had no place here; everything that was unnatural, against his laws, crowded in on him. It drove him faster, as if he were trying to escape the very thing he was seeking. Down the Strand, past Nelson's column, under the arch and into the Mall, the palace shining at the end like a great cake. Sightseers cheered, thinking it some mad fancy dress stunt, while policeman leaped out into the road, waving guns, guards bundling out of their sentry boxes; but the tiger was a match for them all.

The roads flashed by in a blur. Then there were railings and, on the other side, the shadowy expanse of the park. They could hear whistling and clapping and the booming thump of a bass. The tiger gathered himself together and, with a boundful leap, cleared the tall spikes, landing with a thud on the green. He staggered and fell to his knees, gasping for breath. They'd arrived.

A great shout brought them back: fans cheering and clapping and whistling in appreciation. Sylvie and George started to run towards the noise, past the rows of well-spaced trees and deserted pathways. The crowd loomed ahead, moving, shifting, breathing like some many-headed animal. Over their heads they could see the stage, bathed in brilliant light.

'Look!' George cried. 'We're too late!'

The Songman had enjoyed the leisurely trip up to London enormously. The Woodpecker Man and he had carved a corridor of silence across the land, as broad and as permanent as any six-lane motorway. London too now lay shrouded in inexplicable silence, its dogs, its pigeons, its scrawny urban foxes all now bent to his will. No horse whinnied its way down the Mall, no cat meowed for a saucer of milk, no squirrel chattered in the capital's trees. Soon the SongGlasses would be practically obsolete, but there was still pleasure to be had throwing them out, watching the green woodpeckers chase them as they tumbled to the ground. Once in Hyde Park, he had been politeness itself – Daniel's agent, he explained to the organizers, supervising the placing of his strange instruments, overseeing the safe arrival of the glass orchestra. Walter Klopstock had been as good as gold. At the first sign of obstinacy the Songman had simply sung him into a state of dog-like obedience.

'He's ours,' he told Mildred with a smile. 'Our little tousle-haired errand boy.'

Once calmed, the conductor had scurried round, eager to please, examining each new glass instrument as it was unpacked with exaggerated enthusiasm. He wasn't the only one. Any initial doubts the players had on seeing their new equipment were quickly dispelled as they put them to their lips, drew a bow across their strings, struck them with a tentative drumroll. They sounded wonderfully clear, the notes almost made of air. They couldn't wait.

'Just don't drop them,' the Songman said, wagging a good-natured finger. The musicians laughed, delighted. As if they would! He left them to make the final preparations for his own, unforgettable entrance.

The concert began in the early evening, with massive screens on either side of the scaffolded stage; bands from America, the UK, a couple from Zimbabwe, another from Nigeria. The young crowd pressed together, eager, enthusiastic; hands waving, mobiles held open, girls on their boyfriends' shoulders, the press with their cameras and flashlights squeezed up at the front.

By the time the first half had ended, the crowd was good humoured and a little tired. Now came the interval. They didn't expect much. It was a time to get something to drink, to eat, go to the loo, text a friend. They squatted down on the worn grass, the buzz of conversation heady and happy. It had been a good day's music, and a better night was ahead.

As a curtain at the rear of the stage was peeled back, a gasp went up. Raised up on three tiers, the orchestra rolled forward on waves of glittering glass, the instruments shifting in and out of the light as if they were hardly there: violins, violas, cellos and double basses; horns, trumpets, clarinets and bassoons, flutes and oboes, trombones and tubas, a row of kettle drums and, most dazzling of all, the piano, with its glass body and glass legs and a lone black-necked swan, wings outstretched, standing on the raised lid.

'Ladies and gentlemen,' a voice boomed. 'The Orchestra of Light.'

The orchestra began to play – some old songs at first, popular classics, melodies that the audience half remembered. The glass instruments seem to give the tunes a quality that made them sound brand new. No one took any notice when the Drummers appeared on either side of the stage, egg-shaped drums slung around their waists, quietly beating out the rhythm. The music shimmered and danced, fell among them like dappled sunlight; happy memories wafted through the air. The crowd stirred, surprised, entranced, refreshed. They hadn't expected this. They forgot about food, phoning friends: that insistent drumming lay at the back of it all, almost holding them down. No one wanted to move. Somehow it seemed difficult, almost foolhardy. It was much better to stay put, out of harm's way, all dreamy and peaceful. There were nasty things out there, beyond the park, the drumming seemed to warn.

The orchestra played on. The music seemed to fill the park in a way that all the bands with their speakers and light shows and break-dancers couldn't. There was something almost otherworldly about it, as if the audience were being taken to a place they had never seen before, never heard before. They sank back, eyes closed, drifting. And then, through it all, came the sweetest note that anyone had ever heard, floating down from the heavens. They opened their eyes. Gliding over them came a silver balloon pulled by black-necked swans beating their wings in perfect time. The Songman stood with his arms spread wide, his head thrown back, his beautiful throat stretched out, looking like a bird of paradise. The crowd were transfixed. As one, everyone took out their mobiles, holding them high, to show the world what they could see, what they could hear. The Songman sang, his Song shining out like a beam of white light, a song of hope and promise and a carefree future.

Slowly the swans circled, pulling the SongBird down onto the stage. The music died away. The crowd shifted, expectant. There were new instruments on stage now – three strange-looking beasts arranged in a semicircle. The Woodpecker Man stood by their side, dressed in a livid green suit, green birds on his shoulders and on his red top hat. The man with rabbit teeth was adjusting the position of a fourth instrument, consulting a sheet of paper as he wheeled it into place. Mildred Drummer stood to the side, still drumming. The Songman got out of the basket and walked across the stage. Klopstock stepped down from the rostrum and handed him the baton. At the back of the crowd George pulled desperately on Sylvie's arm.

'Come on, Sylvie. We've got to try.'

Sylvie held back. There was something preventing her from going forward: drumbeats circled the periphery, acting like an invisible barrier. She put her fingers in her ears but it was too strong. She needed some help to move forward.

'Give me the SongGlass, George, and start singing,' she said.

'What?'

'As loud as you can. It's my only way through.'

'What, anything?'

'Anything!'

'OK.

'Once a jolly swagman lived by a billabong,
Under the shade of a kooliba tree . . .'

The drumming in Sylvie's head began to clear, the Songman's voice dissolving as George bellowed into her ear with a voice like a stabbed bagpipe. She began to elbow her way through the crowd, treading on people's feet, knocking over their drinks, taking no notice of the shouts and protests that followed in their wake.

'Come on, George, keep singing!' she shouted.

They pressed ahead, the barrier weakening against George's onslaught. Suddenly it gave way. They were through. They barged on, pushing and shoving until they were just a couple of metres from the stage. The man with rabbit teeth was seated at the Furroughla. The Woodpecker Man was standing by the Featherblow, ready to begin. The Songman stood on the rostrum, his baton raised. Sylvie twisted the Song-Glass, her Song flying out, a lone voice in the quiet. The Songman turned, puzzled, then caught sight of her.

'Sylvie?' he exclaimed, his voice raised in astonishment. 'You're here? But how . . . ?'

She jumped over the barrier and clambered up onto the stage. The Woodpecker Man moved forward, but the Songman stayed his hand.

'I had to come,' she said, a little out of breath. 'I couldn't keep away. I had to hear it, your Song, Dad's Note, the animals' songs all together.' She took a step closer. 'You were right. I want to do this with you, be a part of it, a part of history. Let me work the Furroughla's pedals like I did that day. Let me be a part of history.' She held out her hand, palm outwards. 'It'll be stronger if I do it, you know it will.'

The Songman laid the baton on her shoulder, oblivious to the waiting crowd, his eyes searching hers.

'This is not a trick, Sylvie? You will not attempt to destroy it?' He ran his fingers over the Mark. 'You will let the music run its full course?'

'Yes,' she said, looking him straight in the eye.

'You are telling the truth, I can feel it. I hoped this would happen, from the first moment I saw the Mark. Oh, I am glad you have come, Sylvie! Glad! We shall do this together now.'

'Sylvie!' George was down below, his face bewildered, angry. 'How can you? What about your dad, the animals? Don't they mean anything to you?'

'Be quiet, George,' she said dismissively. 'You don't understand. This is the only thing that matters now.'

She turned her back on him and took up her position in front of the Furroughla, one foot on the pedals. The Woodpecker Man hopped up next to her, his black fingernails poised over the Featherblow's leather bellows. The man with rabbit teeth knelt down next to the Shinglechord. In front of them, the Clattercloud stood motionless, waiting. The Songman raised the baton in his right hand once again, his left demanding perfect silence. He paused, held it absolute. Sylvie took a deep breath.

They began.

Quickly the music took hold, the Featherblow's wispy notes drifting through the reeds, out above the low rumble coming from the Furroughla. Gradually the pitch began to rise, the Furroughla hungry for more air. Sylvie worked the pedals hard. If she closed her eyes, she could almost imagine herself back in the hut, Dad by her side.

'Come on,' the Songman urged, beating the air. 'Faster! Faster!'

She began to pump furiously, the Woodpecker Man matching her for speed, his arms working like pistons, his green coat flapping, his face grinning, black insects wriggling out of his ears. The music picked up speed, a low humming taken up by the Clattercloud as the glass bell began to reverberate. The sound expanded, filling the air like dense smoke. The moment had come, just like before, suddenly, without warning.

'Now!' the Songman shouted. Sylvie pulled out the stop as he jammed his hand into the Shinglechord's flap. The Furroughla began to judder as the notes split, one low, one high, circling each other in a spiral of speed.

'It's on its way!' the Songman cried. 'There's no stopping it now! It's mine! All mine!'

Sylvie jumped off the pedals; Dad's instruments shook and shuddered as the vibrations took hold. She pressed her hand against her temple, wincing in pain, the notes swirling ever closer. Her hand began to throb violently. It was time.

She called:

'Come, whirlwind!
I grasp thee,
my strong hand
And cry Deliverance!'

There was a ripple in the crowd, a path streaking through the noise like an arrow. A blur. A flash, and he burst onto the stage – the tiger, his eyes burning, his tail thrashing, his body coiled.

'Back, you brute!'

Brandishing a snatched music stand, the man with rabbit teeth lunged forward. The tiger roared and knocked him clean off the stage with one swipe of his paw. He roared again, his face flecked with rage, then ran full pelt, jumping on the Songman, pinning him to the stage with one enormous paw. He stood over him, his teeth bared, his breath hot, a vicious drawn claw resting on his throat.

'Sing!' Sylvie commanded. 'Sing your Song that unlocks all other Songs! Sing the Song of SongDay, or else . . .'

She pulled on the tiger's ears, forcing his head back. Her head was pounding, her skull stretched like an elastic band, ready to snap. Then it came, a great voice booming through the dread that was thundering down upon them. The tiger! She could hear the words rolling from his tongue, and she knew, from the terror on his face, that the Songman could hear him too.

Oh bloody sky! Oh purple night and crimson morn!
Call thy dark hosts
Hear My Song
I am the terrible destroyer

Let me rent this serpent, rattle his clanking chains
See his writhing neck, his eyelids scale
Perplexed and terrified
Let me fall upon his brain and bowels,
Rip them forth upon the ground
Let blood pour around my feet
Steep his wounds in salt
Let me laugh at my tortures
Let him groan horrible and run about
Drunk with gore.

Behold! I am oblivion!

He pushed his fangs into the Songman's neck, rivulets of blood trickling down.

'Don't kill him!' Sylvie shouted.

Store your rage!

My hand upon thee!

She reeled back. It was coming now, coming fast, the great void, the black collision. There was a rush of air, a spinning tunnel of black, frothing destruction opening its throat, ready to swallow her alive. She was spinning round and round in a vortex, her insides about to explode. It had to be now!

'I can't hold him!' she screamed. 'Sing it, Songman, or he'll rip your throat out!'

The tiger roared again. The Songman opened his mouth, eyes bulging, hands clawing at the stage, as his Song pierced the sky and the notes collided.

The world blinked.

The world blinked and there was silence, darkness: utter silence, utter darkness, the sun blotted out, the moon and the stars no more, a moment when nothing existed, everything suspended in a great wheel of infinite emptiness, a moment of eternity, vast and endless and without pity.

Then light ripped the air, white burning light that shook the eyeballs.

A crack broke upon the wind, splitting the sky in two.

The glass instruments exploded, the songs bursting forth as the shock raced across the land like a tidal wave and carried them away in a vast, cataclysmic pulse. Out they poured, all the animals' songs in the world – the polar bear on her icecap, the dog by his fireside, the great eagle flying over the lonely hills; all the animals, big and small, loud and quiet, fierce and timid, their stolen songs all singing together; and above them all the tiger's, surging over the world as if sung from the highest mountain top. He stood there, his four feet planted proudly on the stage, his great mouth open to the sky while he sang his song of freedom. It was done. The animals were free. And as he ended his song, a thousand howls echoed across the city, taking up his call, as the dogs of London found their voices once again.

A flare. The Woodpecker Man sprang into the basket, pulling on the burners, green woodpeckers circling his hat.

'Stop him! He's escaping!' George yelled. The Songman was sprinting across the stage, his hands stretched out. The tiger whipped round. The Songman jumped, his fingers clutching onto the edge of the basket as the balloon began to climb. The tiger roared again, his body arched, ready to spring, his eyes fixed on his prey.

'No!' screamed Sylvie. 'Leave him! It's over now!'

The tiger turned his great head, eyes blazing. He

had heard her, but he was no longer listening. He had done his work for her. Now it was his turn. This was what he was born to do, to leap and kill, run wild, free from restraint. A tiger!

He leaped with a shuddering roar, the arc of his body stretched to its full rippling length, his mouth a yawning chasm, his long claws raking open the Songman's back. The Songman shrieked in agony as he desperately tried to hang on.

'Help me! Help me!' he screamed, clutching at the Woodpecker Man's coat.

The Woodpecker Man jumped back and began hitting the Songman's fingers with the rim of his hat.

'Please, no! Please!' the Songman begged, but the Woodpecker Man only hit him harder, screeching at his birds as they flew down, their beaks stabbing at the Songman's hands and head. With a pitiful wail, the Songman let go, falling back into the tiger's open jaws. The tiger seized him, his sabre-sharp teeth sinking into the Songman's broken body, shaking him from side to side.

A shot rang out.

The tiger sprang back, dropping the Songman to the ground. At the back of the crowd a policemen took aim again, the bullet missing as the tiger swirled round.

'Go,' Sylvie cried. 'Run! Run for your life! Before they kill you!'

The tiger turned, held her for a moment with his eyes.

Oh sweet lamb
I sing and you reply to my Song
I have seen thee, a spirit in the bright air
I turn delighted
Golden wheels circling.
Seize the harp!
Strike the strings!
Behold! The clouds of ecstasy!

He reared up and, with one last roar, jumped into the crowd and was gone. Free at last.

The Songman lay twisted and crumpled. Blood was seeping through his coat out onto the stage. His body arched up in a sudden convulsion, then sank back to the floor.

'Sylvie? Are you there?'

He beckoned her over with a feeble flick of the wrist. She knelt down beside him. Deep claw marks raked his neck.

'Sylvie,' he croaked. She bent down, trying to hear his words. His face had lost its hardness. He looked more like Uncle Alex again. Uncle Alex! That's who he was. She almost felt sorry for him. He patted her hand. 'That was quite a clever ploy. I don't think I'll be singing any more.'

'No.'

'No.' He turned to look at the balloon sailing away. 'My voice – was it very beautiful?'

'It was the most beautiful voice I have ever heard.'

He coughed, a trickle of blood running from his mouth. Opening her hand, he fingered the Mark. He licked his lips slowly.

'What do they say, the animals, when you hear them? What do they say?' His voice rasped like an empty rattle.

'What do they say? They say, "Let me sing, let me hear my voice." They want to sing their songs, like everybody does, like you want to sing yours, to tell the world that you are alive, and that the world is full of songs.'

'I did not just want to sing my song,' he said, the old vehemence coming through. 'I wanted to sing everybody's.' He looked past her, as if he could see somewhere far away. 'Oh, Sylvie, we could have sung such a song,' he said, 'if only—'

His eyes glazed over. He was gone.

Sylvie rose to her feet and surveyed the scene. The crowd had fled. The man with rabbit teeth lay on the ground, a great gash in his leg, Mildred trying to staunch the wound. The Furroughla, the Shinglechord and the Featherblow lay smashed to pieces, their innards spilled out onto the stage. Only the Clattercloud remained intact, the glass bell still swinging from side to side. She put her hand out and brought it to rest. She felt oddly calm.

'Well,' said George, picking a sliver of glass out of his hair, 'it's all very well the tiger running off like that, but you do realize what it means, don't you?'

'What?'

'We'll have to get the train back.'

A week later George and Sylvie and Sylvie's dad were standing on the station platform. George was carrying his red-tailed kite, Dad was carrying a newly washed spade and Sylvie was carrying a small tree, the roots bundled up with sacking. They were off to collect the fox, and then go down to the animal sanctuary to fly George's famous creation and plant the young oak next to where the old one had fallen.

With the Songman dead, the lighthouse was no longer hidden from view. No one had quite believed their tale of what had gone on there, until they had rowed across and found Daniel still locked away, the animals singing at the top of their voices, delirious with joy. The chimpanzees and the younger gorillas were sent back to the countries they came from, where they would be set free to do what wild animals should do – live their lives out in the open, with all the risks and joys that brought. Only the old gorilla remained. He was too old to travel, too old to learn new ways of living. He'd been behind bars for too long. But Daniel had found him a place in a spacious open-air zoo, not fifty miles away. Sylvie had promised him that she would go and visit him as often as she could.

Thanks to the dog tags that they found jumbled up in a basket, all the stolen dogs had been returned to their rightful owners – all except one: Tillie, the black Labrador cross. They couldn't find out where she came from. She hadn't even had a collar, let alone a little disc. That had soon been put to rights. Tillie Bartram, the name tag read, with Sylvie's address and new mobile phone number on the other side. She sat next to Sylvie now, watching the empty line, happy with her new home.

Suddenly her ears went up. Her tail began to thump. She pawed Sylvie's leg, looking at the others.

Hereshecomes hereshecomes

Tillieround'emup Tillieround'emup

The train was coming up the track. It was a brand-new train, with brand-new rolling stock, and air conditioning and automatic doors and tables for everyone. They got into the third carriage and took their seats,

Tillie's black head poking up inquisitively between Sylvie's knees. There were no Drummers aboard, but on the other side of the aisle sat a man with a polka-dot tie and a woman with a matching scarf. The plump solicitor was sitting at the back, complaining to his friend as usual.

'These new-fangled carriages,' he was saying, 'are not a patch on the old ones. The air's too dry, the tables are too large, and the doors haven't got any handles. Change for change's sake, that's all it is. You know what I'm going to do?'

But Sylvie never did hear what he was going to do because at that moment the man with the bow tie leaned forward. He was reading a local newspaper. INQUEST HELD ON MUSIC TEACHER MAULED TO DEATH BY TIGER, read the headline.

'No school today?' he said brightly. 'Teachers all eaten? Ha ha ha.'

'It's the holidays,' George pointed out. '*Les vacances.* Remember them? Buckets and spades. Nights out with the boys.'

'Holidays!' the woman snorted. 'They're everywhere on holiday. Even restaurants.'

Holidays. In a couple of days Sylvie and her dad and Tillie were driving down to Durdle Door for two weeks. She had a feeling it might be for the last time.

'Dad,' she said suddenly, 'what about Mum? Did you know that she was alive?'

Her father blushed. 'Sort of.' The woman across the way looked at him with deep suspicion.

'Why didn't you tell me?'

'I didn't want to get your hopes up.'

Sylvie looked out of the window. Her hopes were up, that was the trouble.

At the next stop the scruffy lad jumped in, his muddy boots replaced by a pair of green suede shoes.

'Those items on his feet,' said George, eyeing them enviously, 'they're—'

Sylvie held up her hand. 'I know, George. They're serious malarkey.'

They both laughed. The train left the station. Sylvie nudged George and gave Dad a surreptitious kick. They all craned forward. The train rounded the bend. They could see the ledge coming into view. There he lay, the old fox, stretched out comfortably in the sun. She wanted to wave, but she knew she mustn't, knew she didn't need to. He could feel her, just as she could feel him. The fox lifted his face to the sun and sang a long joyful song. Somewhere within it Sylvie thought she could hear Mr Jackson, calling in the distance.

IgoodboyMrJackson ISylvieboygooddog

Therethere therethere

Dear Mr Jackson. How she would miss him.

The fox got to his feet and started to trot off in the direction of the station. By the time they got there and had walked down to the path across the fields, he'd be there to meet them. Somewhere out there roamed the tiger too. There'd been sightings from Land's End to John o' Groats. Sylvie would have to seek him out sooner or later, before he got shot or was caught again. She'd take him to where he belonged, his homeland, wherever that was.

'George?' she said. 'When I get back from Dorset, are you doing anything special?'

'Only a little light algebra and some conversational French. Why, what you got in mind?'

'Nothing much. Just thinking.'

Copyright Acknowledgements